Tunbridge Wells Ghost Stories

James Ward

COOL MILLENNIUM BOOKS

1

A CIP catalogue record for this book is available from the British Library.

ISBN: 978-1-913851-59-0

Cover picture shows the view from Mount Ephraim towards The Trinity Theatre.

This novel was produced in the UK and uses British-English language conventions ('authorise' instead of 'authorize', 'The government are' instead of 'the government is', etc.)

To my wife… and Cedric.

Contents

Aunt Eunice's Hoard

I.

From the age of sixteen until the day I left university at twenty-two, I always spent the same three weeks of each year – the last half of July plus the first seven days of August - staying with my best friend, Charles Forsythe, and his family, in their big Edwardian house in Tunbridge Wells. In many ways, it was a homecoming: I'd been born locally, I'd gone to the biggest of the area's primary schools – which is where I'd met Charles, as a matter of fact – and then to the C of E comprehensive on Culverden Down. After my own parents died in a car accident in 2017, and I went to live with my aunt in Cornwall, Mr and Mrs Forsythe felt demonstrably sorry for me; but they also feared that their only son was set to lose his best, and sole, friend (it undoubtedly helped that the attachment was mirrored on my side). Anyway, their invitations to stay always had a *subpoena* flavour about them – *we expect to see you back here in a year's time, Steven Parsons: consider yourself booked* – and when, every July, in total and utter obedience, I arrived on their doorstep lugging my ten-ton suitcase, they invariably seemed just a little *too* pleased to see me (even elderly Aunt Eunice, who lived upstairs ninety-nine percent of the time, and who, given that she actually owned the house, had no reason whatsoever to play along).

In short, Charles and I were like brothers. We were also what used to be called 'young fogies': we didn't care for flippancy, we weren't remotely fond of parties, and we could sit together for hours on end without much in the way of conversation or face-to-screen time (obviously, we both *had* mobile phones, but we tended to consult them once in the morning, once in the evening, and otherwise, only if someone called). Most of our time together, we read: textbooks, not magazines, or novels; revising obsessively for exams, really, and trying to maximise our subject-knowledge. We both wanted postgraduate degrees, you see, then to take up university posts, and, ultimately, to write ground-breaking academic monographs for prestigious journals. I was reading history at Newcastle-upon-Tyne, Charles, archaeology at Edinburgh.

At the time my story begins, we were both twenty-one. He was tall and stocky, with short, straight dark hair which combed left to right on top, and downwards at the sides, and stayed amenably in place without the use of gel. He also had what novelists sometimes call a 'firm jaw', ie, he looked the sort of man you could rely on in an emergency. I was equally tall, but much thinner. My own hair was uselessly curly and I wore heavy plastic-framed glasses of the kind that had been fashionable fifteen years ago, but which were now commonplace. I'd been told that my hands and feet looked too big for my arms and legs, so I suppose that's worth adding. We habitually dressed in ironed trousers, oxford shirts and jumpers.

As for the other members of the Forsythe clan, Charles's father, Dudley, was in his late fifties, and worked in the City doing something financial. He was nine-tenths bald, but dignified enough not to think shaving off the last little bit would improve his appearance (doubly dignified, perhaps, since everything that remained was grey). At home, he wore T-shirts with the names of long-forgotten rock bands on ('the more obscure, the better', he once told me), faded jeans, and oversized slippers done up to look like dog's faces. He always enjoyed two or three whiskies after dinner. His wife, Corrine, was tall and slim, with long brown hair, and typically wore billowy ankle-length dresses and glittery espadrilles. She had lots of friends, and ran three book groups. Some evenings, she lit a bowl of ecclesiastical incense and chanted the Jesus Prayer in the summer house at the bottom of the garden. She liked wine.

However, the main interest of the house, personality-wise, was the 'aunt' (really a great-aunt, from Corrine's side of the family): Eunice. She had the building's entire third floor to herself - four rooms in total, including a bathroom plus a small kitchen - and, apart from her once-weekly dinner with the rest of the family, she was, for all practical purposes, invisible. Sunday was her family-visit night, and usually involved a traditional roast, cooked on alternate weeks by Corrine (lamb/beef) and Dudley (chicken/pork). She always dressed for the occasion: not showily, or eccentrically, but as if making an impression mattered and the most effective signifiers were small, subtle or both: pearl earrings, an immaculately ironed blouse, a silver bracelet, coiffured hair. She spoke intelligently about current affairs, but mostly, she asked Charles and I about our own interests and listened attentively. She liked to hear about history. Dudley seemed to think she was an amateur local historian, although, as far he knew, she'd never actually published anything, nor did she belong to any of the relevant research organisations, nor did she attend any of the occasional lectures at the local library. Nevertheless, he claimed to know 'for an absolute fact' that her hobby, which bordered on an obsession in his humble opinion, involved the sedulous acquisition, 'by foul means or fair', of documents and artefacts relating to the history of Tunbridge Wells Common. Not the town itself, he emphasised: just the Common. Occasionally, much to his sorrow (though he never said anything to Eunice), he came to hear about some extortionate sum she'd paid for an obviously worthless piece of tat, on the basis of which he inferred that she must have a large collection of such junk upstairs, though he'd never seen it, and doubted anyone else had. Antique dealers, auction houses, and possibly – 'probably', he corrected himself - the black market comprised her happy hunting ground, and, once she'd set her heart on an item, she never let it get away.

None of the family could ever get Eunice herself to confirm any of this, but equally, she never denied it. To add to the mystery, twice or sometimes three times a year, so Corrine said, someone unknown would turn up at the door – a 'fellow collector', was how they usually introduced themselves - completely out of the blue, hoping for an interview with the old lady. Eunice never turned them away, but for some reason they always left fifteen minutes later in a manifestly bad temper. They never returned, although others, apparently on the same obscure mission, always followed.

At this point in the story, Dear Reader, you probably imagine you know what's coming. People always do. 'Ah, yes,' you're thinking, 'the two young men, Steven and Charles: they'll shortly be overcome with curiosity about what Aunt Eunice is up to with all that mysterious hoarding of hers. They'll find some way of breaking into her room and purloining her collection; at which point, they'll find they've bitten off considerably more than they can chew.

Because she won't have been gathering documents and artefacts at all! Oh no, she'll have been patiently summoning some hideously unspeakable creature from the underworld, almost certainly with the aid of black magic! Steven and Charles will spend the last two-thirds of the story wetting their pants and running away across the Common, and, if they're lucky, they'll survive, albeit with white hair and a nasty tic each. In that case, they'll be suitably chastened, and it'll serve them right; the end.'

So… yes (and at the risk of undermining my own, rather different tale) I admit that would make a wonderful story. But the fact is, it wouldn't be very plausible. To begin with, Charles and I had well-developed consciences, and we had unmitigated respect for Aunt Eunice. It would never have occurred to either of us to do anything so obviously contemptible as go through her personal possessions behind her back, no matter how insanely 'curious' we were. Secondly, we had no reason to disbelieve Mr Forsythe's assertion that the sole focus of her collection was Tunbridge Wells Common, and why would either of us be especially interested in *that?* No disrespect to it, of course – I'd often walk there on an evening, sometimes in company with Charles and/or his parents: it's lovely, of course it is – but neither of us would have contemplated writing a doctoral thesis on it.

On the other hand, Aunt Eunice's collection does form an important part of this story, albeit obliquely.

But enough of the preamble. Time to get started.

II.

"Fancy a walk on the Common tonight, boys?" Mr Forsythe asked.

Eight in the evening, Saturday. Outside, the shadows hadn't quite dissolved into the gloaming, and there was sufficient light in the day to suggest the sun had just touched the horizon. I sat in the Forsythes' kitchen with Charles and his parents. We'd eaten dinner two hours ago, Dudley had loaded the dishwasher, and we'd spent most of the time since talking amiably about the sorts of things no one is expected to remember the next day.

"I wouldn't mind stretching my legs a little," I said.

"I suppose it can't hurt," Charles said dolefully. "Might as well make the most of the weather."

"I'm going to watch catch-up, if that's all right," Corrine said. "Before Twitter lets on who got through to the next round."

"I thought we always watched *Strictly together,*" Dudley said, feigning hurt.

"You can watch it tomorrow," she said. "You've got the night off, remember?" She turned to me. "It's Dudley's turn to cook, or would be, only Auntie's away till tomorrow afternoon, and she's already made it clear she won't be joining us for dinner. So, we can have whatever we like. Any requests?"

"Takeaway," Charles said. "I know that sounds like an insult," he added after a pause: "like, *takeaway's better than anything Dad can rustle up*, but I didn't mean it like that. I just meant, let's all have a lazy afternoon and evening. I'll pay."

Corrine hooted. "Mr Moneybags!"

"We could go halves," Dudley said.

"Thirds," I put in.

Corrine sighed jadedly, and took a gulp of Shiraz. "Okay, quarters. We'll all pay for our own takeaways. Fragmentation: the hallmark of the modern world."

"Free choice, I call it," Dudley said.

"Where's Aunt Eunice gone?" Charles asked.

"London," Dudley replied. "To collect another marvellous item to add to her already humongous magpie's stash. This time, she's afraid someone will intercept it."

Charles frowned. "Dad, why do you have to be so dismissive? Aren't you ever curious about what she's collecting?"

Dudley emitted a groan. "We've been through this before, Son. I love Eunice, and I love you, but she won't *talk* about her collection, and I have to keep a lookout for all our interests. True, we're not poor, so, if she lost this house, I dare say we could easily afford another, even here in one of the most expensive property markets in the land - "

"Not counting London, of course," Corrine said.

"London's a dump," Dudley replied. "But getting back to the point, I don't like seeing my beloved wife's beloved Auntie taken for a mug by some of the biggest con men – con *persons*, sorry, dear – in Kingdom Come. Because that's what it is. They've spotted an easy mark, and they're intent on siphoning off as big a share of her life savings as they can... Okay, everyone, paint *me* as the villain for being so 'cynical', but *you're* the real villains. I'm the only one who cares. About her and about us."

"That's unfair," Corrine said.

I could see what was coming. Charles held up both palms, his characteristic way of forestalling a row. Corrine took her wine into the sitting room and switched on the TV. Charles and I went upstairs and changed, ready to go for that walk on the Common. When we came downstairs, Dudley met us in the hallway, still in his dog's face slippers and clutching a double whisky.

"Sorry, lads, I'm going to cry off," he said. "Better watch *Strictly* like a good boy, and hope for some sort of rapprochement on the sofa, if you know what I mean." He chuckled. "Sorry, that came out wrong. I just meant, holding hands, something like that."

Charles nodded. "Understood."

"It's nothing to worry about," he said. "We argue about Eunice all the time, you know we do. Each of us accepts the other has her best interests at heart, so there's never any lasting damage. Quite the contrary." He grinned, apologetically. "Still, bloody Twitter, eh?"

III.

The Forsythes lived in Warwick Park, which is more or less across the road from the Common. Usually, we climbed to the 'summit' (apologies if you don't know the town: 'Mount' Ephraim's actually little more than a geologically interesting hillock), then zig-zagged our way slowly downwards, talking desultorily about anything and everything. Tonight, however, I sensed Charles had something on his mind. He'd seemed unhappy when Dudley had asked him if he wanted to go for a walk, then he'd snapped at him about Aunt Eunice. Now, we were walking in silence.

I knew not to ask what was wrong. Assuming it was any of my business, he'd tell me of his own accord.

"Sorry if I seem out of sorts," he said, after five minutes. He gestured to one of the park benches by the Wellington Rocks. We sat down.

"So what's on your mind?" I asked.

"Believe it or not, an email." He took his phone from his pocket, swiped it, tapped it, and handed it to me.

At the top, in embedded type:

From: Professor Lavinia Trevor
Head of the Department of Archaeology, Edinburgh University.

Then, underneath:

Dear Charles,
I hope you won't mind me contacting you out of the blue like this. Tony Mathers, your tutor, speaks very highly of your work, and I know your grades so far have been outstanding. You would be doing me a huge favour if we could put our heads together sometime regarding a relative of yours who happens to collect historical artefacts, and whose interests overlap significantly with my latest research project. Let me know how this sounds.
Kind regards, L.

"Wow," I said neutrally. I still didn't know whether I was meant to be pleased, curious, sceptical, or something else.

"Stoops fairly low, don't you think?" Charles replied. "I've never met Lavinia Trevor, and she's never hitherto shown any interest in me. She obviously knows Aunt Eunice won't want much to do with her, so she's trying to use me as an entry ticket. What do you think will happen to my academic future if I say no?"

I laughed, or pretended to. "You may be reading too much into it. Whoever 'Lavinia Trevor' is, she's probably not a gangster. I assume you haven't told your parents?"

"Correct. I don't want to rope them in. And I certainly won't be showing Aunt Eunice. Professor Lavinia Trevor can take a running jump for all I care."

I laughed. "Aren't you curious?"

"About what?"

"Well, whatever Lavinia Trevor wants, it must be pretty important for her to 'stoop so low', as you put it. I don't imagine she got to be a professor by putting the heat on every young undergraduate with a local historian in the family."

"So, what are you saying? That I should write back?"

"She only wants you to 'put your heads together'; what's wrong with that? You don't have to respond post-haste with a, *Yes, Ma'am, I'll do everything in my power to get you unlimited access to my beloved Aunt Eunice…* whom the email doesn't explicitly mention, by the way, although I agree, no one else fits the bill."

"Once I reply, I'll be conceding the possibility of assisting her."

"Are you so sure Aunt Eunice would want you to turn her down?"

He sighed wearily. "You're missing the point, Steven. If Lavinia Trevor wants to approach Aunt Eunice on her own, that's fine by me. But if I allow myself to be used as an intermediary, Aunt Eunice is likely to think, 'Well, I'd rather *not* help Professor Trevor, but I *do* want to give my great nephew a leg up in terms of his future, so I suppose it wouldn't hurt for me to bury my reservations, just this once.' Can't you see, I don't *want* her to think like that? And what if Lavinia Trevor turns out to be a crook? What if she takes exclusive credit for one of Aunt Eunice's discoveries, whatever they are? Read *Private Eye*: 'top academic' and 'low-life liar' aren't necessarily exclusive categories."

"Okay, then write back to Lavinia Trevor; tell her it's lovely to hear from her, but if it's about Aunt Eunice, you've a policy of not getting involved; you've no objection to her contacting Aunt Eunice in a professional capacity, but you'd be very grateful if she could keep your name entirely out of it, for all the reasons you've just told me. Make it very polite, a tiny bit deferential, and I'm sure you'll all live happily ever after."

He nodded and took a ruminative breath. "Yes, actually, you're right. You're quite correct. I'll write it tonight when we get in, then sleep on it, and if it still looks kosher tomorrow, in the cold light of day… Would you mind reading it before I press 'send', just to make sure I've got the right tenor?"

"Happy to."

"Well done, by the way. I knew I could rely on you. Two heads are always better than one. Fancy calling in Frampton's on the way back, for a pint? I'm paying."

"Always up for a beer."

I think we were both getting colder, so when we resumed our walk, it was at the kind of pace that might revivify us. We fell into silence again. This time, I assumed Charles was planning what he was going to write.

We'd been going for about three minutes, and we were making our way fairly directly to the main road at the bottom of the hill, when Charles noticed something in the undergrowth, seven or eight feet away.

"What's that?" he said, coming to a gentle halt by way of redirecting his attention.

The most I could discern was a glowing point in the midst of thickets. "I don't know," I said. "Something… luminous?"

"I can see that."

"A child's, or a pet dog's toy? 'Persistent phosphorescence', I think the chemists would call it."

"It's not that kind of glow."

I didn't get time to ask what made him such an expert, because he was already on his way into the bushes. He picked whatever it was up and brought it back.

Not a toy, nor anything similarly mundane. Rather, a four-inch high figurine: a young woman, seated on a rustic throne, with the legend, *Hagne,* underneath in Greek letters.

"Do you know anything about Hagne?" he asked.

"The name sounds familiar. It *is* a name, I assume?"

"Ancient Greece. One of the goddesses of the ancient Messenian waters. Or another name for Persephone, the

Greek goddess of the Underworld. That's a pomegranate she's holding in her left hand."

I laughed. "I hope you didn't plant it with the intention of impressing me with your astounding subject-knowledge? University Challenge: starter for ten."

"What's it doing here?" he asked.

"The Messenian waters," I replied. "So, some sort of connection with Tunbridge Wells and its famed 'chalybeate springs'?"

He clicked his tongue. "No, sorry, that's far too arcane. And why make it luminescent?"

"Well, then, it's a product of the modern-day Greek tourist industry - *Get your glow in the dark Persephones here, just two euros each!* - somehow washed up here, two thousand miles from home. "

He took a deep breath and let it out in a flute of disappointment. "Okay, yes, I suppose that must be it. Something to show off when we get in, I suppose. You never know what's going to turn up on the Common, eh?"

"Do you think it could fetch anything on EBay?"

"I'm not desperate enough to investigate. And I hope the same goes for you."

"I can't promise anything," I quipped lamely.

He slipped it into his coat pocket, and we set off at what, I calculated, was our former brisk pace plus one. I could just see the main road, through the trees. Fifty or sixty yards downhill, then we'd be back in the comforting fold of civilisation.

For some reason, though, I was a little spooked.

By a glow-in-the-dark piece of kitsch? Really? Why would something like *that* spook me?

I'm not certain precisely what happened next. As far as I recall, we were travelling consistently downhill at a steady pace, when, after two minutes, we found ourselves back at our starting point: the same patch of undergrowth to our left, the same pattern of tree trunks, tree tops and mini-clearings above and around us, and, most tellingly, the same view of main road, no closer than it had been a moment ago.

We both stopped walking simultaneously, as the realisation hit us.

Charles turned to me. "Isn't this…?"

"Where we've just came from? It definitely looks like it."

He laughed incredulously. "It *is!* I remember that tree! Look there - those are my footsteps!"

I frowned, as the implications hit me. "Sorry, that can't be right. We'd have to have gone round in a circle."

Charles's expression changed. "Of course. Yes. So what's going on?"

"I don't know."

If this *was* where we'd started from, we'd have to have spent at least some of our time going uphill. In that case, the laws of nature would have to have changed. Or, at the very least, we'd have to have blacked out.

I laughed uncertainly. This had to be a dream.

Only it wasn't.

Charles took my arm, once again attempting to redirect my attention.

Four or five yards to our left, a shadowy figure poked about in the undergrowth. It was darker now than when we'd last been in the same spot, so I could only dimly make out whoever-it-was. A man; sixty-ish, short and rather bulky, dressed in a tweed jacket, wearing a respectable shirt collar with a tie. Clearly looking for something.

"Are you okay?" Charles called.

He looked up. A middle-class kind of face, with a double chin and a large nose. Nothing to be afraid of, but somehow not entirely companionable either.

"I've lost an item of considerable sentimental value," he said gruffly. "A statuette. It glows… in the, er, right kind of darkness."

It didn't occur to either of us, till later, to ask what he meant by this. Charles removed it from his pocket. Neither of us particularly wanted to keep it anymore. "I happened to pick it up right here," he said, "not five minutes ago. No one was about. Obviously, we didn't know it was yours."

He strode over accepted it with something approaching exultation. I suddenly saw he'd been crying. It was apparently all he could do to stop himself kissing Charles's hands.

"I – I must give you a reward!" he said.

"That's absolutely fine," Charles replied. "Just happy to help."

"No, no, you *must* have a reward. Stay here. Please. Just give me five minutes, that's all. I'll be back in *five minutes*. Stay here. Please."

He ran off, or rather hobbled away, in an uphill direction, and quickly disappeared into the general gloom.

Charles and I exchanged terse remarks. Obviously, we didn't want a reward; we hadn't expected one, and we definitely didn't deserve one. On the other hand, it seemed impolite just to up sticks and leave. For all we knew, he might well be going to considerable trouble to find us a 'reward', and if he came back with whatever he'd decided was appropriate, and found us gone, he'd think us churlish. And he'd be right.

We waited five minutes, then another ten minutes. Such was our ludicrous concern for appearances that only after half an hour had passed did we agree to depart. We went directly downhill, crossed the main road, and went home. It was getting late now, and neither of us felt like a beer anymore.

I went straight upstairs to my room and sat down on my bed. Once I was back in among electric lights, soft furnishings and 21st century home appliances, it didn't take me too long to feel detached from what had happened, vaguely unsettling though it had been at the time.

As I removed my coat and hung it up, though, I couldn't help noticing a sag at one side, like it was weighted down. I felt in the pockets, and when my fingers fastened on the cause, I already knew, ominously, what it was… Though how *could* it be? I took it out.

The statuette.

IV.

When I shared the discovery with Charles, five minutes later, he was as nonplussed as I was.

Once he'd overcome his surprise, however, he spent nearly ten minutes closely examining the statuette from every conceivable angle, while I sat in the living room's biggest armchair and tried to stop myself falling asleep.

"What are you looking for?" I asked eventually.

"I'm no expert - archaeology's a massive field, obviously – but it's not what we took it for. 'Flotsam and jetsam from the Greek tourist industry': that was roughly your assessment, as I recall, and I concurred. Now that I've looked carefully at it, however, I'd be willing to bet it's much older than that."

"How much older?"

"A lot."

I scoffed, as politely as I could. "The question is, how did it get back into my coat pocket? I can just about understand it being some kind of highly eccentric practical 'joke', but that would require it to be worthless. However, if it's very old, it must be valuable."

"And from that, you conclude that I must be mistaken about its age. Well, of course, we'll have to get a second opinion."

"Which means you taking it to Edinburgh. I warn you: if it does turn out to be a piece of kitsch, you could end up looking silly."

He chuckled. "You're right, yes. Something else to mull over in the morning."

We said good night to each other.

When I came downstairs at 7am, Mr and Mrs Forsythe were getting ready to go to church. They had specific roles there (sidesperson and prayer reader), so, even on Sunday, breakfast had to be early. We sat around the kitchen table with Weetabix, Shreddies, toast, and three kinds of preserve, while Corrine and Dudley talked about Vladimir Putin, Joe Biden, Boris Johnson, COVID, and the shortage of lorry drivers. Charles said little and looked morose. At 7.35, his parents put their plates in the sink and left.

We spent the next two hours drafting and re-drafting Charles's reply to Lavinia Trevor, trying in vain to strike exactly the right note. Perfection persistently eluded us.

We put our endeavours on pause when Mr and Mrs Forsythe came back from church at 9.30. They made a pot of tea and joined us in the living room to share the *Telegraph*, passing the various supplements between themselves like they were playing some sort of game. Afterwards, they got changed into their 'sports casual wear' (as they called it: polo shirts, chinos and golf shoes), made themselves two rounds of tuna sandwiches and left in the car for the golf club on Benhall Mill Road.

Charles and I resumed work on The Lavinia Trevor Problem. When we'd honed his reply to the point where it was as good as it was ever likely to get, Charles pressed send, then put his phone in his pocket, looking gloomy.

"Any more thoughts on the statuette?" I asked.

"Well, as you said, it must have been a practical joke. Or maybe that that was our 'reward'. Someone came and slipped it into your pocket when you weren't looking."

"Neither seems very likely to me."

"Yet I can't think of anything better, and I doubt you can."

His phone gave a short buzz. He took it out, shook his head and clicked his tongue. "I don't believe it. She's out of the office - for the next week."

There didn't seem to be much to say. I shrugged. "She can't have been that interested then. Or maybe she's changed her mind."

"Or maybe she wrote it when she was drunk. Sorry, that was uncalled-for, but we've just wasted two hours of our lives."

"Perhaps it was a hoax: her message to you, I mean. One of those things where a bot takes over someone's email, and sends out random messages to the address book."

"Except it didn't read like that. It was pretty much tailored to me."

"Okay, agreed. But just because she's 'out of office' doesn't mean she's not checking her email. Given that she's asking you for a favour, she'll probably keep an eye on it."

"The fact that I've turned her down means I'm unlikely to get a reply." He sighed and added: "Which is maybe what I want. Only, I'd rather get it sorted. What if she's the kind of person who won't take no for an answer?"

"Then you'll hear from her within an hour or two."

He nodded, and that seemed to be that. He picked up the *Sunday Telegraph*, and I opened my book. We read for thirty minutes, all the time expecting the return phone call. I could sense Charles becoming increasingly despondent.

Suddenly, he sat up and put the newspaper down. He looked like he'd just read an announcement of his own death.

"Are you okay?" I asked.

"Not at all, no."

"So, what's the matter?"

He blinked slowly. "I, er… didn't tell you this last night, but, well, I had a funny feeling of *déjà vu* about that statuette: as if I recognised it from somewhere. Ever since, I've been telling myself that I must have come across it in some academic textbook or other, one whose details I've now forgotten. After all, as you rightly pointed out, I did seem to know an awful lot about it. I even surprised myself a little. Additionally, however, as if that wasn't enough, I've been growing increasingly uneasy about the whole thing *in general,* for reasons I can't even begin to explain, even to myself."

"Uneasy in what way?"

"As if something horrible is hanging over our heads; as if we caught the interest of something out there, and it followed us back here, and it's watching us, waiting for a chance to strike."

For a moment, the silence was almost overpowering. "I've got roughly the same feeling, I think," I said at last.

"And I've got the weird sense it's much more likely to attack us if we stay together."

"What do you mean?"

"As if it's attracted by our being in one place. It can only strike once, and it needs to dispose of both of us."

I laughed. Our imaginations were running away with us – his especially. "I don't know about that," I told him. "That's no part of what I'm feeling. Anyway, it's - "

"I know what you're going to say: it's nothing to worry about, people feel uneasy about all sorts of things, all the time, this is just a subjective reaction to a slightly disturbing encounter."

"Something along those lines, yes."

"Well, I've just remembered where I last saw that statuette."

"Really? Where?"

He stood up. "Follow me."

We left the living room. He preceded me upstairs.

"Luckily, Aunt Eunice is away," he said as we climbed, "but my parents may be back from the golf course earlier than usual, so we'll have to be quick. We're going up to the third floor. Obviously, I don't want you to let on that we've done that."

We ascended three flights of stairs. We crossed a landing, opened a shabby-looking door and entered what I assumed was Aunt Eunice's living room, given the comfy armchair and the TV, facing each other. The walls were papered in dark blue. A sideboard, a mantelpiece above a fireplace, and a display cabinet in the far corner were the main objects of note, and all three were bedecked with knick-knacks and framed photos.

"Notice anything unusual?" Charles asked.

It suddenly struck me that a significant number of the knick-knacks were variations on the same theme: a young, regal-looking woman, seated on a rustic throne.

The statuette.

"So, what do you think's going on?" I said. "I mean, it must be coincidence, mustn't it? What else could it be?"

"Come on, we'd better go downstairs before Mum and Dad get back. We'll talk about it there. Er, what are you doing?"

I'd picked up one of the framed photos. Of an obviously much younger Aunt Eunice, standing beside a man about fifteen years older than her.

Who looked identical to the man we'd met on the Common.

She had her head on his shoulder and they were both smiling. I'd say she was in her early forties, which meant he –

"Steven, *wake up!* I said, we need to get *downstairs!"*

Instead of obeying, I handed him the photo.

He regarded it with a frown, then his expression changed to one of disturbed bafflement. "Yes, I - I see. My God. Well, we've still got to get downstairs."

We descended briskly and sat at the kitchen table. Charles put his elbows on the hard surface. He rubbed his forehead with his fingertips. "Do you think *the whole thing* could be a practical joke? Obviously, no, because it's not funny, but some *strange* person's *idea* of a practical joke? Just to be clear about the photo, Steven: that guy next to Aunt Eunice - her deceased lover, William Rowston, as a matter of fact – is – I mean, you were thinking that he looked - "

"Exactly like the guy who was searching for the statuette last night, yes."

He sighed. "This should be funny. We should be having a whale of a time. *Wow, whatever next?* That's what we should be thinking. *How mysterious! How exciting!* But it isn't, is it?"

"Maybe we've got to make an effort to get into the right mindset."

He sat up. "Hair of the dog. We need to revisit the scene of the crime. Throw that statuette back into the bushes, then make off at top speed."

"You think it's cursed?"

"That's a bit strong. And melodramatic. But something seriously odd's going on. The other question is, why does Aunt Eunice collect ... Persephone figures? Because that's what they are, as I'm sure you already know. I always thought she was interested in Tunbridge Wells Common. You must remember, I hardly ever go up to her room. None of us do. Not that we're forbidden, or anything;

nothing sinister, or even mysterious. It's just, there's no need, and we're not interested. The last time I did, I was too young to assess its contents."

"To add to the interest, why does she choose to ornament her room with seven or eight nearly identical items? Why not just stash them away somewhere?"

Charles raised his eyebrows in perplexity. "We may never know. We can't really ask her."

"Why not? If we keep the statuette, we'll have something she'll want. We could exchange it for information."

"What do you think she could possibly tell us that would make any of this make sense? No, we've got to get rid of it."

It took me a moment to realise the probable wisdom of what he was saying. "Let's wait till this evening then. If we go back at the same time that we found it, there won't be many people about – it'll be crowded right now: it's nice weather – and we can do a little more investigating. For all we know, there might be an archaeological dig there. In fact," I went on, brightening, "there must be. Which means we'll probably encounter our mystery man again."

"I don't follow your logic at all."

"Think about it: Aunt Eunice is supposedly interested in Tunbridge Wells Common. We happen to know that at least one of the several statuettes we've seen today – namely, the one I mysteriously brought home last night – has a Tunbridge Wells Common connection, because that's where we found it. Remember my original conjecture? You said Messenian Springs, I said Chalybeate Springs. That's the key. At some point in the past, some long-forgotten local entrepreneur decided to connect the two, and they manufactured these Persephone figurines to both underscore the link, *and* make a killing. And of course, it never caught on – it's overly intellectual, and much too obscure for most people's tastes - and, for some reason, when it had definitively failed, at least part of his stock was discarded, or even buried, on the Common. So yes, you were correct to say that the statuette I found is older than I eventually surmised; but I doubt it's more than two hundred years old, at the outside. If we go back tonight, the archaeologist – that's what the man we met must be – might well still be there. Even if he isn't, we should be able to discover evidence of his dig."

Charles considered for a moment, then nodded. "That doesn't solve every mystery here, by any means, but it's a good start."

V.

Mr and Mrs Forsythe returned from the golf club early, looking unhappy and arguing about Aunt Eunice. The problem was, whenever she was away from home, she normally checked in with Corrine at 7.30pm. She hadn't called last night, and when Corrine had tried to ring her, at eight, her phone was switched off. Early on Sunday afternoon, Corrine tried again, with the same result. It just didn't feel right, she said; she had a sixth sense concerning these sorts of things. Meanwhile, Dudley was in full reassurance mode. Eunice wasn't a phone person, he replied; never had been.

Since emailing Lavinia Trevor, Charles had been uncharacteristically checking his phone every half hour.

The gloom between us seemed to be growing, and Corrine and Dudley seemed unlikely to dispel it.

Dudley sat on the sofa, opposite his son. "Since you've got your phone out, Charles, would you mind giving Eunice a ring? She might pick up if she sees it's from you."

"I'm not sure what that's meant to imply," Corrine said indignantly. She'd gone to look out of the front window, into the street.

"I simply meant that if she's in some sort of auction somewhere," Dudley told her, "or she's socialising, or haggling with a dealer, or anything like that, she'll probably have her phone on silent. She looks at the screen," he said, imitating someone checking a phone. "Corrine. *Oh, that's fairly routine. I'll get back to it later*. If she sees Charles's name, however, that's *not* routine. She might think something's wrong. She's much more likely to get back."

"Thus scuppering the deal she's allegedly negotiating," Corrine said.

"I literally can't win," Dudley told her.

"Sorry," she said. "You're right: you're simply trying to set my mind at rest. I'm just worried, that's all."

"Understood. And there's no need to be. Charles?"

"Straight to voicemail," Charles said, putting his phone back in his pocket.

"Bloody technology," Dudley said. "Things were ten times better when people were untrackable." He turned to Corrine. "From what I remember her telling us, she should be on the train back now, anyway. Or even back in town already. She'll probably walk in through the front door in an hour or two… Which I now wish I hadn't said, because it's just more cause for you to worry when she doesn't, and why *shouldn't* she stay over an extra night or two in the capital? She's a free agent!"

"I was actually looking for a taxi pulling up," Corrine said.

"Let's do a bit of gardening. You can do the borders, I'll do the greenhouse and mow a bit of lawn. You need something to take your mind off things. Listen to the radio while you work."

She met his eyes, sighed, and nodded her agreement. "If she hasn't called by nine, I'll get in touch with the hotel."

"Good idea. Give her hell. And a generous helping of extra-red-hot coals from me."

Charles took his phone out and checked it. His parents visibly tensed.

"Sorry," he said. "Not Aunt Eunice. I was just checking something else."

Dudley ground his teeth.

VI.

I spent much of the latter part of that afternoon surreptitiously Googling Professor Lavinia Trevor on my phone. From what I could tell, her research interests – Ancient Roman religious practice in Britain between the second and fifth centuries of the Christian era - didn't seem to overlap much with Aunt Eunice's. But I was beginning to become sceptical on that front. Charles and I only really had Dudley's word that Aunt Eunice was exclusively focussed on the history of Tunbridge Wells Common. In the past, we'd accepted that unquestioningly, but only because nothing hung on it. Things were different now. And really, for all his strengths (and he had many), Dudley was no history aficionado: he could well have got things badly wrong. In that case, he probably wouldn't care much.

Lavinia Trevor's Facebook page revealed an idiosyncratic other side to her: unusually for a top academic, she was into New Age-y stuff: Astrology, Gurdjieff, Ietsism, Theosophy. I wondered how much her colleagues sniggered at her behind her back.

Probably not much. She'd published fourteen significant papers and a book. She had a string of letters after her name, all impressive. She was the sort of woman I could have fallen in love with. Her age and appearance were also conducive to that: she was thirty-five with thin, unkempt hair, nothing discernible in the way of makeup, a severe mouth, an oversized forehead, and heavy glasses rather like mine. At 4.55pm, I had a ten-minute fantasy in which she dropped some books in a library somewhere, I picked them up, we talked, we laughed, I took her to an Italian restaurant, then I helped her write a monograph on Marcus Aurelius. At that point, reality kicked in: she was clearly out of my league, and I promptly forgot all about her.

At 6pm, we all ordered takeaways – contrary to our initial plans, Dudley paid for everything, and we all had Indian – then we sat around and talked. At 7.30, Charles and I announced that we were going for a stroll. As anticipated, Dudley and Corrine poured themselves a drink, then retired into the living room together to watch *Countryfile* on catchup.

Ten minutes later, Charles and I were at the summit of Mount Ephraim. The idea was that we'd retrace our steps of yesterday evening as closely as possible, and pan a little wider, all the time keeping our eyes peeled for anything that resembled an archaeological dig, or anyone who looked like the man we'd met.

I had the statuette in my pocket. To be honest, my earlier gloom had begun to dissipate a bit now (although I don't think the same was true of Charles), and I wasn't sure it would be a good thing just to cast the statuette into the bushes. Doing so seemed not only a bit silly, but also a needless concession to a self-inflicted superstition. On the other hand, I knew Charles hadn't wavered. For his sake, I'd jettison it if necessary.

Ten minutes later, we'd reached the spot. We stopped, and turned to each other.

"This is it," he said. "I haven't seen anything that looks like a dig, and, to be honest, I wasn't really expecting to. There would have been something about it in the papers. And I haven't seen that man either."

"Maybe we should hang about for ten minutes."

He frowned. "What? Like we did yesterday? I've got a very creepy feeling right now. I don't know about you, but… Hang on, I – What's that?"

"What's what?"

But he'd wandered into the undergrowth in exactly the same direction in which we'd found the statuette. At first, I thought he must have seen evidence of professional spadework. Of the two of us, he'd be more likely to recognise something like that.

I didn't follow him: any discovery had to be his own: that was our best hope of solving this mystery. It was getting dark now. He crouched down next to a tangle of bramble branches and fern leaves. He tried frantically to separate them.

"Steven, come here," he said, with a note of panic in his voice.

I strode hurriedly over and went down next to him. The thing I was looking at – because it was so deeply shocking - seemed to gradually assume reality, rather than being fully presented to my senses in one glance.

A body.

A corpse, most likely: it could hardly be asleep, and looking closer, it already appeared faintly putrescent.

The final little piece of reality that reached me completed the revelation: *it was the man to whom we'd returned the statuette yesterday evening.*

But, if that was unsettling enough, what happened next nearly gave me a heart attack. Charles gave an eardrum-piercing yelp, and scuttled back swiftly on all fours, and didn't stop until he'd reached the footpath, at which point he scrambled clumsily to his feet, and stood looking as if he wanted to run, but couldn't remember how to. I followed him backwards at a slower speed, almost equally panicked. For a second, it was all we could do to stop clutching each other.

"What was it?" I demanded indignantly.

"Oh, my God," he said.

I made to return to the thicket. He clutched my arm and almost pulled me over in his attempt to stop me.

"We've got to *go!*" he said. "We've got to *get out of here,* Steven. *Right now.*"

He all but pulled me along with him, downhill and away. I wasn't particularly reluctant, to be honest. He could explain later – he'd *have* to, and we'd have to call the police – because, to be honest, I was glad to be leaving. There was something much more than the regular murder-scene or site-of-unexpected-decease about that place. Something I hadn't noticed first time round, though I think it had been there all along. Something unambiguously evil.

Charles looked ghastly. We didn't stop walking until we got back to his house. But then, at the front door, he did an about-turn, and we began walking towards the High Street, about two minutes' away.

I didn't need him to explain: in our present condition, neither of us could possibly have faced Corrine or Dudley: they'd have known at once that something was wrong, and Charles didn't look capable of explaining, and I still didn't really know the exact details. He needed time to calm down.

We walked up Mount Sion and entered The Grove Tavern on Berkeley Road. Being Sunday evening, it was quiet, with only four other customers sitting quietly at the bar. We bought a pint of bitter each and sat alone together in the corner.

"So, what happened?" I asked, after a minute had passed, "and, er, I don't want to sound pedantic, but oughtn't we to have phoned the police about five minutes ago?" I lowered my voice to a whisper. "That *was* a corpse we just saw, wasn't it?" A genuine question: I was as shocked as he apparently was.

"Steven, I don't know how to put this. Apologies, before I start 'explaining'. Which I can't, so treat that word with a massive pinch of salt. Okay, let me tell you what scared me. Okay, here goes, yes. Underneath that – *corpse* – there was… something alive. Big. About the size of a dog, really. *Alive,* definitely. Shaped – I don't know – like a worm. But with hair." He cackled. "Oh my God, yes. Segmented. Hairy. Black. No head, or limbs. Like – this is going to sound like a new level of weirdness – like – like a person who's been alive for a million years, and they've gradually collapsed – reduced, like liquid in a heated pan - into something utterly, *utterly horrible.* Evil. That's it. Yes, and it was feeding on him – 'him': the corpse." He retched. "Repulsive. Sorry, Steven, sorry."

"Wow." I had to tread carefully here. "And you got all that from – what? – a glimpse? Because it can't have been more than that."

He laughed humourlessly. "Yes, I see. I see what you mean, yes."

"So?"

"More than a glance. Or, yes: a glance. But not visually speaking. An accurate intuition."

"'Truthful, you mean? But how can you know? We're wasting time here, Charles. We need to call the police. They'll investigate, then if there's anything 'weird', they'll find it. Then you won't be alone."

"Listen to you. You think I'm delusional."

"You've had a nasty shock, that's all. But it's well within the realms of the natural. It was a corpse, that's all."

He downed the second third of his pint and turned to face me. "*Was* it? Think about that, for a moment. Here we have the tail-end of the event that began yesterday evening. That event contained a number of unpalatable 'facts', some of which, if taken at face value, would literally require the basic structure of reality to have changed. Such as how, when we left the scene, we were continually walking downhill, and yet five minutes later, we arrived back at our point of origin. And how we divested ourselves of the mysterious object, yet when we got home, you found it in your pocket. And to cap it all, when we go back tonight, there's a corpse - "

"I see what you mean. I - "

He laughed. "Shall I tell you what *else* I intuited out there, tonight, Steven? Just this: that that corpse *didn't exist*. It literally *didn't exist*. There *is* no corpse, not that we saw! If we call the police, we'll be a laughing stock! There's *nothing there*, not for anyone else! What we saw was some kind of – I don't know; It was *meant for us*. Look," he continued, before I could get a word in, "here's what we're *actually* going to do. We're going to go home, and we're going to tell Mum and Dad, or one or the other or both, that we found something disturbing out there on the Common, and would they please come and check? *We don't want to give any details away before you've had a look for yourselves, just humour us, please*. If they find a corpse, fine: we'll call the police. But they won't, no, they won't! And I'm telling you now: that'll be far, far worse."

I finished my beer. "In what way?"

He stood up. "That – thing feeding on the 'corpse': it learned who we are. In the moment I touched it, Steven, it learned everything about us. Both of us. And it's not the only member of its species. They've already marked us out."

I gave an unconvincing laugh. "Marked us out for what?"

He grimaced. "My God, it was utterly *loathsome.*" He swallowed, retched, and downed his pint. "Utterly! *Utterly!*" We'd attracted the attention of the landlord and the other customers, but Charles seemed oblivious. He applied his hands to his face and pulled the flesh down. Tears suddenly rolled from his eyes. "Which is as much as I know." He put both palms on the table and leaned forward so his face was almost next to mine. For a second, he seemed completely bewildered, as if he had no idea what to do next, then he said: "Good enough?"

"I suppose it'll have to do," I said, as calmly as I could.

VII.

We had another pint before leaving. We drank it quickly. I suppose we both needed Dutch Courage. We walked down Mount Sion in silence, keeping an eye out for neither of us knew what: we each had the distinct sense of being watched by hostile eyes, and more than two, or four… or twenty. *They've already marked us out.* We almost ran the last five hundred yards.

Dudley stood up as we entered the kitchen. He was alone. "What's up?" he said. "What's going on? You look scared. Are you all right? What's happened?"

Charles gave me a look: *we should have rehearsed this, why the hell didn't we?*

"We found something out on the Common," he said. A reversion to the script, such as it was. His words sounded stilted, his body language looked artificial. "We'd like you to come and check."

Dudley frowned. "What? What have you found?" He seemed to realise that Charles was the less *compos mentis*: "Steven: what's going on? What's my son talking about?"

"I, er – Charles and I found a man asleep on the Common," I told him. "He's asleep, that's all. We couldn't wake him up. Charles thought he was dead. He's not dead. We agreed we'd have to ask someone. Sorry, I know it's an imposition. Charles and I have got a bit of a bet on. Two pounds."

Dudley sighed, as if he'd been on the verge of believing his son was about to get interesting, and this was yet another nail in the coffin. "I'll get my coat. Don't tell your mother, she's enough on her plate. She's upstairs listening to Shostakovich and waiting for Eunice to call. "Pretty macabre bet, by the way. Two pounds for a man's life?"

He was right, of course. I'd let my inventive skills run away with me.

"Do you think we'll be able to find the spot again?" Charles asked, apparently by way of changing the subject.

"I'm sure," I said. "Then, if he really is dead, we should call the police. And I'll, er, be two pounds better off. Which I'll give to charity, of course."

Dudley went to get his coat. He returned wearing a puffer jacket and holding a heavy-duty torch. We set off without speaking, Charles and I leading the way. Five minutes later, we'd reached the spot.

"You're quite sure this is it?" Dudley asked. He passed me the torch. "Woods always look similar everywhere to me, and it *is* dark."

I swept the surrounds with the beam, and looked down towards the road, mainly to reassure him. "This is as near as the path gets. The 'corpse' is over there."

"In that case, lead the way," he said.

I advanced cautiously, without Charles, to the spot where we'd left the apparently dead body.

But there was nothing. Not only that, but there seemed to be nowhere it *could* have been. None of the undergrowth showed the slightest evidence of having had a body upon it.

Dudley appeared at my shoulder. "This is where you think you encountered him? I must say, he doesn't seem to have left much of an impress. Are you *sure* this is the spot?"

"Certain."

"And he was asleep? Well, of course, he must have been, otherwise he'd still be here. Unless the murderer's removed his body, of course. But if he'd been killed, there'd probably be some sign of it. There'd be bits of fabric snagged on the thorns, or traces of blood, or a trail where he'd been dragged away."

Charles and I remained mute. We wanted to speak – just for the comfort of hearing our own voices - but we had no idea what to say.

"Well, anyway, there's nothing here now," Dudley went on. "He was probably drunk, or on drugs. I don't think we should call the police. We may need their help."

"With what?" Charles asked.

Dudley put both hands in his pockets. "Your Aunt Eunice, of course. She was due back this afternoon, and she still hasn't called. We're not panicking yet, although we *will* be, depending on what your mother learns when she calls the hotel. Anyway, if we need the police to help us locate her, we can't risk putting their backs up by sending them on a wild goose chase tonight. No, as regards your sleeping-stroke-dead guy, let's wait and see what happens. Keep an eye on the local news, eh? I take it you got a good look at whoever-he-was?"

"Yes," I said.

"And you tried shaking him? Silly question. Of course you did. In which case, he can't have been in a state of *rigor mortis*. Anyway, there's nothing we can do. So, for all practical purposes, mystery solved, as far as I'm concerned. We'd better get home. Your mother will probably need us."

When we got in, ten minutes later, we found Corrine sitting at the kitchen table in her overcoat, with what looked like a fully packed suitcase by her side. She looked livid.

"Where have you been?" she said.

"What's going on?" Dudley asked her.

"We found a man sleeping on the Common," Charles said. "Steven and I differed as to whether there was anything the matter with him. We called Dad out for a second – third – opinion. He'd gone when we got there."

"Corrine, what's going on?" Dudley asked again. "Why are you wearing a coat? And what's that - ?" He seemed to twig. "I take it something's happened to Aunt Eunice?"

"She's 'gone missing'," Corrine said. "That was the hotel manager's best, and only, explanation. She was due to check out at 10am this morning. She'd paid them to look after her luggage for three hours, then send it her at Charing Cross, so she could get on the train at one. From what I understand, she was going to spend much of the morning shopping."

"So when exactly did she 'go missing'?" Dudley asked.

"That's still a matter of conjecture. No one saw her leave the hotel, and she didn't hand her room key in at reception, as you're supposed to; but when the maid went to make up the room, at ten-thirty this morning, ready for the next guest, she found all Aunt Eunice's things still there. Just as if she'd walked out to go to the local shop for a moment."

"Why didn't they contact us?"

"She didn't give them our details. They've got her home address in Warwick Park, and her phone number, but they haven't got my number, or yours. They've been ringing her, of course, just as we have, but they've no reason to suspect foul play. She's old, perhaps she's forgetful: that was the manager's take."

"I hope you set him straight on that score," Dudley said.

Corrine put her fingertips on her face. "Where can she have gone? Do you think she might have had some sort of breakdown?"

"She might still be on her way here," Charles said. "If you go to London - "

"I've got a very bad feeling about this," Corrine said. "I've had an awful sense of foreboding *all day,* and it's getting worse."

Dudley sat down opposite her. "I - "

"This is what we're going to do," she continued. "*We*. I can't do this alone. And we're going to need your help, Steven. Are you okay with that?"

"Absolutely," I replied.

"Dudley and I and Charles are going to London," she said. "I've already checked us all into that hotel. Charles, you'll have to help me look for Eunice. Dudley, you'll have to go to work tomorrow, I know that's non-negotiable, but if you stay in London, that gives you the whole evening to pitch in. Steven, all you have to do is stay here, in case she does return. Don't go out. Keep listening for the front door, even at night. There's enough food in the fridge for a week, and you can go online to Sainsbury's Delivery if you need anything else."

"What about the police?" Dudley said. "I'm not trying to get out of doing my share, but shouldn't we be relying on them?"

"The manager's already called them," she said. "A detective will meet us there. Maybe: because that's only what I've been told by the hotel to expect. Which may be vastly over-optimistic. The police probably have other things to do. Or think they have. Anyway, the hotel manager's retrieving the internal CCTV as we speak. He should have it ready for us to look through once we get there. Or ready for the police. Or us *and* the police. Hopefully." She was shivering.

"I'll pack my things," Charles said.

VIII.

Corrine was adamant: she had to be in London, nothing else would do. Which meant Charles and Dudley would have to accompany her.

Neither of them put up a struggle. Dudley was in London most of the day anyway, and although Corrine's insistence meant he'd have to do a bit of 'helping out' in the evening, on the plus side, he'd avoid his daily train and tube ride, and he'd get to eat in a good restaurant at night. Eunice notwithstanding (and he didn't seriously believe anything bad had happened to her), it could even turn out to be a mini-break. As for Charles, he just wanted to get as far away from Tunbridge Wells Common as he conceivably could. If he'd been told Aunt Eunice had gone to Scotland, I think he'd have been even more pleased. I recalled him telling me that it was necessary for us to separate. *I've got the weird sense it's much more likely to attack us if we stay together* was how he'd put it.

I suppose I should have minded, but he still hadn't convinced me he was entirely right in the head. Probably everything that had happened to us so far had a natural explanation. Okay, so we'd seemed to be going physically downhill, yet we'd ended up in the same place, but that didn't mean anything: we'd just switched off a little, for a while, that's all: we'd both been tired. The statuette in my pocket? Maybe that old man had been a professional 'street magician', determined to freak us out. Which would also explain his 'corpse' and his subsequent disappearance. Given enough time, he'd probably turn up with a TV crew and reveal his identity. At which point: laughs all round.

So there it was.

Or maybe I simply told myself that because I was scared, I don't know. The point is, once I'd agreed to help, I no longer had the slightest choice in the matter. Everyone fell in with Corrine's plan, and the family made a dash for the railway station. At eleven o'clock that night, I was alone in their house.

Which isn't how it felt. I'd never noticed before, but the whole place seemed plagued by unexplained creaks and soft, inexplicable bumps. Remembering my pledge to listen for a knock on the front door, I realised I'd have to sleep on the sofa. If Aunt Eunice came home, and she'd lost her memory for some reason (which was what her predicament sounded like), then she almost certainly wouldn't have a key. I needed to be alert.

I didn't sleep well that first night. The feeling that I wasn't alone got stronger however, and by Monday evening, it was much more intense. None of the Forsythes had called to see how I was doing, or update me on developments, and I took that to mean that they were busy, and nothing had changed. I considered calling Charles, but decided against it for the same reason: they'd be busy. However, the absence of human contact must have helped erode my already fragile nerves.

The sense of not being alone gradually evolved into an ominous sense that something awful was about to happen. At first, I thought it would arrive in the form of news: Aunt Eunice had suffered a heart attack, or a stroke. But then I realised it was deeper and closer at hand than that. When it happened, it would be something *within this house.*

Monday night was very little different to Sunday night in terms of the amount of sleep I got, but the noises in the house seemed to have grown in volume just enough for me to register the increase. The creaks had become more infrequent. The soft, sinister bumps – as of a large cuddly toy falling from a height in an adjacent room – more regular.

The consummation, if I can call it that, occurred on Tuesday night, in two separate incidents, one immediately after the other.

It began at 8pm with my phone ringing. I dropped it twice in my haste to pick up, a measure of just how unnerved I was. *Charles.* I was sitting in the large armchair, facing away from the window. Powerful beams from the sinking sun illuminated the far wall.

"Charles?"

"I haven't much time," he said, in a weird hurried monotone. "Mum and Dad – I don't know where they've gone. Or rather, yes, I do. They've disappeared. Gone the same way as Aunt Eunice, I suppose, obviously. And that thing I encountered on the Common: there are more of them. I keep seeing them, which… so do *you*, probably, don't you?"

He sounded crazy. I didn't want to further upset him by telling him: no, I hadn't seen anything. "Where are you?" I asked. "Are you in Tunbridge Wells? Should I come and meet you?"

"I'm in *London,* Steven. I'm still in London! I went to the police, that's what. I reported Mum and Dad missing. They want to keep me in for questioning. Well, no they didn't. I *persuaded* them to, actually. I daren't leave. Listen,

Steven. Have you seen them? You must have. Where are you?"

"In your house. Where you left me. Waiting for Aunt Eunice. - Hang on, you're in a – police station?"

"She's not coming. Are you alone? You mustn't be alone."

"Well, that's what we agreed. I haven't seen anything and I'm - "

"Lavinia Trevor's coming to help. To you, I mean. She's been here, to me. She arranged everything. She won't be long. Hold tight. That's what I'm calling about, really, Steven. To tell you. She knows everything. She knows what to do. I'd get out of the house, if I were you. Or stay… but, no, no, not if you can't. Rambling, I am, yes. Forgive me." He laughed manically. "Not a phrase I'd ever have used before, is it? *Forgive me*. Like the twelfth century! Get out, Steven. Don't worry about me. Worry about *yourself*."

The line went dead.

I mentioned earlier that the room was flooded with sunlight. During the time I'd been talking, it seemed to illuminate two particular points on the leather sofa opposite me, where the buttoned backrest met the cushions. The brown leather glared with reflected sunshine, but I got the clear impression that, as the light in the room slowly diminished, those two spots – buttons, they must be - were getting brighter.

As soon as Charles hung up, both disappeared, and I suppose the immediate memory of them must have been affectively stronger than their actual presence, because I suddenly formed the conviction that they weren't buttons at all; rather they were a pair of *eyes*, and they'd been gazing at me.

The realisation can't have been accompanied by fear, otherwise I could hardly have done what I did next. Telling myself that I mustn't fall prey to stupid delusions, I walked over to the sofa and thrust my hand down the back.

What I felt there still inhabits my nightmares. Something large, bristly - and hideously alive. The simple act of physical contact somehow conveyed that it was nothing belonging to this world, nothing remotely congenial or wholesome; more, that it could easily have swallowed me whole – an event which would, in no way, have been the end of me, for beyond the ingestion lay an infinity of horrors, all too appalling to imagine.

I half-pulled the cushions off the sofa in the violence of my recoil. I managed to turn my back on what I'd probably uncovered, but I suddenly had the conviction – like awaking from a too-pleasant dream - that the whole house was full of them, and had been for some time. I grabbed my coat as I opened the front door. I lurched into the street and began to run along Warwick Park in the direction of the Pantiles.

It suddenly struck me that I was also running towards the Common. For reasons that are probably obvious, the mere thought of ending up there petrified me, to the point where I almost double-backed. Not to return to the Forsythes' house, I should add.

But what would any sort of turning around achieve? I needed to be in proximity to other people. Going the other way would take me farther away from that. The Common might lie in front of me, but so did The Pantiles, so did the

High Street, so did the railway station. I checked my coat pocket. I had my wallet. I could get somewhere far away.

But where?

I also had the statuette.

It suddenly occurred to me that maybe that was the problem. If this had been fiction, Charles and I would have appropriated something that didn't belong to us, and the nameless things I'd encountered in the Forsythe's house would be trying to make us give it back. The solution would lie in total surrender. As in, *Oh Whistle and I'll Come to You, My Lad,* where Parker throws the whistle into the sea, and whatever it is that's been stalking him immediately desists.

I frowned and ran a hand across my hair. A few days ago, that would have seemed insane, now it felt undoubtedly worth a try. Throw it away on the Common, yes.

First, however, I'd have to overcome my terror of the Common. And terror it was.

It would be almost deserted now. Even so, mightn't there still be one or two people making their way across it? Visiting the Pantiles maybe, and parked way above, on Mount Ephraim?

Possibly, so I'd have to keep an eye out. And I'd need courage. Which, things being as they were, meant a drink or two. The Duke of York on The Pantiles, that was a good bet for plenty of people. And wasn't there also a hotel within a stone's throw? I took out my phone.

Yes, The Tunbridge Wells Hotel. Or One Warwick Park. So I could stay in either of those, and throw the statuette away in the morning, in broad daylight.

A hotel wouldn't necessarily protect me, though. It certainly hadn't protected Charles, who, as far as I could make out from his garbled report, had voluntarily incarcerated himself in a police station. I wondered if he was as secure as he thought he was, even there.

I crossed the busy Frant Road, entered the Pantiles and walked briskly to The Duke of York. Fifteen or sixteen people sat around the bar - wood panelling, leather upholstery, floorboards, and a brick hearth - in discreet groups. I ordered a pint of Harvey's, and turned around to face my fellow drinkers, seeking a morsel of reassurance in the everydayness of their faces.

It took a second to dawn on me but – that was – wasn't it? – Aunt Eunice sitting by the door? On her own, with what looked like a glass of sherry? Our eyes didn't meet. She finished her drink, stood up, and walked out.

I consumed as much of my beer as I possibly could – about half: even in my present state of mind, I didn't like to waste it – and exited. When I got outside, The Pantiles was a lot busier than it had been a few moments ago. And I couldn't see Aunt Eunice anywhere.

She must be on her way home, which meant I had to intercept her. If I ran ahead, I couldn't credibly fail. From here, there was only one route to the Forsythes' front door.

Then I saw someone else. The man from the Common; to whom Charles had given the statuette; for whom we'd gone looking, afterwards. Dressed in a tweed jacket and brogues, he looked to be in a hurry. He was heading in the opposite direction to the one Aunt Eunice would be taking… assuming she really was going home.

It didn't immediately occur to me how much of a strange coincidence this was, but then I caught sight of Aunt Eunice again. Going in the same direction as the man. Something different about her: she'd changed her clothes. In The Duke of York, she'd been dressed in a camel coat; now she was all in black.

Then I saw her again, further away, towards the shops.

There were two of her.

Then three. And the man again, dressed in a gabardine.

… All apparently oblivious to each other's existence.

I'd reached the point where I simply couldn't take any more. My head span. It occurred to me, absurdly, that I shouldn't have had that half-pint of beer, as if that was the principal culprit. I needed something to cling on to.

My phone rang. It hit me like an alarm. I removed it from my pocket, glanced at it – *Unknown Caller* – and picked up. Someone with a brief to sell me insurance would be more than fine right now. Any human voice.

"Steven?" A woman's voice.

I swallowed. I'd found my way to a bench. "Speaking." I sat down. "How can I help?"

"This is Lavinia Trevor. I believe Charles told you to expect me. Where are you?"

Someone well-intentioned. I almost cried. "I – I'm in Tunbridge Wells… The – the Pantiles. I'm sitting down. On a bench."

"You sound as if you've had a nasty shock. Are you okay?"

I was frantically scanning my surrounds for Aunt Eunices. "Not really."

"Do you know Framptons? The bar? On the corner?"

I nodded. Then I realised she couldn't see me nodding. Was she even real? Was any of this? "Er, yes," I said at last.

"Make your way there, if you can. I'll meet you inside in ten minutes."

IX.

I decided to stop thinking, stop looking around me, and just make a beeline for Framptons. When I got in, I ordered another beer, more out of habit than because I wanted one (realistically, I'd probably have preferred a strong coffee), and sat on a hard chair at a table next to the window. On the opposite side of the bar, Aunt Eunice sat sipping a sherry. I realised for the first time that she couldn't see me. She couldn't see anyone, as far as I could tell.

Probably because she wasn't really there.

She gradually stopped being scary, and became merely disturbing: a symptom of my own mental unravelling. I downed my pint, went to the toilet and came back and ordered a second. I didn't want a coffee now. If Aunt Eunice wasn't there, why should Lavinia Trevor be? Only, without her in the frame, I didn't have a plan. The brush-things I'd encountered in the house were after me. If they were real, I didn't stand a chance.

But that was wrong. I suddenly remembered that I *did* have a plan. I'd already thought it through. Go up onto the

Common and throw the statuette as far away as I possibly could.

Which would be much easier with, say, five beers inside me.

At that point, a young woman in a raincoat and a navy blue beret entered the bar in a hurry. Lavinia Trevor. I recognised her from her Facebook profile picture. She looked around, made eye-contact with me, and seemed to relax slightly. She went to the bar and ordered what looked like a white wine. I was too fazed to go over and welcome her. What if I'd misidentified her – and she me? Right now, anything seemed possible.

She walked over and sat down next to me. "You're Steven, I take it? Charles's friend?"

"Steven Parsons, yes. You must be Lavinia Trevor. I spoke to Charles on the phone. He said you could help. Maybe you could begin by telling me what's happening? I don't mean that in a confrontational way, obviously. You don't owe us anything. But I'm beginning to think I'm losing my sanity."

"Charles said you found a statuette on the Common. Do you have any way of getting to it?"

I took it from my pocket and put it on the table.

Her eyes lit up. "I must say, I wasn't expecting it to be this easy. I thought you'd have left it somewhere." She picked it up and examined it closely. "Do you have any idea how old this is?"

"I don't mean to be rude, but how can you tell? You've only just set eyes on it."

"Believe me, I can tell."

I chuckled humourlessly. "I don't really care how old it is. I don't really care about it at all. Quite the opposite. Had you not called, I'd probably have flung it away on the Common. That was my plan."

She laughed. "On the *Oh Whistle and I'll Come to You* hypothesis? Cursed object, return to sender?"

"Exactly that, yes."

"You'd effectively have been condemning yourself - and Charles. Have you a coin to hand? Any denomination, doesn't even have to be British."

I took my wallet from my coat pocket. "Are you – I mean, what's your interest in this?" I handed her a two pence piece. "Will that do? Do you want to buy it? The statuette, I mean? Because if that's the case - "

"I've no intention of taking it out of Tunbridge Wells. It's got to be destroyed. By which I mean, ground to dust." She used the coin to scrape Persephone's arm several times, and produced a tiny quantity of powder on the table. "Follow my lead," she said. She licked the tip of her index finger, put it in the powder and transferred it to her tongue. It couldn't be poisonous, and I'd have been willing to do anything at that point, obey anyone if I thought they could help. I followed suit.

She smiled, apparently gratified by my compliance. "Okay, that makes us both immune. I won't lie to you, Steven. I've been watching Charles's 'Aunt Eunice' for over a decade now, patiently waiting for this very opportunity."

"Immune to what? And what opportunity?"

"Immune to attack. You must have encountered those 'hairy' things by now, surely? Charles certainly has. Loathsome, yes? Well, no, actually. They're simply what theologians call 'wholly other', and biologically, we're not equipped to deal with that: we've evolved to find it repulsive. Because maybe a lot of the time, it *will* be hostile. Best to err on the side of caution, eh?"

"So you know about the 'hairy things'?"

"The important thing, from your point of view, is that I know exactly what to do to get you out of this mess." She stood up. "Come on."

"Where are we going?"

"Charles's house. Or rather, the person who used to be Charles. His house."

We left Framptons, Lavinia Trevor leading. "I don't know what you mean."

"Charles has disappeared," she said. "Just as his parents disappeared, early yesterday morning; just as Aunt Eunice disappeared on Saturday night. In Charles's case, the police are frantically asking themselves how he can have escaped from a locked cell. It's not that important, of course: he's hardly an arch-criminal. Still, they're bound to wonder."

"Disappeared where?"

She smiled. "Going somewhere else doesn't qualify as disappearing in my book. Disappearing means being literally nowhere. Of course, that's set to happen to you soon, unless we do something drastic. Which is why you're lucky you've got me."

"I keep seeing Aunt Eunice. I hardly think *she* can have disappeared."

"You're almost certainly seeing echoes of her. Which is interesting. Listen, Steven, I wouldn't normally bother to explain all this, but since you're a historian, you might find it interesting, and you'll probably understand, even though you might find it hard to believe. About two thousand years ago, the Romans came to Britain. What the history books don't record, because most of the relevant primary sources were destroyed by the Christians, is that they came to this country in search of the goddess Persephone, whose portal they'd learned was here, beneath what is now Tunbridge Wells. Having located it, they established the so-called Way of Truth, in which an initiate descends into the Underworld, and a 'space beyond space, a time outside time, and an admixture of the necessarily real with the metaphysically impossible', as one second century devotee apparently put it, according to two different medieval copyists. The whole thing was described by the Ancient Greek philosopher, Parmenides, hundreds of years before Rome came into existence. Anyway, William Rowston, Aunt Eunice's long dead lover, discovered hard evidence for its existence. He published his findings, but the tide of academic opinion turned against him: the whole thing would have required major chunks of ancient history to be completely rewritten, a lot of people's life-work would have been rendered utterly redundant, and who knew what knock-on effects all that would have? No, the academic world is the most hidebound of all worlds, and it wasn't ready for a paradigm shift. After some sort of unauthorised dig on the Common - very embarrassing for his employers – he left for the continent, where he died in mysterious circumstances. Afterwards, Aunt Eunice made it her life's work to vindicate him – and re-join him in the 'space beyond space'. She's been collecting related artefacts ever since, all undoubtedly genuine. What she seems to have grasped, that he didn't, is that the thing that was there in Roman times is still present today, and it no more wants to be disturbed now than it did then. The Romans must have known that, of course: but they had ways of bending recalcitrant things to their will, if the prize was worth the effort. Which it undoubtedly was. Immortality. Not the sort of bog-standard immortality that you get by living for an unlimited duration, but the genuine out-of-time, everlasting bliss variety.

"Anyway, what went up for auction in London was a seventh-century piece of text, Byzantine, on fine parchment, which Aunt Eunice and I both realised contained valuable information connected to William Rowston's researches, and which may even have been owned by him at one point. Its possessor would – with sufficient number of other tokens in place: viz. those statuettes – gain access to The Way of Truth. Her bid beat mine, but then I didn't need it any more. I'd arranged with the auction house to view it in advance, and I realised that having it in one's possession – especially if you also owned a number of genuine first century AD Persephone figurines – was likely to place you in great danger."

We were almost at the Forsythes' now. I was becoming increasingly uneasy, especially given the speed of our approach.

"Hang on," I told her, "we're not going inside, are we?"

"We need to retrieve all those figurines from the top floor – Charles told me all about them, but I've known for a while anyway – then we're going to reduce them to powder. Which won't be as difficult as it sounds. Then we're going to mix said powder with water, then we're going to pour it on the Common while I recite something from my photograph of that fine parchment I just told you about. Simple as that. Hey presto: you get Charles and Charles's family back, *and* you get to rid yourselves of Persephone's hounds, as I like to think of them. Meanwhile, I literally get to be a goddess. Sorry, that should be: I get *to become God*."

It was the most incomprehensible plan I'd ever heard. Yes, she was completely insane, but at least she was company, and by way of a bonus, she was company-with-a-plan. Which was as much as I wanted right now.

Then everything seemed to switch about. The world literally seemed to turn over. I sidestepped and lost my balance. I landed on the pavement on my knees and elbows.

"Feeling okay?" Lavinia Trevor asked. She chortled, without warmth. "I forgot to tell you: that powder we ingested has strong hallucinogenic properties. In my defence, it's our only way of protecting ourselves. I say 'hallucinogenic', but I'm afraid it's not entirely subjective. We're about to enter the same world. Get up, Steven. I can't do this without you. Be a man. Think of the Roman general, Magna Magissipus. Think of Protulus of Gerasa or Anatolius of Smyrna."

All at once, it was as if someone had injected something into my brain. I had the overwhelming feeling – which the reader, if she really must, may attribute to the power of suggestion - of having entered Persephone's realm, deep underground. Her malevolent stare seared my back. The sky turned red and filled with the hairy things I'd encountered in the Forsythes' house, only now they had wings. They journeyed from east to west, thousands of miles overhead, in huge flocks, singing praises to their queen. I no longer had the sense that they were repulsive or loathsome. They just seemed to … *be,* in the same sense that I was.

Lavinia Trevor grabbed my hand. She pulled me to my feet and we ascended a soaring helical staircase. We entered Aunt Eunice's living room. Lavinia Trevor ecstatically scooped up the statuettes – I suddenly realised she was enjoying herself - while I stood idly, noticing all sorts of things that simply hadn't been there on my first visit: models of anatomically impossible creatures, arcane laboratory glassware, maps of unknown countries, exquisitely cut jewels of all colours, astrological charts.

We descended the staircase and pounded the statuettes to dust. I don't know where we were when we did that, or even how we did it. Then we mixed the dust with water in a large, antique-looking jug that seemed to come into existence out of nothing. Suddenly, we were both naked in a way that felt, weirdly, *holy*. Set apart, cleansed.

We joined hands and ran to the Common faster than I thought anyone could move. Faster, perhaps, than anything at all: suddenly, we were just *there*. Lavinia Trevor kissed me – nothing particularly erotic about it, as I recall, just part of the programme – then slowly emptied the jug and recited her words.

The earth seemed to erupt. The entire Common bulged and took on the shape of Persephone. I lost sight of Lavinia Trevor as I was sucked into the Earth. Then I was belched out of the other side and rose ninety-three million miles into the air. The Sun swallowed me like a long-overdue homecoming. At which point, I suppose I must have lost consciousness.

But I don't know that for certain. All I do know, is that that is where my memory ends.

X.

I awoke naked and alone on the Common at around 4am. When I looked around, I realised I was in exactly the same place Charles and I had found the corpse of whoever-it-was (William Rowston?) that Sunday night. More, I was lying in an identical bodily position. I stood up with considerable difficulty, self-inflicting a plethora of minor cuts and abrasions. It didn't even occur to me to look for Lavinia Trevor. I knew with certainty that she'd *gone* in the same sense that, only a few hours ago, she'd told me Charles and his parents and Aunt Eunice had gone. I later learned that she'd handed in her resignation at Edinburgh University, and that she'd left a note warning her friends and family not to come looking for her. As far as I know, no one ever did.

Obviously, I was traumatised. I had no idea what to do. I couldn't very well go back to the Forsythes': I'd locked their front door behind me, and I had no reason to believe reality would be otherwise in that regard.

Which raised the question, how much of the last ten hours *had* been real? Had Lavinia Trevor? Had my visit to Framptons? Had The Pantiles, even?

I didn't know.

A police car picked me up – after I flagged it down - on Saint John's Road, standing at the crossroads in Southborough. Its two officers took me to the station, gave me some clothes to put on, and locked me in a holding cell, seeming to consider my predicament slightly funny. After several terse questions - and once they realised I wasn't drunk or hung over - they began to feel sorry for me.

In the morning, a middle-aged policeman entered my cell in an airy manner and asked me a few of the same questions. Once he realised I wasn't going to be a smart aleck, he softened. He became sympathetic. I gave him the Forsythes' address in Warwick Part – I couldn't remember any phone numbers, not even my Aunt's in Cornwall – and somehow he managed to track down Charles and his parents. They arrived to take me away in the car five hours later: 'as soon as they could', they said, and I believed them.

We left the police station in gloomy silence. I hadn't even been cautioned. We went back to their house. Charles sat awkwardly on the sofa. He seemed overjoyed to see me – he'd almost cried when we shook hands - but embarrassed to show it. Mrs Forsythe hugged me. Dudley stood around looking as emotional, if not more so, than his wife and son. He went into the kitchen and poured himself a large whisky.

Aunt Eunice had been found undressed and unconscious in Whitechapel. At the time Mr and Mrs Forsythe picked me up, she was 'recovering' in St Thomas Hospital, although the long-term completeness of that was very much in the balance. She died five days later.

For over a week, the Forsythes seemed relatively estranged from each other and from me. I mooted the idea of returning to Cornwall, but they wouldn't hear of it, and I knew why. Something inexplicable had happened. In some ways, it had established new bonds between us. But it had also broken old ones. A time would inevitably come when we would start communicating, and I held a crucial part of the jigsaw puzzle.

I can't recall the first time we had a frank conversation, but I have a feeling it took place around the dinner table. That would be characteristic. It turned out that they'd all undergone roughly the same thing I had, which is to say they'd all awoken naked somewhere, with no memory of how they'd got there, or even what had happened during the last ever-so-many hours.

We talked at length, but without reaching any conclusions. After a week, I went back to Cornwall.

Though the Forsythes kept in touch, it was ten years before I got another invitation to stay with them. After twelve months, I learned that Charles had dropped out of university; then I heard that he'd become a manager in Tesco; then I heard he'd got married and become a father. A little girl, whom he and his wife had named Eunice.

Meanwhile, I had 'problems' of my own. Not the sort you might imagine: no PTSD, no flashbacks, no nightmares. Rather, it was as if I'd got a glimpse of an exponentially better world, and, by comparison, nothing I could achieve in this one could conceivably mean anything. I might as well do one thing as another, and nothing at all as well as either. It took me slightly longer, but, like Charles, I dropped out of university. My Aunt in Cornwall died. We'd never been close: she left all her money to her daughters, which struck me as eminently fair; I certainly wasn't going to contest the will. I wandered up and down the country on foot for a while, telling myself I was a liberated spirit, before the truth sank in: I was tediously homeless. Which didn't bother me either. Like everyone, my time on Earth was limited; we were all going to die. I took to drinking. To begin with, it gave me access to that other world… then it just became a way of living.

The next I heard about Charles, a decade had passed. By now, I was living in various hostels, on and off (in between sleeping rough), and he was apparently looking for me. How much effort he was putting into it, I don't know. He might even have seen me and not recognised me: I'd aged prematurely: thirty-one, looks sixty-one, so people said.

Anyway, from what I learned, Charles had long since given up on Tesco. Unsurprisingly (to me, though it may surprise the less imaginative of my readers) he'd become an Anglican vicar. I didn't run towards him, but neither did I run away. One rainy afternoon in mid-December, he and his wife (and his ten-year-old daughter, plus his five-year-old son) found me – I don't know how - on a park bench in Liverpool, nursing a can of lager.

The upshot was that his parents wanted me to come and live with them in Warwick Park. All the Forsythes (and they were quite a clan now) knew about my 'decline and fall', to put it in worldly terms. They knew I was an alcoholic, for example, but they were sure they could help me in that regard. We ate Christmas dinner together that year. For some reason, we'd all independently become vegetarians, so it was a nut roast. We went to church as a group, and, after that, for reasons I won't bother to explain, I started to spend a lot of time in church, mostly alone.

The rest can be told in a few sentences. We ate together every week. Charles had a parish in Sevenoaks, so he was always on hand. I gave up drinking. I went to live on the third floor of the Forsythes' house in Warwick Park, becoming a new Aunt Eunice, without the arcane paraphernalia. I became a 'better' person, if by that is meant, a kinder, more charitable individual. I still look forward to dying.

Sometimes, I gaze out of the window. You can see a lot of Tunbridge Wells from here. Its beauty never fails to astonish me.

Also, sometimes, I go for a walk on the Common. Do you believe in ghosts? Because I've seen Aunt Eunice and William Rowston there, many, many times, walking arm-in-arm like the lovers they obviously are. And I've seen Lavinia Trevor. A goddess now, apparently. She looks happy, but not as if the novelty won't wear off some day.

I'd like to say I look forward to joining them. But theirs is a lesser bliss. Charles is right: there's a vastly greater good than Persephone. You can't see it, you can't touch it, but it's waiting for you on the flip side of what we consider real. And it's never more than a hair's breadth away.

The Hermetic Woman

I.

Public records, other than those to which members of the public have had access before their transfer, shall not be available for inspection until they have been in existence for fifty years, or such other period as the Lord Chancellor may prescribe.

— The Public Records Act, 1958

Thirteen years after the end of the Second World War, the police report concerning the event which forms the pretext for this story was finally made public. Viz. on June 21st, 1901, five members of the Tunbridge Wells Freemasons' Lodge were found murdered in an upper room in Calverley Park. The manner of their deaths suggested something considerably 'out of the ordinary'. All had been stabbed through the heart, at the exact same entry-point on the chest, and with such violence that the blade had gone through the body and exited at its full width through the victim's back. The weapon itself resembled a medieval sword, and had been abandoned, propped up, apparently casually, against the wall opposite the door. Most astonishing of all, however, the evidence showed that none of the victims had offered the slightest resistance.

The reason the murders remained hidden from the public for so long was that they were immediately deemed to fall under the auspices of The Official Secrets Act of 1889. Obviously, they were not the work of a single individual, they had none of the hallmarks of a *crime passionnel,* and they didn't look to be motivated by parochial concerns.

Rather, they looked as if someone wanted to send a message.

Suspicion fell upon the Germans. The Second German Navy Law of 1900 presaged Britain's maritime rivalry with that nation, and certain members of the civil service (farsighted, as it turns out) feared an escalation. A well-funded, rival 'Freemasonic' organisation – an *Academia Masonica,* to give it its proper designation - had just been unofficially founded in Saxony, and the contention was that this organisation might be motivated by an ecstatic nationalistic fervour, of the sort to which such bodies are regrettably prone. In other words, it might be both announcing its credentials to the world, and simultaneously signifying its loyalty to the *Kaiserreich.*

Terse communications were exchanged between the Foreign Office and the Imperial German embassy in London, but without shedding the slightest light on the matter. The Germans denied any knowledge of the 'Ordo Templi Orientis', as it was called, and, to be fair, the British evidence for the organisation's involvement was piteous; *a priori* deductions, that was all.

In fact, as it now turns out, the Foreign Office was barking up entirely the wrong tree. The founder of the OTO was a wealthy Austrian - not German - Industrialist, and it had its origins on the Austro-Hungarian border, far from the obvious German power-centres in Berlin, Frankfurt and Leipzig. And although it is true that Germany and Austria-Hungary were allies in World War I, in 1901 their foreign and domestic policies diverged.

Since the release, in 1958, of the various official documents relating to the five murders, a number of amateur detectives have offered halfway plausible theories, in books, in newspaper articles, and on the radio, purporting to explain what happened. The Freemasons always make good fodder for a conspiracy theory, poor old Aleister Crowley has (as usual) been implicated, and I believe even the extraterrestrials have been drafted in, especially in the USA, where two paperbacks on the subject have lately appeared.

However, I can state with authority that not one of the hypotheses so far advanced is remotely correct. I have a personal link to the story, in that my uncle was one of the five men who died horribly in that upper room. But my connection goes much, much deeper than that.

In a word, I can explain everything.

It has been difficult for me to write this account. What strikes me now, with the benefit of hindsight and nearly sixty years' life-experience, is just how deeply, and how frequently, I was deceived. *Lied to,* to be blunt. By my two guardians, by my own sister, by the woman at the centre of this story - by everyone. And lied to fairly systematically. I was kept firmly on the outside right to the very end.

But I bear no one ill-will. Were the culprits here to defend themselves, they would undoubtedly claim they did it *for my protection*.

Being, as I hope I am, an understanding and impartial judge, I cannot honestly say I would disbelieve them.

II.

Cytherea Holmes was at least a 'Magister Templi', and may even have been an 'Ipsissimus'; either way, she belonged to the third, and highest, echelon of a now defunct organisation called The Hermetic Order of the Golden Dawn. Together with her much less dazzling fiancé, Robert Collinson, she arrived in Tunbridge Wells on June 17th, 1901, shortly before the first of the scandalous events that subsequently became a landslide, and ultimately led to the Order's demise.

I would date the beginning of our brief association to the moment when, at breakfast on the morning of June 18th, my uncle announced that he would be taking the entire family – four of us, including himself - to a 'spectacular' party on the Calverley Estate that evening. He must already have discussed the whole thing with Aunt Gloria, but Mildred and I were taken completely by surprise. The party's pretext was that a celebrated couple named Cytherea Holmes and Robert Collinson had just arrived in Tunbridge Wells. I had never heard of them, but then women of my age – I had just turned twenty-one - were kept in the dark about all sorts of things in those days. For reasons my uncle did not specify, our local dignitaries thought it would be an honour and a privilege to extend the pair a lavish welcome. By 'local dignitaries', it later transpired, he actually meant Freemasons.

At this point, I may as well introduce my family, since they all play a part in what follows. We lived in a large town house on the edge of Rusthall. Looking today at the two photographs I had taken that year, I was perhaps conventionally 'pretty', but I certainly didn't see myself that way then: yes, I had my positives, but I also had a pile of unruly black hair, a longish neck, and slightly round shoulders. Mildred, my older sister by eleven years, looked like an older me, but with brown locks and less of a smile. She had her own house now, following the death, in 1900, of her husband, Joseph, in the Second Boer War; but she occasionally returned to live with us.

Uncle Gordon and Aunt Gloria were our guardians; our natural parents had died when I was very young. Uncle Gordon was tall, physically upright, habitually aloof, a shopkeeper, the town alderman, and a proud Freemason. I never recall him wearing anything other than a suit. Aunt Gloria was the family Napoleon: much smaller than the rest of us, and rarely content with life, she seemed to take pleasure in devising complicated new rules and issuing impromptu decrees on matters of minor importance. Something in her childhood had made her averse to religion, and she only tolerated Uncle Gordon's Masonic involvement because she supposed it to bring measurable material benefits. She wore black as a matter of course (although Uncle Gordon was rarely even ill, let alone dead), and she preferred the styles of the 1870s. Her eyes were perpetually alive. She had thin, belligerent lips. She customarily referred to Mildred and I as 'you children', even though Mildred was thirty-one.

My uncle had hired a carriage that night, and the four of us set off for the Calverley Estate at half past eight. It had been a beautiful day, and on either side of the long road, a wide expanse of grass, dotted with elms and mature oaks, was illumined by the setting sun. I suspect only Mildred and I were genuinely excited about what lay ahead. As far as Uncle Gordon was concerned, it was merely a social function, yet an inferior one, since not only did it *involve* women but was actually in *honour* of one. Aunt Gloria also saw it as second-rate, but for the opposite reason: because it involved Freemasons. I had been seduced by the word 'spectacular', meaning… nothing like the outings I was used to (ie, Thursday night dinners with the Forsythes, back-and-forth perambulations on the Pantiles with a friend or two, Whist evenings at the parsonage with the Rev. Bates and his uncommunicative older sister and elderly mother).

Mildred was excited for a completely different reason. Since Joseph's death, she'd quietly been attending séances, both in Tunbridge Wells and farther afield, in the hope of receiving some sort of message from beyond the grave; she knew enough about Cytherea Holmes to expect a sympathetic hearing, and perhaps even advice about how to progress in her otherworldly endeavours. She was therefore quietly desperate for an introduction.

"I'm sure this 'Cytherea Holmes' and her fiancé are considered very important in some circles," Aunt Gloria said, "but in my humble opinion, it's a shame to waste such a lovely evening indoors."

"We should have walked," I ventured, as a way of getting into the conversation. "At least some of the way."

Aunt Gloria frowned. "It's important to show one can *afford* a carriage, Ada, and to do what everyone else is doing. How many other guests can you see on foot?"

"None," I said, chastened.

"It may *extend* onto the lawn, for all I know," Uncle Gordon said. "I wasn't involved in the fine detail of the planning. Anyway, it'll be dark soon, and the temperature will drop. Unless the whole place is properly heated – and *you* may not know Munro House, my dear, but *I* do, and I can tell you it's draughty! – we'll probably be cold enough to begin with."

"I didn't know we were going to Munro House," Aunt Gloria said. "I thought Munro House was empty; had been for years, I thought; so I heard."

"That's precisely why we've requisitioned it," Uncle Gordon replied. "No one wants the *personal* expense of hosting Cytherea Holmes. This way, we can share the cost and - "

Aunt Gloria interrupted him with a hoot. *"No one wants the personal expense?* What about 'the honour and the privilege', as you put it at breakfast this morning?"

"Ah, well - "

"Well?" Aunt Gloria burst out. "Well! Well! Well! Who *is* this young woman and her – fiancé? You still haven't really *told* us! You probably *think* you have, Gordon - I mean, knowing you: how cerebral you are - but you *haven't!"*

"It's a Masonic matter," he said shortly. "It's not something I'm necessarily at liberty to share."

"Do so anyway," she replied equally curtly.

He sighed. "All I can tell you is what everyone knows, and no more. She's a high-ranking member of a secret society with Masonic origins. That's all."

"I thought women weren't even *allowed* to be Masons," I put in.

"I didn't say it *was* Masonic," he replied: "just that that is where it had its origins. We have a continuing interest in it. Or some of us have; London has; the Master Masons have. No, they're not part of our organisation, but they're investigating things with which, historically, we've always been deeply concerned."

"'Always'," Aunt Gloria said sardonically. "Since 1717. Hardly 'always'."

"The Masons are far older than that," he told her. "And that's the end of the discussion, Gloria. I know how you feel about Masonry. I'm not prepared to argue with you."

Mildred leaned forward. "By 'things that, historically, we've always been concerned with', Uncle, you mean… magical practices."

Uncle Gordon scowled like he'd been given castor oil. "I'm not sure I'm actually permitted to confirm - "

"It's a matter of public knowledge," Mildred informed him gently. "They've been in *The Strand Magazine.*" She turned to face me. "The Hermetic Order of the Golden Dawn, they're called, Ada. And they *do* have women members. *We* could join!"

Uncle Gordon and Aunt Gloria exchanged weary looks. Aunt Gloria expelled ten ounces of air. "I'd steer well clear of them, if I was you," she said. "They sound exactly like the Freemasons to me – but with all the *silly-billy* bits and none of the advantages! It always amazes me, children and dearest husband, the way some people pine for bygone ages of superstition and stupidity. We're in the twentieth century now." She fixed her eyes on Uncle Gordon. "I suppose the idea that this woman is allegedly a - *magician* is connected to you and your 'dignitary' friends entertaining her in Munro House?"

"I'm not sure what you mean," he replied.

"The fact that it's reputedly haunted."

"Is it?" he said airily. "I wasn't aware. Anyway, I'm not sure what connection you discern."

"Superstition added to superstition," she replied. "Double superstition; men's pig-headed credulity times two. Or times three, if you add this... woman, who, I wouldn't be at all surprised to find, is 'startlingly beautiful', whatever *that* assessment means."

"As I remarked earlier," he replied, "I know how you feel about Masonry. I'm not prepared to cross swords with you. Not in front of the children."

Aunt Gloria harrumphed. We 'children' looked at each other, then at the floor. The carriage ran over a rock. We all bounced briefly in the air. The driver called a perfunctory sorry, then we fell into silence.

III.

In some ways, it was one of the oddest parties I have ever attended; in others, dully conventional. Cytherea Holmes was its centrepiece. She wore a high-collared, red lamé dress from (so I was told) an expensive *modiste* in Paris. She wore jewels everywhere it was possible for a woman of taste to wear jewels: even her shoes had diamonds, emeralds and rubies. She looked to be about Mildred's age. Her face was thin and its features well-spaced. Her eyes were brown, and her hair lustrous, silvery blonde and immaculately styled. None of which conveys the powerful impression she made on everyone present. As if to fulfil Aunt Gloria's prophecy, I continually overheard people declare she was the most beautiful woman they'd ever seen. For some, her 'loveliness' was quite literally unearthly.

I say the whole thing was odd: for a full hour she stood alone on a low podium at the front of the ballroom. The guests queued in couples, or families, to meet her, as a master of ceremonies introduced everyone in turn. The closer people got, the more nervous they became. Face to face with her, they seemed vaguely obsequious, and when their little audience was over, they looked relieved. (Much later on, I read a novel called *The Master and Margarita*. In Chapter 23, the heroine appears as the principal attraction at a ball, in a somewhat similar pose. Bulgakov's chosen title for the chapter: 'Satan's Rout' is also relevant. More about that later … maybe.)

Anyway, because we all approached her in order of social rank (it was that kind of party), and because Uncle Gordon was considered a prominent member of the local business community, my family was amongst the first to make her acquaintance. She exchanged a few words with my aunt and uncle, then with Mildred. When my turn came, she asked me how old I was. I told her. She smiled, as if she was pleased I was precisely that age. At which point, the attendant official discreetly moved me beyond her radiance.

A moment afterwards, I couldn't help wondering where her fiancé, Robert Collinson, was. I'd been looking forward to seeing *him* as much as her: they were supposed to be an illustrious couple, and, in my view, therefore, mainly worth seeing *as* a couple. Meeting her on her podium had been nice, but vaguely pantomimic, but I now assumed that he'd be at least as fetching as she was, and I didn't want to leave without confirming my prediction and congratulating myself on how clever I was.

Then I saw him. Ah, yes. Probably the handsomest man in the room, about Cytherea's age, standing alone in the far corner, just a few yards from his fiancée's left hand, with his hands clasped low behind his back. Neat brown hair, an aquiline nose, a well-defined mouth and eyes that seemed to be looking for something or someone. I wondered why no one seemed to be talking to him.

Mildred appeared at my side. "What did you think of her? Wasn't she *wonderful?"*

"She *looks* wonderful," I said. "As to whether she *is,* I don't know."

"What did she say to you?"

"She asked me how old I was."

Mildred looked at me as if, well, that was entirely my fault. "And what did you tell her?"

"I've learned always to tell the truth," I replied facetiously, "no matter what the provocation."

She clicked her tongue. "Don't you want to know what she asked *me?"*

"What your name was?"

"Don't be contrary, Ada. I don't like you when you're contrary. No, she asked me about *Joseph.* Whispered, so no one else would hear, I assume. And she asked me about him before I'd even had chance to tell her anything at all. She didn't mention him by name, of course. She said she'd heard I was looking for news of my deceased husband, and that she might be able to help me."

I was surprised enough to be momentarily lost for words. I'd obviously underestimated Cytherea Holmes: maybe she really *was* wonderful, after all, and here was the proof. "Really?" I said. "That's – well, that's astonishing! How could she have known *that?"*

Then I realised. Of course. Uncle Gordon must have told her, probably unintentionally, along with some other more important information, possibly even before tonight.

Before I could relay this, though, Mildred began expounding her own theory. "Didn't I tell you," she said, "during the ride here, that she's involved in *magic?* When I suggested to you that we could get involved In the Hermetic Order, I was utterly, utterly serious." She laughed. "Did you see Auntie and Uncle's faces, at that moment? No? Well, like I just said, I'm serious. Fiddlesticks to them. Women, in this world, have little enough power as it is. But imagine if we could bypass all the social hurdles, all the petty prejudices. Not *overcome* them, Ada, *bypass* them! Gain the power to literally *bend the laws of nature to our advantage!"*

I looked around for Robert Collinson, mainly as a pretext for changing the subject. But he'd gone.

"Where do you think Robert Collinson is?" I asked.

"Who?"

"Robert Collinson. Her fiancé."

The smile – or at least, the animation – dropped from her face. In lieu of pointing, she swept her eyes towards the French windows. "He's the one standing alone," she said quietly. "Don't let him catch you looking at him. From what I've heard, he possesses a terrible temper, and very little sense of what's appropriate at a social function like this."

To my dismay, he wasn't the man I'd seen earlier. Nor did he even resemble him. Suddenly, I didn't feel so clever after all. The real Robert Collinson's suit looked as if it had been handed down through three or four generations, none of whom had treated it kindly. His hair was dark, thin and unkempt. His features were what used to be called 'coarse', although today we'd probably call them weathered and somehow intrinsically disgruntled. His legs were noticeably short. He looked to be at least ten years older than his fiancée.

"How interesting!" I said. And I meant it.

IV.

After Cytherea Holmes's rather peculiar personal reception, there was lots of dancing and conversation, and people began peeling off from the ballroom to wander around the house. I lost sight of Mildred, but Elijah Scott, the butcher from Southborough, asked me to dance twice, and we ended up touring the grounds together. Elijah was five years older than me and four inches taller, with a long black beard and overgrown eyebrows. Aunt Gloria disapproved of him because he was a 'tradesman', but that was an affectation. (How could it be anything else, given that she herself had married a shopkeeper? Besides, she couldn't reasonably believe I had the slightest chance of marrying into the landed gentry - even had that been my desire, which it wasn't: I was a nobody.)

In any case, the evening was made more exciting by our playacted need for secrecy: the self-consciously adopted notion – as fictional as it was thrilling – that we had to prevent Aunt Gloria and Uncle Gordon seeing us together. We took liberties we would never normally have dreamed of taking: holding hands, peeping into side rooms (in one of which, I saw Mildred and Cytherea Holmes talking animatedly: was my sister's wish coming true?), running up and down dark staircases, exploring corridors, blowing out candles so we could gaze out of windows, and finally climbing a rickety old ladder to the roof, where, magically, we were able to see the lights of Tunbridge Wells.

"I love this town," Elijah told me as we stood against the parapet, gazing into the dark distance. "All I want to do is cut joints of meat for everyone living here, for ever and ever!"

I laughed. I may have been fickle – I knew he was joking – but I believe that was the point at which I started to go off him. Perhaps I did have a future with the landed gentry, after all. "That's nice," I said.

"With you there beside me, I mean," he added. "To support me."

"What did Cytherea Holmes say to you?" I asked, in a bid to change the subject. "I assume you met her?"

"I was at the front of the queue," he said proudly. "Three or four families behind you. Oh, we had a long talk. Can't divulge the details, of course. Freemason's honour."

"What did you think of her?"

"Very beautiful. Very cerebral. So, I've no idea what she's doing with someone like Robert Collinson. And I'm not the only man here tonight who thinks that."

"What's wrong with him? – Come along, it's getting cold up here; we should re-join the others."

"You're right. People may be looking for *me*. Truth told, this isn't just a social occasion."

"Oh? What is it then?"

We'd reached the top of the ladder, ready to descend. "I'll go first," he told me. "That way, I can catch you if you fall. Or if a rung goes through because it's rotten – I don't know what we were thinking, coming up here, really – I'll be the one who suffers."

"Thank you," I said.

"To answer your question, it's as much of a Masonic *meeting* as it is a social occasion. We're here – or some people are – to assess Miss Holmes. Well, I'm pretty sure she's passed the test, whatever it is; don't ask me; I won't be able to tell you; I'm not sufficiently senior. Anyway, all the men think she's both amazingly attractive and highly intelligent. And I believe one or two may even have set their caps at her, despite Mr Robert Collinson."

He'd reached the bottom of the ladder. I followed him without difficulty. We stood facing each other.

"You suggested there was something wrong with him," I said. "Robert Collinson."

He chuckled. "I didn't quite put it that strongly, Ada. And keep your voice down. It's just... well, *she's* all sweetness and light, and *he's* the polar opposite. Which one could almost understand, were he rich or attractive, but he's neither of those things, and he's not particularly pleasant either. From what I've heard, he spends most of his time in her company sulking."

"Still waters run deep. And he may be the jealous sort."

"He has good cause to be, from what I've heard tonight. But I've already told you that. As for him being 'deep', well, I don't know. He must have *something*, so perhaps you're right."

"I must be," I told him.

He laughed. "Ada Pearson The Infallible."

"Ah, there you are, Elijah!" A moustachioed man in his late fifties appeared from around the corner, dressed in a red jacket and black trousers. "We've been looking for you! Martin wants your opinion on, er," – he cast a sidelong glance at me - "something. Excuse me, my dear," he said, addressing me in an unnaturally indulgent tone, as if I was a child, "but you won't mind if I requisition Elijah for a while, will you?" He linked arms with him without waiting for my reply. "Come along, Elijah. Wait till you hear *this!"*

Elijah left without even the pretence of putting up a fight – being a Mason meant as much to him as it did to Uncle Gordon: both lived in perpetual fear of causing offence to other Masons – and suddenly I found myself alone. I wondered if every single Mason was like that: afraid of upsetting all the others.

The corridor into which he and I had just descended was long, dingy, and slightly dilapidated, with sullenly closed doors on either side. I shuddered; I could well believe this had been an empty house before tonight, and I could well believe it was haunted.

I needed to get back to the other guests. Apart from any other consideration, I might have been missed – people might be looking for me - though I didn't consider that very likely.

To my frustration, however, the house seemed to have become a maze. Corridors that I was sure I'd been along with Elijah were cul-de-sacs, and two sets of stairs simply led to a ceiling, like in a folly. More, I got the disturbing impression that, whenever I was forced to go back the way

I'd just come, the physical geography of the return route had subtly altered.

The temperature dropped, and I admit, I became afraid. I hadn't encountered another person for several minutes; and I couldn't hear any voices. Presumably, I'd strayed into some remote section of the house. My only question was: whether to attempt calling someone?

But I wasn't sure whether I could keep the panic out of my voice. And I didn't know how hearing my own distress would affect me.

But then, I had the much more unpleasant sense that no, I wasn't actually alone, after all. Not only that, but my invisible attendant wasn't lurking around any corner like a mischievous person, but was actually *beneath my feet* in the manner of something wholly unknown and possibly unknowable: the floor seemed slightly springier than it should have, and warmer – I could feel the heat through my shoes. A pungent smell arose. My instincts read it as the exudation of something not only living, but bent on killing.

And then – how can I put this, without sounding insane? – the floor seemed to open up in front of me. What I beheld through the ten-feet-wide fissure was a cavernous pit with a black creature at the bottom, like a flat fish of some sort, only hundreds of times larger.

For a moment, I thought it was going to devour me. Then, in a trice, as if in some kind of preternatural revelation, I saw it wasn't remotely interested in me.

It was interested in - Cytherea Holmes?

"Ada! What are you *doing?* Where have you *been?"*

Uncle Gordon. In the act of swivelling around, my vision evaporated. Not only was normality restored, but the memory was erased. I remembered nothing whatsoever of what I'd just seen, or intuited, until later.

"You can't wander round on your own!" he said irritably. "Who knows what might happen to you?"

Even at the time, it seemed an odd remark.

V.

The ballroom was still packed with guests. The dancing had long since finished, but no one looked ready to go home. The string ensemble ploughed doggedly through Mozart's Haydn Quartets, though only a few slightly inebriated souls seemed to be listening. I couldn't see Uncle Gordon or Aunt Gloria or Mildred. I couldn't even see Elijah. I went to the side of the room, as I'd been taught to do when I was 'lost', and sat alone on a chair with its back against the wall. The conversational roar was deafening. The lights stopped just short of being blinding. It was hot.

Someone stood over me. "Are you quite well?"

I looked up into the face of the handsome man who'd been standing in the corner earlier. His face expressed considerable concern.

"Oh, yes," I said. "I'm just a bit warm."

"We haven't been introduced. My name's Michael Bowling. I'm here on business, really. Should I – could I bring you a glass of water?"

"Thank you, I just need a moment's rest."

"May I sit down beside you?"

"Oh, yes, please do. I'm Ada Pearson. My Uncle helped organise all this. Not that's that's anything to boast about."

"I'm not personally acquainted with your Uncle, but I know your Aunt fairly well."

I was about to ask him how, when our attention was diverted by the sight of Robert Collinson on the other side of the room. This time, he was arguing. Three men were nervously trying to calm him down, but they didn't seem to be having much success. I recognised the portents: a 'scene' was about to develop, and possibly even a minor scandal. I tried to tune my ears beyond the nuances of the wall of conversation, to see if I could glean any clue as to what was going on.

It didn't take me long. Cytherea Holmes had disappeared. Uncle Gordon and one or two other senior Masons – including Elijah, I guessed: that was probably the real nature of the 'something' he'd been called away for – had gone looking for her.

I turned to Mr Bowling. I suppose I was about to express my concern.

But he was no longer there.

I couldn't see him anywhere. More to the point, I couldn't see *anyone* I knew.

And then I did see him. He was on the other side of the room, and, like Robert Collinson, he looked to be involved in an altercation, with the difference that he was apparently trying to calm his three antagonists down.

It suddenly struck me: they were intent on ejecting him from the premises! He held his palms at shoulder level in a conciliatory gesture, then allowed them to march him towards the exit.

What on earth was happening? It didn't really concern me – this wasn't my party, nor did I have even the slightest stake in it – but I couldn't help feeling disorientated, in the way one necessarily does when unexpected, inexplicable and obviously unpleasant events start to multiply before one's eyes.

I don't know what put it into my head – possibly the heat, the proliferation of strange events, and the lack of air – but I suddenly became convinced that Cytherea Holmes and my sister had *run away together*. Why couldn't I see Mildred? Just as importantly, why couldn't I see Aunt Gloria? She might well have gone looking for Mildred, especially if she'd heard that the two women were together. Which they definitely *had* been: at one point at least: I'd seen them.

I felt slightly ill. The vision beneath the floor hadn't helped: a lesser woman would have required smelling salts! I got up and made my way across the room, edging inelegantly past the guests – none of whom seemed to register my existence - to the nearest door.

I found myself in a corridor very similar to the one I'd been in when Elijah had deserted me. Only, much less stuffy.

I could breathe again.

I cast a final look back into the ballroom. And there they were: Mildred and Aunt Gloria, sitting on chairs against a distant wall, just as I had been. They didn't look as if they were missing me. As far as I could tell, they weren't even talking to each other. They looked bored.

Suddenly, I wanted more than coolness and fresh air. I wanted to be alone. I strode along the corridor, climbed two flights of stairs and wandered along a landing to one of the windows I'd gazed out of earlier. It opened easily, and I took three deep breaths.

The darkness here was almost complete, but I felt none of my former anxiety about ghosts.

Then a door opened at the end of the corridor, filling the landing with a weak light from within the room. A woman appeared, partially silhouetted. One I vaguely recognised.

Cytherea Holmes?

"Ada," she said. "Come here. Come inside, quickly."

VI.

"Chop-chop!" She closed the door on us the moment I was inside and put her fingers to her lips. "Whisper," she told me. "Sit down on the sofa." She turned the key in the lock. "We should be safe in here."

Unlike just about every other room I'd looked in tonight, this one had furniture: an armchair and a sofa. It felt much warmer than the corridor, though I could see no sign of a fire in the grate or anywhere else. Four short candles burnt on the mantelpiece. The slight gust as Cytherea Holmes closed the door made their flames and our shadows wobble.

I established myself on the sofa, as commanded. She blew out all the candles except one, and came to sit next to me. "Otherwise, someone will see the light under the door," she said. "They'll know I'm in here."

I didn't know how to respond. Or even how to behave, really. "Are you hiding?" I ventured, at last. "I mean, is it a game?"

"Hide and seek, you mean? No, it's deadly serious. And I'm relying on you to help me. Mildred said you would."

"Mildred?"

"Your sister."

"I meant…" I didn't know what I meant. Probably: *what on earth's happening?*

"I don't expect you to understand, Ada, not fully anyway, but I've made a breakthrough; I'm a true hero of the spirit, a *Thirthankara,* a ford maker. Yes, in brief, then: I've discovered a magical way for humans to overcome old age and death. And I've been abandoned precisely because of that. All the men here think they can replicate my findings, then claim the credit. Including *villain number one,* my 'fiancé', Robert Collinson."

I still had no idea what was unfolding. "That's terrible," I said, abstractedly.

"Yes, isn't it?"

"Are – are you – is this a joke?"

Suddenly, she was on her knees in front of me. She grasped both my hands. She brought her nose to within an inch of mine. "I know it's dark," she said. "But look into my eyes. This isn't me jesting, Ada, it's real. Robert Collinson doesn't love me. On the contrary, he hates me. He's following me until such time as I tell him what he wants to know. And when I finally break – which I definitely *will,* eventually: I'm not made of steel, Ada: no one is – then *poof!* I'll be dragged down to Hell like poor old Dr Faustus!"

I was beginning to get a sense of what was happening now. She was mad. "I'm not sure what I can do," I said.

She stood up. "We all live in a bubble of self-satisfaction," she said. "Every last one of us. Created by the wrathful God as a prelude to our destruction. A God who enjoys killing – and yet is still God! The Jews in Clifford's Tower: his own children! Aaron's sons – Aaron the *priest,* whose sons used *the wrong sort of fire! He delights in destroying us!"*

"I think, yes, I think I may have read that story - "

My incoherence was interrupted by a knock at the door. It sounded like code: two long raps, three short ones, followed by two long ones. Cytherea sprang up, turned the key, ushered the visitor in, then closed and locked the door again – all so swiftly that it seemed like a single motion.

The net result was that, suddenly, Mildred was standing in front of me. "Ada, it's me," she said. "Mildred."

I laughed. I couldn't help myself. *As if I might not recognise my own sister!* I was probably close to having hysterics, if I'm honest. "What's going on?" I asked.

Now it was Mildred's turn to fall to her knees. Just like Cytherea, she grasped my hands and attempted to crush them. "I've never asked anything of you, Ada, as I'm asking this. *Help me help Cytherea!"*

I swallowed. I looked from Mildred to Cytherea, then back to Mildred again. Something inside me temporarily surrendered. I was outnumbered by maniacs.

"Tell me what you want me to do," I said.

Cytherea wandered to the door, leaving centre stage to Mildred. She made a show of putting her ear against it, as if listening for incursions from the corridor.

"Cytherea needs to be hidden," Mildred said. "She needs to get away from everyone who's trying to exploit her – by whom, I mean *everyone;* the whole world!"

"The whole *male* world," Cytherea put in, from the background. "Although given that men hold all the power, and the power *is* the world, I suppose 'the whole world' is entirely accurate. Apologies for interrupting, Mildred. Go on."

"We need to hide her. Especially from Robert Collinson. Who wants to kill her, by the way."

"*Will* kill me, if I ever divulge my secret," Cytherea said. "Which, given the amount of pressure bearing down upon me, I will. How can I not?"

"So, it's up to you and me," Mildred said.

"Tell me what you want me to do," I said, for the second time, though partly as a result of Cytherea's rather farcical asides, I felt even less biddable now.

"Our plan," Mildred said breathlessly, " – Cytherea's and mine - though it's yours now, since you've agreed to join us; that is what you're saying, isn't it, Ada? that you're with us, not against us?"

"Yes," I said simply.

"This is our plan," she continued. "We're going to hide Cytherea here! Right *here,* in Munro House! It'll be empty again after tonight, and who'll ever think of looking for her in the very place she so publicly abandoned? I've been listening to everyone downstairs. They're split between thinking she's halfway to London, and thinking she's halfway to Dover or Folkestone! No one's even *begun to suspect* she's ten feet above them! Nor will they, not anymore. They stopped searching the house twenty minutes ago. Robert Collinson's left for the capital. Tomorrow, Uncle Gordon and a few of his friends will come back. They'll do a bit of tidying up, but not much, because they're men, then they'll lock it up, and after that, they'll forget all about it. It'll go back to being 'the empty house', the 'haunted' House that no one wants!"

"I can't stay here indefinitely, of course," Cytherea said. "I just need a week's grace. Then I can disguise myself and head for the coast. I have friends in France. *Real* friends, who'll hide me for as long as I like."

"We've just got to bring her food," Mildred said. "And as much news as we can discover."

"That's all I'm asking," Cytherea said.

"We've already agreed a secret signal," Mildred said. "So, we just knock at the window, and Cytherea lets us in."

"Where are we going to get food from?" I asked stupidly.

Mildred laughed. "I'm a thirty-one-year-old widow, Ada. I have my own means, and I've a degree of independence. I don't really need you at all. But you're my sister. I love you, and I want you to be my accomplice. It'll be good for you, make you more independent. And it's only for a week."

All at once, it occurred to me to ask what *she* was getting out of the arrangement. I'd remembered what she'd told me earlier, that Cytherea had *heard I was looking for news of my deceased husband, and said she might be able to help me.* Where did that fit into their 'arrangement'?

But I bit my tongue. It didn't matter. Cytherea Holmes was a mad woman, and clearly my sister was equally deranged. They'd formed an instant bond because they were as alike as two peas in a pod.

I remembered Aunt Gloria's assessment of the Freemasons: *superstition added to superstition*. Well, this was surely a parallel case: insanity added to insanity.

How long had Mildred been out of her mind without me noticing? Probably since Joseph's death. She might have fared better had she been able to tell herself that he'd been killed in a heroic conflict, but, as far as she knew, and as she often told me, the Boers were simply farmers; they weren't tyrants or megalomaniacs. To die defending the British Empire from a ragtag assortment of rural smallholders, five and a half thousand miles away? It didn't seem glorious; quite the opposite. No wonder she was suffering.

She was my sister, and my duty was plain. I had to resist the temptation to indulge her. I couldn't save both women. I might not even be able to save one of them. But Mildred was my flesh and blood, and she had a moral claim on me. Harsh as it sounds, I owed Cytherea nothing.

I therefore had one option only. I was obliged to broach the matter with Aunt Gloria. I had to reveal everything. As a consequence, Cytherea Holmes would be ejected from Munro House in the morning, and then, if she really did need to run away, she could probably do so with ease: according to what Mildred had said, Robert Collinson was in London. If he decided to pursue her, she'd have several hours' start on him at least. In the meantime, we could coax Mildred back to reality.

The alternative didn't really bear thinking about. Cytherea had plainly intuited that Joseph was Mildred's Achilles Heel. She'd string her along with 'messages' from 'the other side' – Spiritualists did that all the time - then she'd leave her. At which point, Mildred would probably be in a worse state than ever.

I'd made a decision. Now I needed to take it home with me.

The carriage ride home was very similar to the one there, except that no one spoke. From Uncle Gordon's point of view, Cytherea's abscondment had turned the evening into a disaster, and, although Aunt Gloria was unsympathetic, she certainly hadn't enjoyed herself. Mildred and I were full of our own thoughts. Mildred seemed distant enough from the three of us to be hardly present at all.

I fell to thinking about Cytherea, specifically when she'd cast herself on her knees and put her face next to mine. At the beginning of the evening, when she'd been perched on that ridiculous podium, I'd imagined she was about Mildred's age. Close by, however, she looked significantly younger than that; indeed, no older than I was.

Which was absurd! But then I remembered: the first occasion had been accompanied by brilliant illumination, the second by candlelight.

So, the difference between the two signified nothing.

VII.

The next morning, my bedroom was full of sunlight. I seemed to snap out of sleep, and in the same instant, was fully awake. I crossed the floor and threw the window open. The birds sang, the sky was azure, the cool breeze on my face smelt faintly of honeysuckle, and beyond the nearby woods and the adjoining fields, deer grazed. Almost beneath my nose, a bumblebee buzzed past. I felt shockingly alive.

The events of the previous evening came back to me in a rush, but with all their values wonderfully revised or reversed. Mildred and I and Cytherea were young. We were of a piece with this summer's day. By contrast, Aunt Gloria was late autumn, if not winter. What on earth had made me consider allying myself with *her?* Who was *I* to decide that Mildred was insane? Surely, she knew her own mind!

In conclusion, I hadn't necessarily been in the moral right last night, and probably only a certain sanctimoniousness of attitude had allowed me to think otherwise.

Added to which, supposing I betrayed Mildred's confidence: what thanks would I get?

However, something else was on my mind, just out of view, manifesting itself, for the moment, only as a subtle alteration to my normal mood.

Something good?

Hard to tell, but it couldn't be something bad, because there was no uneasiness about it. In my experience, uneasiness always precedes a gloomy realisation, and usually well in advance.

It had to do partly with Elijah. Yes, I was finished with him. The way he'd simply abandoned me! But that was typical of the Freemasons, at least in my limited experience. They were overgrown boys, perpetually on the lookout for childish pleasures and very little else.

But yes, the other side of the coin - was Mr Bowling. Mr Michael Bowling.

Which was utterly irrational, of course. I'd spent two minutes in his company, we'd exchanged a couple of inconsequential remarks, and I knew nothing about him. Since he'd apparently been ejected from the premises, he might not even be a good or decent person.

On the other hand, he might simply not be the boyish type.

As I got ready to go down to breakfast, I tried to put the whole thing out of my mind. Mr Bowling only appealed so vividly to me because I'd gone off Elijah, and the place Elijah had occupied in my affections – my aspirations, really, more than my affections - had to be taken by *someone*, at least temporarily. A place-marker.

I arranged my toilette, and got ready for breakfast. Half an hour later, as I went downstairs, I could hear Aunt Gloria and Uncle Gordon discussing something loudly.

As always, I tried to shut my ears: eavesdropping was supposed to be wrong, but experience had taught me that if they were ever talking about anything interesting, they tended to keep their voices down. Strange as it may sound, the loudness was partly for my benefit, a means to my edification.

Mildred sat on the edge of the big armchair in the drawing room, daintily holding a teacup and a saucer. "Don't close the door," she said listlessly, when I came in. "I want to hear what Aunt and Uncle are saying." She gestured to the tea-set on the coffee table. "Pour yourself a cup. The pot's still warm."

I took her advice, and we sat opposite each other, exchanging eyes, sipping and listening.

"How was I to know the sort of woman she was?" Uncle Gordon said. "How were *any* of us? She came with the highest *recommendations,* and not from just a single lodge, either! From *several!"*

"It didn't take *me* long to work it out," Aunt Gloria said. "and I'd never even heard of her before yesterday at breakfast!"

"How? *How* should I have known?"

"Your own words, in the carriage last night? I believe they were: 'No one wants the personal expense of hosting Cytherea Holmes. This way, we can share the cost.' And you're *really* claiming that nothing struck you as remiss about that? I saw it *instantly!"*

"I mentioned it merely to show how *miserly* some of the brethren are!"

Aunt Gloria scoffed. "Equally, maybe some of the 'brethren' knew far more about her than you did. Such as, how she's supposedly up to her eyeballs in debt."

"Hardly 'supposedly'. In any case, they *couldn't* have known that: they'd have said something. What possible motive could any of them have for concealing it? I mean, any Mason have for concealing it?"

"The Masons are men, my dear. They want to fawn on a 'beautiful' woman. Some of your 'brethren' are so wealthy, they probably considered whatever financial contribution they've stumped up to be a sound investment. And of course, they may have had even baser motives. You said yourself – although you really didn't need to: I had my ear close enough to the ground last night – that, pathetically, several were plotting to elbow Robert Collinson aside and replace him with themselves."

"*He* was as much of a fraud as *she* was!"

"Of course he was! And he'd probably have been happy to be 'elbowed aside'. The two of them were looking for wealthy men to leech off. I'd be very interested to see these 'recommendations' from prestigious lodges you spoke of. I'll wager they were forged. They must have been."

"I hadn't considered that. My God, you're right."

She chuckled. "What would you do without me?"

"I'll raise the possibility of their collusion at the meeting. I'll have to."

"Assuming that meeting's well-behaved enough for you to get a word in edgeways. My guess is that it'll be one long catalogue of accusations, recriminations and denunciations. Panic will preside from start to finish. You'll get nothing done, Gordon. Not today."

"I can but try."

Mildred frowned. She noticed me noticing. She leaned over to me and whispered, "I'm trying to discover how they 'found out' what they mistakenly think they've discovered: that Cytherea's a fraud. Do *you* know?"

"I've no idea," I replied. "What makes you say it's mistaken?"

"I told you last night, Ada, just as I told them: I've read about Cytherea Holmes in *The Strand Magazine*. She's a *bona fide* member of The Hermetic Order of the Golden Dawn. *The Strand Magazine* doesn't lie, and it doesn't make crass mistakes either. And of course, if she is merely a high-class courtesan, then what was that conversation she had with us last night?"

"She might simply be a high-class courtesan who wants to get away from Robert Collinson."

"Do you think she couldn't have persuaded any number of men there last night to *kill* Robert Collinson, if she'd wished? *And* to give her all their money? She doesn't need a puppet-master!"

"We must tell the children," Aunt Gloria was saying, "although I'm sure they'll have overheard most of it. I believe they're in the drawing room. *Mildred! Ada!"*

"Don't argue with them," Mildred whispered to me. "We can use this to our advantage."

We put our teacups down and filed into the parlour. Aunt Gloria sat languorously in her black dress, looking as if she was having the time of her life. Uncle Gordon stood by the window in his grey suit, clasping his hands behind his back. He wore a grim expression.

"You may have overheard what we were discussing," he said.

During family conferences, Mildred usually spoke for both of us. I was normally expected to remain quiet. "Some of it," she said. "We couldn't help it, I'm afraid."

"It would be funny if it weren't so serious," Aunt Gloria remarked.

Uncle Gordon drew a deep breath. "To summarise. It turns out that we were all deceived. Cytherea Holmes is not what we took her for. According to what we were told, she was a respected scholar – 'respected', that is, for a woman - having published a significant paper on Renaissance history, and, in addition, an investigator into, well, such spiritual matters as have always interested the Freemasons. She'd recently achieved a 'breakthrough', so we were told."

"Only, it now appears that we weren't 'told' that at all," Aunt Gloria said, with a slight smile. "Or at least, not by whom we thought 'told' us."

"As I've just conceded," Uncle Gordon continued tetchily, "we were deceived. Cytherea Holmes is a would-be fine artist, also an actress, from Camden - "

"Which is just outside of London," Aunt Gloria put in.

"And she owes a lot of people an awful lot of money, which she is unable to find. In short, she's drowning in debt, and a prime candidate for prison, if anyone ever manages to get their hands on her, which I doubt they will: Cytherea Holmes probably isn't her real name. We were all fooled last night, but luckily, The Grand Architect of the Universe" – he paused involuntarily as Aunt Gloria rolled her eyes – "was overseeing us - "

"Is that orthodox Masonic doctrine?" Aunt Gloria said. "I thought the Grand Architect was a non-interventionist?"

Uncle Gordon clicked his tongue and scowled.

"Can I ask you how you found all this out?" Mildred put in meekly, as if she was merely introducing a diversion to prevent a row.

"Found *what* out?" Uncle Gordon said. "I'm, er, not sure what you mean, my dear."

"That Cytherea Holmes is a charlatan," Mildred went on. "She seemed perfectly nice to me. And as I said, she's been in *The Strand Magazine*."

"You can mention that at the meeting, Gordon," Aunt Gloria said. "If *The Strand Magazine* was fooled, that makes our credulity far more forgivable. Ergo, why shouldn't the world and his wife be?"

"What meeting?" Mildred asked.

"There is an extraordinary meeting of the senior members of the Tunbridge Wells lodge at eleven o'clock this morning," Aunt Gloria said. "Which brings us to the point. I think you've told the children enough now, Gordon. It's time to tell them how they can help."

Uncle Gordon drew himself to his full height: five feet and ten inches. "This morning, I spoke to the editors of all the local newspapers. Some of them belong to the lodge, so they understood the problem well enough. If it gets out that there was a party on the Calverley Estate last night, and that the Freemasons hosted it, and that it was in honour of a well-known - *prostitute,* and her 'handler', or whatever they're called, we'll be a laughing stock. Not just locally, but internationally; amongst other lodges. We'll also have done the cause of Freemasonry incredible harm. The point is – and this is behind what I'm about to ask you – no one must ever know there was a party at Munro House last night. Virtually everyone present will therefore deny it. You must never mention it, do you hear? If asked about it, you must state categorically that it never happened."

"Certainly, Uncle," Mildred said.

"What about you, Ada?" he asked. "Will you do likewise?"

He must have been very upset to consider asking me in my own right. "Of course," I said.

"But can I simply repeat my earlier question?" Mildred said. Without waiting for a response, she repeated: "How did you find out that Cytherea Holmes is a charlatan? *Someone* must have revealed it!"

Aunt Gloria and Uncle Gordon exchanged looks. Then nods.

"Ultimately, Robert Collinson confessed," Uncle Gordon said. "After we agreed to give him safe passage in return for the truth. But luckily for us, there was also a well-informed interloper on the premises last night. I'd actually met him on one or two occasions before, because he's a Freemason, only from London. He's also a leading light in an organisation called The Society for Psychical Research, which specialises in hunting down swindlers and exposing them. Anyway, we were all set to eject him unceremoniously, when he revealed his hand and told us what he was doing there. So it was that, over the course of twenty minutes, we learned all about Cytherea Holmes, with him providing documentary evidence to substantiate his accusations. Very pleasant young fellow. I believe you actually met him at one point last night, Ada. Under normal circumstances, I'd already have mentioned it, but, for what it's worth, he seemed *rather taken* with you. Name of Michael Bowling. If he comes calling - which I think he may – please pretend that you remember him, and don't let on too hastily that your heart belongs to another." He smiled weakly and gave a valiant wink, as if things were just as they'd always been. "We're relying on you and Elijah – Mr and Mrs Scott soon, God willing - for those prime cuts of meat."

VIII.

Once our cooperation had been secured, we sisters were free to do as we pleased. Mildred suggested we go for a walk. I could see she was agitated, though she was judicious enough to know she had nothing with which to reproach me: I could no more have realised who Michael Bowling was than anyone else in my position could; and the simple fact that I'd met him couldn't reasonably count against me. No, she wanted information, that's all. And guarantees.

We donned our shawls – despite the early morning's promise, the day had turned cloudy – and set off briskly for the woods. Ten minutes later, we sat side by side on a tree trunk under a tall, leafy canopy. We savoured the silence for two minutes, then Mildred began to question me. To begin with, she wanted to know how I'd met Michael Bowling, what sort of an impression he'd made on me, and how I intended to behave if he 'came calling'. I told her I didn't think he was a mischief-maker. "Uncle Gordon said he had evidence for his accusations," I added.

She let out a despairing groan. "Mr Bowling's obviously in cahoots with Robert Collinson! You heard what Cytherea said: they're trying to destroy her. Put it this way, Ada. Uncle Gordon and his friends took just *twenty minutes* to assess that evidence before declaring it valid. Does that sound like a thorough appraisal to you?"

"I suppose it depends how much evidence there was." I could see I was irritating her. "And what sort."

"I read about her in *The Strand Magazine! The Strand Magazine* isn't written by imbeciles! Evidence that she's an actress from Camden? None. Evidence that she's deep in debt? None. Evidence that Cythera Holmes isn't her real name? Not an iota. And, finally – most egregiously of all – evidence that she's a *prostitute? Less* than none! Don't you *see?"* she continued, "it's exactly what they all *wanted* to believe all along! Because a woman's *not allowed* to be very beautiful *and* very successful! There *must* be something suspicious going on if she's both of those things, because the combination's unnatural!"

"But if Michael Bowling's a member of The Society for Psychical Research, he can't be a simple villain."

She smiled indulgently. "Do you actually know what 'The Society for Psychical Research' is, Ada?"

I conceded that I didn't.

"Nor do I," Mildred admitted. "But I'm inclined to think it's a made-up organisation. Admit it: if neither of us knows what it *is*, we can't very well know that it's *real*, can we?"

"But nor can we just assume that it's make-believe," I said. "Uncle Gordon would probably know. The Freemasons are interested in the entire realm of the supernatural. Some of them would know. They must have known."

Mildred brought her eyebrows together and said nothing.

"It must be a real organisation," I went on, pressing my advantage, "and it must be highly respectable."

"'Highly respectable'? What makes you say that?"

"As you just pointed out, twenty minutes wasn't enough time to assess a wad of documentary evidence. Which must mean that such an assessment was unnecessary. Why? Because its possessor had enough authority in his own right. They took his word for its reliability. Which must in turn mean that the Society is real, and that it's reputable, and that Mr Bowling isn't a villain."

Mildred was faltering now. "But of course, he might be *mistaken*. He, himself, may have been duped."

"It is possible," I said, "but isn't the opposite equally so?"

She sighed. "Very well then, let's imagine, for the sake of argument, that he's right. So, here we have an ex-actress from Camden, a woman deeply in debt; a woman tightly controlled by a brute of a man, a repeated victim of the worst depravities, and who wants to escape from all that; from a life of perpetual depredation and virtual slavery. Do you think we should *help* her, or do you think we should just wash our hands of the whole business?"

"I think we should probably help her," I admitted reluctantly. "Especially given that we've already promised to do so."

Mildred nodded. "Of course, I'd forgotten that." She frowned, and put her hands together beneath her nose. "But I don't believe she *is* a swindler, Ada; I don't believe that at all. I believe she's everything we all believed she was during the carriage ride there; everything *The Strand Magazine* says she is. Yes, don't forget *The Strand Magazine* – I bet Mr Bowling doesn't even know about that! Anyway, if she really was a swindler, there'd be easier fake identities to adopt than that of one of the top representatives of the Order of the Golden Dawn! And given that she'd managed to fool the entire Tunbridge Wells lodge, why wouldn't she go a bit farther afield - and try her luck in America, say? Why stay here, virtually on Camden's doorstep?"

"I can't answer that," I said. "I don't know how her mind works. Or anything about her. Maybe she couldn't afford a boat ticket."

"Last night, she took me aside and spoke to me for half an hour. *Half an hour*. And she knew everything there was to know about Joseph and I. Things I've never told anyone! She couldn't have known I'd even *be* there. Besides, I'm a nobody, just the older, plainer daughter of a rural shopkeeper. Why would she seek to impress me?"

"So that you'd help her escape?"

She clicked her tongue. "We've been through this, Ada. There were a dozen or so besotted men there last night who'd have fallen over themselves to do that. And they'd have been far more useful to her. Men have the power to open doors. Thirty-one-year-old widows don't."

"Well, I don't know then," I said honestly.

"Just keep an open mind," she said. "Tonight, we'll take her some food. We'll sneak out in the early hours. Leave it up to me. I'll get the provisions, I'll wake you up, we'll go there together. Believe me, Ada, you won't regret it. You'll see how wrong your Mr Bowling is. At some point during the next few days, I truly believe we're going to witness an undeniable *miracle."*

IX.

At two o'clock the next morning, Mildred quietly opened my bedroom door and beckoned me. We crept downstairs, let ourselves out of the house, and only put our shoes on when we reached the garden gate. It seemed funny, at that point, that our feet were already muddy. We were young! I thanked God that I'd listened sympathetically to my sister a few hours ago. I was always late to realise the possibility of actually *living* my life, instead of merely letting it run down like a half-wound clock – witness yesterday morning when I awoke - but, thank God, so far never *too* late.

We crossed three fields, traversed the woods in almost complete blackness, and passed through a succession of narrow gaps in three hawthorn hedges. We were too excited to talk. After about a mile, Mildred signalled for me to stop. I obeyed. She reached down into what looked like a ditch, pulled out a bulging sack and held it up in the moonlight. "Vegetables," she said. "She's a vegetarian. Like a lot of mystics," she added, as if she needed to ram home the morning's lesson: *she's not what you think she is*. "I'll cook us a meal when we arrive."

I didn't know what I was expected to say. But I wanted to be supportive. "Would you like me to help?" I asked.

"No, I'm an expert in the kitchen. I want you to get to know her. I'll stay out of your way. Just keep an open mind."

I giggled. As I've just said, I was excited. "It's two o'clock in the morning. Will she even be awake?"

Mildred frowned. She set off at speed, and I struggled to keep up with her for a while, until at last, she seemed to flag. She'd been punishing me for asking a stupid question, and possibly for giggling.

She put the sack down, stood with her feet wide apart, and put her hands on her knees. "Well!" she said breathlessly.

I laughed. "Shall I carry your bag?"

"I'm not old yet. But yes, you're right, let's sit down. A few minutes won't hurt."

We sat and sweated. Women's clothes in those days were ridiculous. I think Mildred had actually been involved in the *dress reform* movement at one point. Not that most of us ever believed, in those days, that things would really improve in that regard. A few brave spirits, that's all.

"I have to tell you something," Mildred said suddenly. "I've been trying to muster the courage."

I reacted with a self-conscious grin. How much courage did it take to broach something with *me?*

"You're a good person, Ada," she went on. "In a way that I'm not. I've never told anyone this before… but sometimes… I'm actually *glad* Joseph is dead." She crossed herself. "I know that's sinful. He was never very nice to me. And since he died – like I said, I've never told you this before – I've learned he wasn't very nice to the South Africans, either."

"I think that's reasonable," I said. In all honesty, I'd never much liked Joseph either. "Why should you feel guilty for not grieving a husband who showed you so little love?"

"You may not believe what I'm about to tell you, but I swear it's true."

"There's something else? Well - "

"This is nothing to do with Joseph," she said, apparently reading my thoughts. "It's about Cytherea. And Uncle Gordon."

"Uncle Gordon?"

"Probably not principally him. But the local Freemason's lodge, in which he's a 'leading light' - insofar as a Tunbridge Wells shopkeeper can ever be a 'leading light', anywhere, in any meaningful sense of the term."

"Cytherea and Uncle Gordon? Are the two of them… romantically involved?"

Mildred hooted. "Really! Can you imagine Uncle Gordon being *romantically involved* with anyone, ever? He's never been young! He was born sixty-one-years-old!"

"What then? Debts?"

"Stop trying to guess, Ada. Just sit quietly and let me speak. It's a lot odder than that. I said you might not believe what I'm about to tell you. That was an understatement. What I should have said, is that *no one* might believe it! It's literally beyond credence."

I was impatient now. And slightly troubled. "Well, what *is* it?"

"The truth is, I haven't been entirely honest with you about all this. I mean, what we're doing now, and why we're doing it. Neither was Cytherea, last night. We thought we might scare you off if we introduced the astonishing truth too early. We considered it might be too much for you to stomach."

"I don't, er – So what is 'the astonishing truth'?"

She scoffed. "Mind you, Uncle Gordon hasn't been honest with *anyone*. That tawdry little drama, this morning, about how Cytherea's this, that and the other, and she's let everyone down: it was all theatre, feigned indignation with not an ounce of genuine emotion to support it. And I'm as certain as I can be that there was no 'meeting at eleven o'clock this morning'. It was utter flimflam, designed to pull the wool over our eyes; and Aunt Gloria's, for what that's worth."

"I really, really don't understand."

"The Freemasons planned all this. They orchestrated the whole thing. They know Cytherea hasn't gone to London, or anywhere else. They know she's in Munro House. They arranged the entire thing with a view to establishing her there, and I happen to know she's fully complicit."

"So – I'm not sure I follow what you're saying. – They *know* she's in Munro House? And she *knows* they know?" I laughed nervously. "To what end?"

"There's something - "

I put my hands on my temples. "Sorry, before you answer that question, I need to ask a more fundamental one. How do you know all this?"

She sighed through her teeth. "Partly because, Ada, I'm an unattractive, probably un-re-marriageable, widow living, on an occasional basis, with her step-parents. Uncle Gordon and Aunt Gloria have no interest in me. As far as they're concerned, their duty was fulfilled when they packed me off with Joseph Wilde and a 14-carat gold ring. Nowadays, they don't even see me. I pass through the house invisibly, like a ghost. So, I read their letters, even the highly confidential Masonic specimens; I listen to their conversations, even their most private ones; I pass through walls, I fade into the upholstery, I become transparent. In short, I can enter rooms where they are, without them looking up, or registering my existence on the most basic level. As far as they're concerned, I might as well be lying in some unmarked grave in the Orange Free State." She wiped her eyes. "Which is what he deserves. Joseph, I mean."

"I heard what you just said about feeling glad that he's dead, but until just now, I thought you wanted to see him again. I thought you'd been to séances."

"Yes, I have. I did. Because that's what's expected of someone in my position. *The inconsolable widow*. It's to Cythera's credit that she made me realise just how much I despise that role; how much I hate him."

"I thought - "

"You thought I was looking for some message from him. Well, yes, I was. Something like, *Sorry, Mildred, I deeply regret being so thoroughly horrid to you*. But I don't want him to be in Hell, either. He doesn't deserve that. No one does. I'll do anything to get him out of there. Not because I love him, but because I want to be a good person. Like you, Ada. Cytherea can help me."

"I'm mystified, then. You said the Freemasons 'know she's in Munro House and she knows they know'. That *was* what you said, wasn't it?"

She smiled. "Unfortunately, you side-tracked me. I believe my last relevant statement was about to be, 'There's something under the floorboards.' I mean, obviously, in Munro House. A creature of some kind, but not one you might meet in a book of zoology, as far as I'm aware. Unique, evil, unspeakable. They've put her in Munro House to test her, and she's accepted the challenge. Like in an ancient myth. If she succeeds in destroying the whatever-it-is, she'll be literally unassailable, as far as anyone on this Earth's concerned. Even the Freemasons will have to bow down to her. If she fails – and the Freemasons are hoping she will – then, from their point of view, the world will have been spared a tyrant of the first rank; worse than

Robespierre, worse than Nero, worse than Genghis Khan! Because she may be nice now, but people change. Time changes them, which is why immortality is good for no one, except under God's rule. They become more intolerant."

"And you got all this from Uncle Gordon? It doesn't sound like the sort of thing he'd ever broach with Aunt Gloria. She'd laugh him out of the house and into the street!"

"Not from anything he told her; from supposedly 'confidential' conversations with his friends; from letters and memoranda, things I've been given to 'put on the fire'. It can't have escaped your attention that they frequently use me as a maid, despite the fact that I have money of my own, and materially, I don't really need them. It suits me periodically to play along with them, so I never complain."

"Does Cytherea know you know?"

"Of course. She told me last night. She recruited me on that basis. And now I'm recruiting you. *Re*-recruiting you, because you agreed last night, but to a semi-fiction. Now you know the truth, you're free to reconsider."

"So, the Freemasons intend to destroy her? That's their thinking?"

"It all depends on the monster. Whether she can defeat it."

I stood up. I was on the verge of going home. "Mildred, this is deranged. Even if Uncle Gordon and Cytherea Holmes believe it - "

"Cytherea told me what happened to you last night. I mean, after you got lost in Munro House. In fact, she *made* it happen."

I was about to protest that I had no idea what she was talking about. Then, in a rush, the memory returned: wandering along those long, disorienting corridors and then the floor opening like some kind of wound. "I – " My throat was too dry. "I - "

"You *know* what I mean," she persisted. "She *made* you see it, because she knew it would make you more amenable. You'd remember nothing afterwards, that was the idea. Until now, of course. Just think: it's been there in your unconscious all along! She did it through 'animal magnetism', if you want to know. Oh, I know no one believes in that anymore, but she does!"

"I don't understand what we're doing!" I burst out. "I thought you wanted to see Joseph again, but now you tell me you don't! I thought she was trying to get away from Robert Collinson, but now it turns out she isn't! And there you are sitting next to a bag of vegetables, ready to cook for – for – *Why does she need our help at all?* If the Freemasons know she's in there, and they're happy with the fact, and she's happy with it, presumably she's *got* food! It'll be the *least* they'll have given her!"

"You're right. The food doesn't matter. Cytherea wants us because she wants friends. Robert Collinson is a man of no importance. He's simply a fool who's infatuated with her, and also knows something about her, since he's also a member of the Golden Dawn. She effectively got rid of him last night, with the collusion of her Freemason friends: 'put him out of danger' is how she'd put it, since she undoubtedly loves him… I mean, in the sense that one might love a dog or a cat. As for why *we're* involved, well, Ada, we're going to try and save her. She doesn't need to confront any monster. She has power enough as it is. It's a man's plan: victory or defeat, because that's the only way men are capable of seeing the world. One or the other, never compromise. And she *is* a scholar, by the way, despite what Uncle Gordon says. She wrote a book. I've seen it. You should ask her about it. Oh, and while we're on the subject of six impossible things before breakfast, I might as well tell you something else: she's four hundred years old."

I felt like crying. I ran my hands through my hair. I dearly wished I'd adhered to my original plan now, and told Aunt Gloria. How, *why* had I allowed myself to be dissuaded by something as trivial and irrelevant as a sunny summer's morning?

Because I hadn't realised quite how insane Mildred was, that's why. I'd thought she was only mildly so.

A new course of action opened up, although it wasn't one in which I had much choice: it was purely the product of necessity. We'd proceed as planned to Munro House, we'd go through the motions of supporting Cytherea (whatever that involved), then I'd tell Aunt Gloria in the morning. This time, I wouldn't be deflected.

In the ten minutes or so that Mildred and I had been seated, the sense of something unwholesome had crept up on me. It suddenly became present to my awareness: by which I mean, I was all at once conscious of my consciousness. The restoration of my memory of the thing under the floor – if that's what it was, and not some vivid auto-suggestion – had probably forced it into view. I could tell, from a few sweeping glances at my sister, that she felt it too.

"Should we go?" I asked.

We clambered to our feet simultaneously.

She drew close. "We've been followed," she whispered. "We're being followed."

"Perhaps - perhaps it could be Uncle Gordon?" I half hoped it was.

"Had it been him, we'd never have reached the garden gate. Look, there's Munro House, right in front of us."

We looked downwards across the landscape at the moonlight silhouette of a squat building in the far distance, small enough from here to be little more than a black shape. I knew immediately, as if by instinct, that she was right: yes, that was Munro House.

Then it struck me how odd that was. As far as I knew, there was no location sufficiently elevated to look down upon Munro House from this angle, and definitely not from this distance. True, the High Weald is full of ridges and folds, so that one can rapidly find oneself at unexpected heights, or sunk in equally sudden depressions. But not like this.

Where *were* we?

My disorientation, and the sense that we weren't alone, combined to produce an overpowering wooziness… if that's the right term: it certainly wasn't a pleasant feeling.

But then something happened that amplified the whole thing.

Footsteps. Someone really was approaching.

Before we even had chance to confirm the fact to each other, much less formulate a plan, a man came lumbering through the darkness. He stopped a few feet before us with a terrible expression.

Robert Collinson?

He looked every bit as surprised to see us here, as we were him. We'd probably have yelped had the shock been any less intense. I think he would too. As it was, Mildred and I were too paralysed even to grab each other.

"Have you seen her?" he asked. He looked exhausted, defeated and teary.

"Who?" Mildred asked in a croak, though it was obvious he could only mean Cytherea Holmes.

He took off without answering; downhill, in the direction of Munro House.

Any relief we might have felt was short-lived. It quickly became apparent that he was being followed. Not by a person, or even an animal, but by the thing I'd seen in Munro House – a long fluid *lump*. It moved with horrible determination, in ripples, overtaking its victim just before he reached the bottom of the hill. He hollered, and kept hollering, but the sound became increasingly faint.

I think at that point, I must have lost consciousness. The next thing I knew, I was lying down, it was dark, I was cold. My sister was cradling my head in her lap. Silvery clouds raced across the sky. I tried to recall how I'd got here. The journey from the house, Mildred pulling that sack from a ditch –

Suddenly, Cytherea Holmes came into view. "Thank you for coming," she said sombrely. "It's rather chilly out here. Shall we go?"

X.

I wasn't entirely sure what I was doing on the ground, but I also knew it wasn't something into which I particularly wanted to enquire. Mildred pulled me to my feet, threw the sack over her shoulder, and took my arm. Cytherea held my hand. We walked briskly downhill, in silence.

The closer we got to Munro House, the darker, more forbidding and derelict it looked. Just before we reached the front door, Cytherea stopped and pointed upwards.

I raised my eyes. The sky was brimful of what looked like comets swirling around a central point. It was impossible to tell how distant they were; somewhere between the tallest tree and the farthest reach of the universe, I thought light-headedly.

"Angels," she said. "My present and future. Don't worry, I'm not forcing them to stay. They're here because they love me. Shall we go inside?"

She opened the front door with a proprietary air, as if she'd lived here all her life. We stepped into the long hallway, and she shut us in. I could see why. The light in here was absolutely brilliant. If it should escape, people might realise that the house was occupied.

But wait - how *could* it be so intensely illuminated? From outside, it had looked undeniably abandoned!

"Welcome to The Interpreter's House," she said. "You've read *Pilgrim's Progress,* I take it?"

"Why couldn't we see any light when we were approaching?" I asked.

"Thick curtains, Silly," Mildred said. I think she realised the moment the words left her mouth that some of the windows didn't even appear to *have* curtains.

"It's magic," Cytherea said wanly. "Oh, do you really have to *cook,* Mildred? Can't we eat your vegetables raw? I just need sustenance. I don't need a meal."

"I won't lie," Mildred said. "I'm not really here to cook you a meal, though of course I'm happy to do so. Ada and I are here to dissuade you." She turned to me. "Ada, you've seen the thing under the floorboards. Do you really think Cytherea can defeat it? Be honest."

I laughed. I looked from one woman to the other. I blushed. I laughed again, less confidently. This pushed all the insanity across a line into farce. Two deranged women about to argue about whether one of them should go out and do battle, like St George (or perhaps Don Quixote), with a twentieth-century dragon (or perhaps a windmill).

Then I remembered Robert Collinson. My blush became a blanch. "What was the question again?"

"It's decided," Cythera said imperiously. She ignored me and rounded on Mildred. "You saw what happened to Robert tonight. I have to rescue him. The die is cast, as they say."

"There will be other occasions!" Mildred said. "Conciliation, not destruction: that's the correct way."

"There's no conciliating it. But we should talk alone. Follow me. Ada, stay here."

Cytherea walked to the nearest door, threw it open and held it grimly for Mildred to enter. It felt like a headmistress ushering an unruly prefect into her office for a scolding. She closed me out. I heard them arguing.

It suddenly struck me that there was much more to Mildred than she'd divulged, even now. Despite her recent protestation of complete transparency, she was still hiding things from me. Specifically, the way she'd just spoken to Cytherea suggested their meeting at the party last night hadn't been their first; that perhaps they were approximate equals, engaged in a project in which they both had an incalculable stake.

I felt very alone.

But then, maybe that was why I was really here. They really did want me to join them, and the truth could only be dispensed in increments. *The Hermetic Order of the Golden Dawn*. I smiled inwardly: it sounded very fine. I liked it. I thought of Michael Bowling again. What would *he* say? Would Elijah Scott be happier with it? Which of them was more likely to want to be my consort? And merely that?

Such thoughts shocked me – in a happy way!

Or such fantasies. Viewed from another angle, I was becoming as mad as I already believed Cytherea and Mildred were… or as I *had,* an hour ago.

The door to the headmistress's study opened. Cytherea led the way out, followed by Mildred, who didn't look as cowed as I expected. I knew in that moment that my surmise had been correct: in some ways, they were equals; at the very least, they were old acquaintances. They were putting on an act for my benefit, just as Uncle Gordon and Aunt Gloria had this morning. Was *anyone* prepared to tell me the truth?

"Mildred's going to cook us a meal," Cytherea announced. "I'm going to show you around the house." She beamed happily and grabbed my hand. "Come on."

Mildred faded into an adjoining room. Cytherea pushed open one of two double doors in front of us, revealing what I vaguely recognised from last night (the décor had completely changed) as the ballroom.

The entire floor had been cleared. Three concentric circles stretched to the walls, with the smallest only a foot or two within the others, and enclosing a heptagram.

"The Holy Trinity," she announced. She laughed. "Unless you were expecting astrological symbols or the Ptolemaic system. Nothing can be achieved outside the Christian religion. In combination with magic, of course; *magia naturalis*. Have you ever heard of Jacob Böhme? He's the key to everything here, and to the whole of reality. Look" – she increased her pressure on my hand – "let me show you something even more remarkable! You remember the room where we first met, last night? I mean, *properly* met, not the idiotic introductions with me on a confectioner's display stand."

"I think so," I said. "But to be frank, the house was a bit of a maze last night."

She laughed. "Follow me."

We went upstairs. We crossed a landing. She opened a door and ushered me into the room in which we'd first encountered each other. I recognised the chair and the sofa, the height of the ceiling, the relative position of the window, the candle stubs on the mantelpiece. But there was a hole in the floor with a tree growing through it.

"I shouldn't imagine you recall this!" she said.

"Is this a different room?" I asked. "Sorry, that was a silly question. Or – or was it?"

"Dissimilar, yes," she replied, "inasmuch as it contains this tree. How did it grow so tall in the space of a day, I hear you ask? Magic, that's how." She plucked a leaf and proffered it for my examination. "Maidenhair. Ginkgo, as the Chinese call it. The oldest tree on Earth. Look at the leaves, see how they're in two identical halves: male and female, good and evil, above and below, alpha and omega, black and white, Heaven and Hell, yin and yang, war and peace, sense and sensibility, crime and punishment, Gargantua and Pantagruel, Tweedledum, Tweedledee, oh dear, what can the matter be? And these veins that run through them – see? Rays, *comprenez?* Rays from on high! Here, take your left shoe off. Hand it to me."

Perhaps because I was so utterly disorientated, I was completely under her power now. I obeyed.

"You're very beautiful," she told me. "I don't mean that you *look* beautiful, that's for the poets to judge. Look, I'm slipping this leaf into your shoe so that tomorrow, you'll know this was real."

"How couldn't I?"

"Because after this, you're going to wake up in bed, and they'll tell you it was 'all a dream'. Now, put your shoe back on and come with me."

She kissed my cheek. We left the room and mounted another flight of stairs, then another – then another. At some point, the intervening landings disappeared, and the staircase gradually became helical.

"Lean over the bannister," Cytherea said. "Look down! Then up!"

We'd stopped, so I could do as she asked. I already knew we'd been climbing for far longer than the house itself could conceivably allow: I'd been on the roof with Elijah just a day ago; plus, I'd seen it from a distance. At most, it had three floors, so it must be about forty feet tall.

When I leaned over the rail and looked down, however, I might have been looking down into eternity; equally, when I looked up. I felt dizzy.

"Follow me," she said again. Somehow, a landing had materialised to our left. We crossed it and passed through a door and found ourselves outside, on a platform bounded by a parapet. "Come and look!" she yelled above the gale.

Of course, it was too dark to see the ground – even had I wanted to – except for a few clumps of light, unevenly spaced.

"Right down below us," Cytherea said: "that's Tunbridge Wells!" She pointed. "That's Crowborough. Heathfield! In the near distance: that's London!"

"Are you sure?"

She laughed. "Isn't it *amazing?"*

"What's that on the horizon? That vague purple glow, with the yellow flashes?"

"Ah, you don't want to know. Suffice it to say that, from here, one can see into the future. Forget that. If we go up a few flights more, we can see Paris and Berlin. Even New York, if you go high enough! Would you like that? I warn you, though: the farther you ascend, the more everything looks the same."

I couldn't take it any longer. I decided to seize the bull by the horns. "What's going on? Mildred says you've got to fight some… monster?"

She readjusted. "That's right. The one you saw. But then, as I understand it, she told you everything."

I had to remind myself that I'd actually *seen* the 'monster'. Unless, *I* was insane, *she* couldn't be. But was *I?*

"You want to know what it is," she said.

"Yes, I suppose so. Yes, definitely. Is it real?"

"It's much more than real. But then, you'd have to have read Plato to understand that. It's God."

"It's – er, *what?"*

"God."

"I don't know what you mean. What I heard - did you just say - ?"

"The *Ungrund,* as Jacob Böhme put it. As a consequence of Lucifer's unsuccessful rebellion, this world of time and change was created, in which God appears as a grotesque, angry creature, in conflict with the forces of light. Our purpose, as human beings, is to reverse the Fall, and be reborn as beings of light. Thus we regenerate nature – our nature - and help God return to his pre-creation, original state of goodness and truth."

"I see."

She laughed. "Of course you don't!"

"Who is this …Jacob Böhme? Is he a – I don't know. I was going to say, a Freemason? Who is he?"

"He died in 1624. I met him on two occasions."

"In the seventeenth century."

She smiled. "I was born in the fifteenth century, Ada, in Constantinople. Though 'merely a woman', I accompanied a man called George Gemistos on a mission to the West, whose purpose was a resolution of the differences between the Orthodox Church and Catholicism. We wanted the West to believe in *theosis,* the possibility of oneness with God. If we could get them to accept that, we thought, unity would follow. Broaching it too directly wasn't possible. So, we presented them with Zoroaster and the Chaldean Oracles as a way of introducing it gradually. A man called

Marsilio Ficino was to be our Trojan Horse. The plan would have worked, had it not been for the Reformation, which seemed to ruin everything for a while. But then, along came Jacob Böhme, a pious Lutheran cobbler. And here we are, today."

"I don't know much about history – I've never heard of 'George Gemistos' or 'Jacob Böhme': I - I still don't understand what's happening! You're going to fight… you say *God*. That's a – a *big* battle. Shouldn't you be practising?"

"I don't need to. I know I'm going to win."

"Against God."

"When we approached Munro House tonight, you saw those angels. I showed them to you, do you recall?"

"You told me that's what they were."

"I've got their unanimous support. They love me. They love me as no being's ever been loved before, possibly in the history of the universe. Well, excepting perhaps the love the Father has for the Son, but that's for another day. They love me, and I love them. On His deepest level, God wants to be defeated. It's his salvation, within which, He begets the Son. Afterwards, I'll become the chief angel. They all want it. God – that creature - wants it. The angels want it. Even Lucifer wants it, since, as Origen says, he can't be allowed to suffer eternally. And then, there will be a new heaven and a new earth." She grasped both my hands. "Feel it, Ada. *Feel* it. The *love* surging through this house! Oh, I know what you've been intending to ask, all along: what do you want *me* for? Little *me*, little Ada Pearson? Well, Ada, you're 'merely a woman', in a way I once was. I *don't* need you. Not at all. I love you. I love everything and every being in the entire universe, and in a few days, you'll be sitting at the right hand of God." She giggled. "No, sorry, that's me. As an angel, I'll be a lot, lot taller: ten, maybe twelve feet in height! But you'll be sitting at *my* right hand. Or somewhere. The banquet, that's right. The Messianic feast. We'll sit *together*, holding hands – my huge hand, your normal-sized one - how does that strike you?"

"I thought you were a member of The Golden Dawn," I said, in an attempt to re-rail the conversation. "That's what Mildred told me."

"They're my friends. I quickly advanced through their ranks, as, of course, I would. It's where I met your sister."

"Well, she never mentioned it."

"Look, Ada! Look! Tonbridge, Sevenoaks, Orpington, London – and you've seen the stairway: you *know* I can take you even higher. That 'purple glow', by the way: that's the end of the world. This is magic. Magic is *real!* Tomorrow, we'll be at the feast! Just believe me."

I surrendered and laughed. Yes, suddenly, astonishingly – for no reason! - I *did* believe her!

She held my arms. "The angels actually live in a city greater than any city that ever has been, or ever will be! The Shard, The Empire State Building, Burj Khalifa, but redeemed! Beauty, *beauty."* She stared into my pupils. "Apologies: you've never heard of those places, have you?"

"Maybe. I don't think so. Are they in *The Strand Magazine?"*

"Oh, the angels' city – if I could only show it to you, Ada!" Her demeanour became serious. "The angels are forever trying to dethrone God. They're forever destined to fail. God is forever destined to be in the wrong, the angels in the right. God is forever destined to win, the angels to lose. Until now. Look at how cruel God is, Ada! The book of Leviticus, or Numbers: *stone him to death, she must be killed, drain out its blood like water, take a heifer and break its neck, destroy everyone: men, women and children, do not permit a single member of that community to live*. That's the creature; that's God. It has to die, and it wants to."

"I hope you win, although it feels a bit, er… *blasphemous* to say that. But what happens if you don't?"

"Nothing at all. Everything stays as it is. So, there are wars, and there are murders and diseases, volcanoes erupt, earthquakes destroy cities, tidal waves crush villages, there are rapes, and dismemberments, and torturing and slavery, and dictatorship, and triumphant lies, and, to sum up, the creature continues its rule."

"In that case, good luck."

She laughed. "Luck!" She raised both my hands to her lips. "I have to practise! Stay here a while and enjoy the view. You may never see it again."

She left me alone on the platform.

I took another look at 'the end of the world'. Yes, I could really believe that's what it was. Strangely, it was wonderful.

I didn't want tonight to end. Or rather being up there: I didn't want that to end. Despite everything I'd experienced since stepping outside at two o'clock in the morning, and for all the ferocious wind, I felt happier than I think I'd ever felt before. And, truth be told, happier than I've felt since.

I stayed on that little balcony until I was numb with the cold. Then I walked slowly back to the staircase and descended. I was dog-tired.

When I re-entered the ballroom, it was full of indifferent-looking men in suits and top hats. Cytherea had her skirt wrapped around her waist, and she was pointing and repointing a heavy sword, of the sort I'd seen crusaders wielding in pictures. Mildred stood to one side, apparently commenting at length on her technique. She looked faintly ridiculous to me, like something from a Wagner opera. I certainly couldn't imagine her killing anything.

No one seemed to have noticed me. I went to the window. The fact that it was dark beyond the pane and dazzlingly light in here should have made the glass opaque. But I could see everything outside. Those swirling lights in the sky were much closer now, and yes, they did look a little like angels. Not that I was remotely qualified to judge that, but, well, they looked exactly like all the angel pictures I'd ever seen, and I couldn't imagine what else they could possibly be.

I wondered why Mildred thought she was capable of assessing anyone's swordsmanship. But then, Mildred was a proven dissembler, and none of this was real, I knew that now. I sat down in a heavy wooden chair, like a throne, with its back against the wall. I fell fast asleep.

XI.

When I awoke, I was lying on my back in bed. It took me a few moments to realise that this was my *own* bed, at home, and that my head was propped up, and that I was dressed in my night clothes. The room was filled with sunlight, however, just as it had been when I'd awoken yesterday.

The very next thing I noticed was a young man, apparently sitting on my left, and an old woman on my right, both of whom I failed to recognise. All their attention was fixed on me. They looked concerned. Their expressions changed, as they apparently registered my entry to consciousness; they became relieved.

"Go and find Mr Pearson," the man said. "Tell him she's reviving."

Mr Bowling. The speaker was *Mr Bowling*.

The old woman left in a hurry. Mr Bowling put his palm gently on my forehead. I tried to raise myself on my elbows. He told me not to exert myself. "You probably won't remember me," he said. "Michael Bowling. We met very briefly at the Munro House ball, three days ago. It so happens that I'm a medical doctor as well as a psychic investigator. Your Aunt Gloria insisted on me attending to you. She and I are members of the same freethinkers' society. Actually, I'm not sure your Uncle approves of me – he certainly didn't seem pleased to see me at the party – but we've managed to see eye to eye, so far today, thanks to your Aunt. And, of course, *you've* brought us all together; concern for your welfare, I mean."

Uncle Gordon entered with his hands folded behind his back, like a chief surgeon. He wore his usual suit and a grim expression. The mysterious old woman followed him. He sat down next to me. "Elijah sent us a big joint of beef when he heard what had happened," he said. "I've already conveyed our thanks, but be sure to underline our gratitude when you next see him, will you? I've nevertheless told him to stay away for a day or so: we don't want you getting over-excited."

"What happened? How did I get here?"

"Thank your lucky stars you're even alive," he replied airily, then, apparently realising this wasn't much of an answer, he went on: "A farmer found you lying in a field next to a sack of vegetables. From what we've been able to deduce, you were sleepwalking. You'd probably have died from the cold, had one of his old sheepdogs not been commendably inquisitive. Have you any memory of what happened?"

"None," I said, which may have been true. Nothing that made sense of my lying unconscious in a field. And that sack of vegetables – hadn't Mildred picked it up?

In the dream; yes, of course, that's what it had been.

But – no, no, it hadn't.

"Where's Mildred?" I said.

"At home, presumably," Uncle Gordon said. "She only came to stay with us the other day because of the party. Do you remember the party, Ada? At Munro House? Two nights ago? Anyway, she's back in her own house now. We sent word of what had happened to you, as soon as we could. She'll probably be along later, although obviously I can't promise anything."

Aunt Gloria entered. She stood behind Uncle Gordon wringing her hands. "We'll have to keep a closer eye on you," she said emotionally. "You could have died! Fancy sleepwalking!"

"She didn't *know* she was sleepwalking," Uncle Gordon said, by way of defending me.

"When will it happen again?" she went on, "oh, that's the question! You might not be so lucky a second time!" She turned to Mr Bowling. "Thank goodness we've a competent doctor to hand! And nurse," she added, turning to the old woman.

"This is Eunice, my assistant," Mr Bowling said, belatedly, indicating the old woman.

"Would you like a little glass of milk?" Aunt Gloria asked me. She turned to Mr Bowling. "She can *have* a little glass of milk, can't she, doctor?"

"I'm sure a little glass of milk wouldn't hurt," he replied.

"I don't really feel like a little glass of milk, Auntie," I said.

"Not even a *very* little glass of milk?" she said. "Not even *warmed up?"*

I suddenly realised – in a way I never had before - that she loved me. "Perhaps later," I said.

"Let's leave her to convalesce," Uncle Gordon said. "Come on, my dear. We don't want to tire her out."

They left. Mr Bowling dismissed the old woman, Eunice, saying she should go home and rest. I fell into a doze. Ten minutes later, Aunt Gloria crept into my room and left a glass of milk on my bedside table. "It's only a thimbleful," she whispered.

"I'll see she gets it as soon as she wakes up," Mr Bowling told her.

The moment she'd left the room, however, I was wide awake. I sat up.

"Er, there's no need to exert yourself," he told me for the second time. "You should sleep."

"I need to see Mildred," I said. "I don't care what Uncle Gordon said. Fetch me my shoes. The shoes I was wearing last night."

"I – that's a peculiar request!"

"Just indulge me, please."

"I wouldn't know where to find them. I didn't undress you, obviously. That would have been Eunice and your aunt. As for your sister, I've no idea where she lives. That's none of my concern."

I looked at him for a moment, my thoughts seeming to go in all directions. I put my hands on my face, then my hair. "I don't expect you to understand this," I said, "but I've got to get to Munro House. That's where Mildred is. She's in there with Cytherea Holmes, who pretended to leave for London, but didn't."

He blinked slowly. He took a deep breath, stood up, put his hands in his pockets, and walked slowly to the window. For some reason, my words appeared to have affected him. "I know," he said softly, still with his back to me.

The room seemed to fill with electricity. "Know what?" I said.

He turned to face me. "You may or may not be aware, Ada, that I'm a member of The Society for Psychical Research. That doesn't mean I'm an atheist, in the sense that your Great Aunt believes I am. Free thinking isn't atheism. Not necessarily."

"That's very clever-sounding, but I don't know what bearing it has - "

"I'll come to the point then. I *know* Cytherea Holmes is inside that house. And I can well believe that your sister is with her."

"So then - "

"It may surprise you to know that Mildred belongs to an organisation called 'The Imponderable Academy'. I don't know much about it; though, believe me, that's not for want of trying. You may know more. Cytherea Holmes is a high-ranking member of the same occult cabal, and she belongs to at least one other, called The Hermetic Order of the Golden Dawn. They're working together to bring some terrible mischief into the world. And they intend to use the house for that purpose. Munro House."

"That's not true."

He laughed humourlessly. He nodded. "Yes, I know you know something about it, Ada. You've been talking in your sleep. True, I'm a doctor, but I probably wouldn't have stayed at your bedside had I not thought we could help each other."

"Help each other? To do what?"

He took a deep breath. "Cytherea Holmes has to die. Tonight. And that house has to be torn down so completely that there's not one brick left standing upon another. You can help me achieve that. In return, I can help you save Mildred."

He might as well have thrown a bucket of muddy water over me; the effect would have been the same. "You're – you're suggesting I help you *murder* someone?"

"I know it sounds insane. But - "

"Oh, it – yes, it certainly sounds *insane*," I replied as indignantly as the shock would permit. "But that's the least of it! Why - why shouldn't I tell Uncle Gordon? And the police? Are you - serious?"

He chuckled. "Deadly serious. And the answer to your first question is, well, partly because they won't believe you."

I ran through the various different informing-scenarios in my mind. He was right. Apart from the fact that I was a woman, and thus latently 'hysterical' (in the way all women apparently were), I was now a sleepwalker.

We allowed a few moments of silence to pass. Despite my unqualified opposition, he seemed to realise I needed time for the full implications of what he'd said to sink in. He was right.

"And what if I *won't* help you?" I said softly, at last.

"Obviously, it would be easier for me if you would. They trust you, and, of course, you know things about them – your sleep-talk has given me snatches, but I know you can tell me much more – that could mean the difference between success and failure. However, to answer your question: if you won't help me, I'll just have to do it alone. The future of humanity is at stake. I can't *not* act."

"How noble of you."

"I fully intend to give myself up afterwards. After which, I'll almost certainly be hanged. Does *that* make me noble?"

I scoffed. *"We'll* be hanged, you mean. If I help you, in the eyes of the law, and in reality, we'll be collaborators. And that's not why I'm appalled, by the way." I shook my head. Was this actually some grotesque delusion? "I can't believe you're even considering it! Please, don't! *Don't!"*

"Even so: two individuals, versus millions."

"Please! Listen to your own words!"

"I have. Many, many times. And I like them no better than you do. But that's completely beside the point. I'll wait by your garden gate at eleven this evening. If you're not there by eleven-thirty, I'll assume you're not coming. In which case, to Hell with you, Ada Pearson. I'm giving you time to reconsider entirely because I happen to know that, buried in your unconscious, here" – he tapped his left temple – "is the knowledge that, however 'insane' I might sound, I'm actually right. I'm counting on you to recognise the truth in the next few hours." He strode to the dressing table and picked up his hat and cane. "I'll inform your Aunt and Uncle that you're sleeping, and that my presence here is no longer strictly necessary." He was on the verge of leaving the room, but then he paused, and turned back. "I will, however, also tell them that, in the little bit of conversation we *did* exchange, you weren't making much sense. If you *do* decide to join me tonight, and we're successful, then at the trial, that might count as 'mitigating circumstances'. Good day, Ada."

XII.

I couldn't sleep - it was morning, and nothing was really wrong with me – so I tried to consider my next move. Obviously, I had to get to Munro House before Michael Bowling did, but not until nightfall, since it was obvious nothing could happen till then. If Cytherea and Mildred were there now, they'd probably be asleep, and no amount of knocking would rouse them: they probably had unsolicited visitors all the time; large houses usually did, empty or not. I needed a plan.

Perhaps my best option was to play along with Mr Bowling – *Doctor* Bowling, really, I suppose - then somehow turn the tables when we reached our destination: grab his weapons and run away, or trip him up, and knock him unconscious.

Or I might be able to dissuade him *en route*. If I told him what Cytherea had told me, that she was literally on the side of the angels…

But no. I'd met men like Dr Bowling before. Once they got an idea in their heads, they were implacable.

On the other hand, he'd given me the perfect pretext to simply leave the house and set off on my own. Under normal circumstances, such a course of action would have been unthinkable… but not if I was sleepwalking. In an unconscious state, I could probably get away with anything at all - including striking Dr Bowling's head with a rock, if need be!

The problem was, I'd almost certainly be under strict observation. Aunt Gloria's *When will it happen again? You might not be so lucky a second time!* almost certainly meant someone would be assigned to keep an eye on me: probably Eunice, since Aunt Gloria herself hated bedside vigils.

But that couldn't be the case. If Dr Bowling was half counting on me to join him at the garden gate, he had to be confident I wouldn't be impeded.

Which presumably meant he'd arranged with Eunice – it would have to be her – to turn a blind eye. How could he have done that?

Well, Eunice would 'doze off', making it as obvious as she could. I'd get up, swiftly get dressed, slip out of the house somehow, and after ten minutes – enough time for me to be well on my way – Eunice would 'awaken', then she'd 'panic', then she'd rouse Aunt Gloria and Uncle Gordon with a tearful, *I only closed my eyes for a second, Sir, Ma'am, and she was off like a bolt of lightning!*

Yes, of course. That's why she was old and so apparently frail: Dr Bowling had selected her on the basis of those very qualities, to make the whole thing excusable. Whoever she really was – she almost certainly wasn't a nurse - Dr Bowling would make sure she was amply rewarded afterwards. How Machiavellian!

Wait a moment. There was another alternative open to me, whose beauty lay in the fact that it was equally devious. I could lie. I could tell Uncle Gordon that Dr Bowling was infatuated with me, and that he'd begged me to elope with him, and that he'd promised to meet me at the garden gate at eleven, and that Eunice wasn't a nurse, but his collaborator. *I can prove it Uncle,* I'd tell him. *If you hide in the vicinity of the garden gate at eleven, I'll come out, and then see if he rushes joyfully towards me.*

But what would I do afterwards? Well, once Dr Bowling had been apprehended, I'd scream. I'd run away. Because, well, maybe Dr Bowling had an accomplice. (Presumably, he had a manservant? Yes, yes, it was him. But thank God, I managed to dodge his clutches.) I ran for my life. I hid. Then I must have fainted.

In terms of what needed to be done – saving Mildred and Cytherea - I had no idea whether this was more promising than sneaking out with a complicit Eunice in the background. Its superiority consisted solely in the probability that, this way, Dr Bowling and Eunice would both get their comeuppance. I didn't like either of them.

I slipped out of bed and put on my slippers. Time to speak to Uncle.

XIII.

At twenty to eleven, Eunice fell asleep. I got up and dressed, making no attempt whatsoever to do so quietly or cautiously. I even hummed a tune. I could find no sign of a Maidenhair leaf in my shoe. I drank the little glass of milk Aunt Gloria had left for me. I went downstairs.

Aunt Gloria herself sat in the kitchen in a ruched bonnet. She looked ready to give someone a whipping. Hopefully, it wouldn't be me. It hadn't occurred to me until now that Dr Bowling might have reconsidered: he might have decided my refusal to help him wasn't to be overturned.

"Elijah is down in the garden with your uncle," she told me.

"Elijah?"

"Mr Bowling's a young man, Ada. Likely, your uncle's no match for him. Mr Pattinson's down there too. Stanley Pattinson, the fishmonger."

"What will they do to him?"

"Bring him in here, give him a bit of a talking-to, maybe threaten him with the law, tell him to stay away from you. They won't hurt him, I'll see to that. I take it the old crook upstairs is still pretending to be asleep?"

"She's probably looking out of the window now. Mr Bowling and she have probably agreed a signal."

She looked at the clock. "It's one minute to eleven. You're a good girl, Ada. I've always said that. Now, you'd better get going."

Suffice it to say, everything went according to plan. I walked into the garden. I called to Mr Bowling. He emerged happily from the shadows by the garden gate and came towards me. His three ambushers broke cover. I screamed. I turned full circle and ran through the front garden. Within a few minutes, I was well on my way to Munro House.

At that point, I remembered something – or seemed to. Yes, Mr Bowling had come towards me; yes, my three defenders had rushed to seize him; yes, I'd screamed and run away. So far, so good, but given that my scream had produced, as it was intended to, the impression of an additional, more proximate danger, how radically had my rescuers paused to take stock of it?

And had Mr Bowling slipped away in the confusion? What if he had?

I couldn't afford the luxury of assuming otherwise. Nor should I underestimate Mr Bowling's powers of persuasion, nor his ability to lie in his own defence. For safety's sake, I should assume that all four men, and possibly others, were now on their way to Munro House with a view to intercepting me.

To make matters worse, I had no idea what I was going to do when I reached Munro House. Nor what I might find there.

Maybe nothing.

But that seemed unlikely. Mr Bowling would hardly be so insistent on going there *right now;* and Mildred had told me that Cytherea was in Munro House not only on her own initiative, but at the behest of the Freemasons. *Something* would be happening. As for the creature, that might not even exist, however much Mildred and Cytherea and Mr Bowling and possibly the Freemasons seemed to believe in it, and however much I might think I'd seen it. Delusions were contagious, as everyone knew.

I don't know how long I was walking, because I was in a hurry and thinking hard, but I soon found myself on the mysterious ridge where Mildred and I had met Mr Collinson last night, and from which we'd looked down towards Munro House. Now, just like last night, the building appeared as a black shape.

But then I noticed something else about it. It was moving. The building was *moving*. And much bigger, somehow.

Or was it?

No, it wasn't! Rather, it was completely enveloped by a much larger entity of indeterminate shape, which was itself gliding over and about it like a monstrous globule. Whatever it was, it built up speed, and eventually cleared the house, leaving its outline fully visible. Then it accelerated and took to the air. It flew for a few seconds, and seemed to evaporate.

I picked up my skirts and suddenly I was running, with no thought of personal endangerment, my only concern being for the two women inside. I had to arrive before Mr Bowling and my Uncle and whoever else; because I knew for certain that they all were on their way now. I'd never been clever enough to outwit them, not for long. Why had I imagined this time would be any different?

I reached Munro House with my lungs bursting and my legs ready to give way. It had been obvious for five hundred yards at least that there had been a catastrophe of epic proportions. The outer walls seemed to glow with a sickly, pale blue light, and, as far as I could tell, the windows were all smashed, every single one. Even from afar, I could hear screams. I shoved the front door open and went inside. The darkness should have been virtually complete, but the same unhealthy radiance as bathed the exterior allowed me to navigate my way with relative ease.

I rushed headlong into the ballroom. Mildred lay on the floor, in the innermost of the three circles I'd seen on my last visit here, shrieking at the top of her voice and beating her head on the ground. In the far corner, Cytherea sat propped up against the wall with her eyes open and a look of intense shock on her face. The sword I'd seen her wielding last night had been thrust through her chest, and presumably deep into the wall behind her. Only its hilt was visible.

XIV.

Is it possible for a person to be in two places at once? Perhaps not an ordinary person, but what about someone like Cytherea Holmes? I ask only because of the account I've provided above, in which I described her final posture. Michael Bowling, however, who arrived ten minutes later, told a very different story. He claimed to have seen her leave the house at speed, obviously in terror. She quickly outran him. Half an hour later, he came across a wooded grove in which a withered old woman lay dead in the midst of ten or twelve unnaturally tall men, whose skin and attire seemed luminous, and who were weeping hysterically. He recognised her from her dress.

Mildred was unable to stop screeching. She died in an asylum six months later, apparently from nervous and physical exhaustion. Uncle Gordon was killed in the mysterious circumstances I outlined at the beginning of this account. Following the catastrophe at Munro House, he became obsessed by the thought that he'd 'sinned', that divine retribution was in the offing, and that, when it came, it wouldn't be pretty. I know the other men who died in that room shared his presentiment. Aunt Gloria followed him to the grave six months later, apparently defeated by the loss. By that time, I was engaged to be married to Elijah Scott, not because I was in love with him – I wasn't, though I certainly didn't dislike him – but because I could see Auntie was declining, and I thought it was something she hoped for, and I wanted to save her. Alas, it appears I am not the kind who can save others.

Michael Bowling? Oh, he more than survived. His sort always does. He married a duchess, I think, and went on to become an MP. Or it may have been a countess. Either way, he's dead now. And he became incredibly boring. I've read his book, *Personal Reflections on the Marconi Scandal* (1915), which was long out of date, even when it first appeared. I don't rate it (except as a cure for insomnia), not even in terms of style.

As I mentioned at the beginning, I'm an old woman now. I've had a lot of time to think about what happened and what it meant. The first, and perhaps most clichéd, interpretation – that Cytherea Holmes's fate was a warning to others about the dangers of hubris – is, in my opinion, utter rubbish. A universe in which we all 'know our place' is medieval. Our place is with God, assuming such a being exists. Abject submission is not the way to get there: as the theologians never tire of telling us (but mainly when they're considering the problem of evil), if God had wanted to populate his creation with puppets, he could easily have done so. And we're not puppets. Moreover, doesn't Jesus talk somewhere about the virtues of 'forcing' the Kingdom of God?

As part of my preparation for writing this account, I spent some time in the library of the British Museum. I went through every issue of *The Strand Magazine*. Nowhere is there any mention of The Hermetic Order of the Golden Dawn, much less of a 'Cythera Holmes'. At first, I tried to err on the side of generosity: maybe Mildred was mistaken. Perhaps the article had appeared in *The Contemporary Review* or *Macmillan's Magazine* or *The Illustrated London News* – or some similar periodical. But now I know: it was just a lie. Well-meaning, maybe, but a deliberate falsehood none the less.

Still, as I said at the beginning: if the culprits were here to defend themselves, they'd probably claim they did it *for my protection*. Maybe *that's* where I've got to err on the side of generosity. And I do. I've made my peace with that particular excuse.

Over the years, I've read a bit of 'Jacob Böhme', the writer from whom Cytherea Holmes claimed to derive her inspiration. His books don't make much sense to me, and when I spoke to the local vicar, he'd never heard of him. But I understand that there *is* a respectable Christian mystical tradition within which he belongs – it would include such obscure figures as 'Pseudo-Dionysius the Areopagite', who claimed that nothing at all can be said about God. So I assume that what Cytherea and Mildred were doing was consistent with some version of Christian orthodoxy. Their ends may have been horrible, but their ends may not have been the end... if that makes sense.

Indeed, I have good reason to assume the very opposite is the case. I asked above whether it is possible for a person to be in two places at once. Let me modify that question. Do you think it is possible for a person to be in *three* places at once? Four? Ten? An infinite number? Every so often – not very frequently, but frequently enough – I seem to catch sight of Mildred, or Cytherea, or both of them. They turn up in the most everyday places: on the Common, in the Pantiles, on Calverley Road, outside the library. Put it down, if you like, to the demented sanguinity of an old woman, although obviously I haven't always been this old. A flash, that's all, and they're gone. Always out of the corner of my eye, never directly, but the sight is always accompanied by a strong sense of *knowing* it's them.

They're both a lot taller now.

The Standing Stones

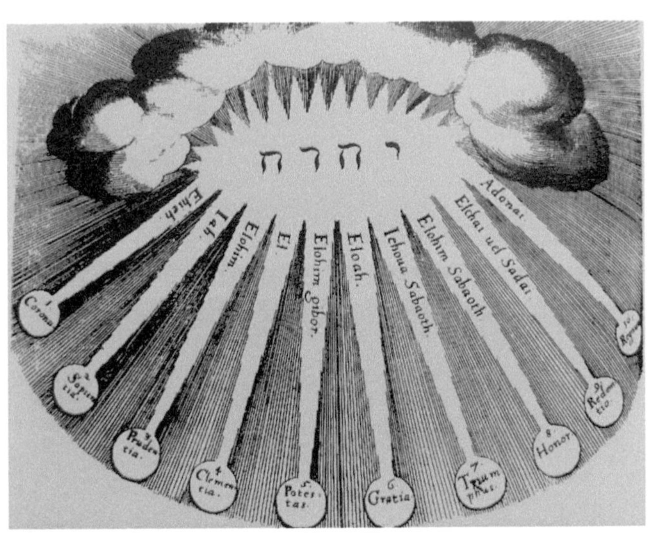

I.

What follows is an attempt to reconstruct the final months of the life of one *Hermione Portcher*, a university lecturer by profession (before she was 'let go' – more about that later), using her personal notebook, plus eyewitness statements from the night of her disappearance. Exactly what occurred that evening, in terms of what people said they saw, is mostly a matter of indifference now, but a dedicated group of local historians obtained eyewitness accounts from various on-the-spot individuals a few days afterwards, and these can be found archived in the central library in Tunbridge Wells. Whether or not the prosaic interpretation proffered by the local intelligentsia (then almost universally swallowed by everyone else), is accurate, I will let the reader judge. Also: it may seem a pernickety point - so it might as well be made here, at the beginning - but her notebook is really a diary, with the difference that it is not always arranged by date. Mostly, it details her daily life. Unfortunately, it becomes increasingly arcane towards the end.

When my narrative begins, she'd recently been diagnosed with a terminal illness, and she probably needed something to confide in. She didn't tell anyone human at all, I don't know why; perhaps because she thought there was nothing anyone could do; perhaps because she didn't want to become the focus of everyone's well-meaning consideration; perhaps because she couldn't find the opportunity, or the words. The fact is, in hiding it from others, she also managed, to some extent, to hide it from herself. Of all the writing she produced during the final short period of her life (and there was a lot), she rarely alluded to it, and even when she did, it was as an aside. At the time she began keeping her notebook-cum-diary, she had just six months to live.

Dr Portcher was always a good lecturer, and consistently conscientious as a tutor. When she disappeared, she was thirty-nine. Somewhere along the line, she'd ended up reluctantly alone. Perhaps the academic life does that to you, especially if you're female. Maybe if you don't meet someone during your undergraduate years, your hopes of finding a partner become progressively slimmer as you become older and smarter. Before you know it, you're ever so slightly 'intimidating'.

I myself will not appear in this narrative, at least not in the first person. Even though my testimony was one of the main reasons Dr Portcher lost her job, I was not responsible for what happened to her afterwards. Besides, I am not primarily penning a confession, but trying to make sense of a small slice of history. If I expiate a small quantity of guilt in the process, that will be a bonus. Either way, I do not want to obscure the central facts with facile snippets of autobiography.

I say 'what happened to her afterwards.' But the fact is, what that was remains a complete mystery.

II.

According to what I've been told, it all began one cold November evening, when eighty-five-year-old Gregory Portcher ordered his three middle-aged children, Ray,

Callum and Hermione, out of his five-bedroom house, 'Beulah Cottage', and onto his seven-acre collection of fields, where Tunbridge Wells fades into the countryside. Since Gregory was apparently in decline (he'd had two 'falls' recently, and he was beginning to confuse the past and the present), his children were happy to humour him. They were here because every fourth week, on the last Sunday of the month, they always had a family 'get together': the three of them and their father. On Sundays one, two and three, they each visited the old man separately. This was very much an end-of-life arrangement: prior to the fateful falls, their visits were much more *ad hoc*; they only ever met as a group at Christmas, always as part of a much larger family gathering, and rarely for more than three hours at a time. They lived within twenty miles of each other.

Hermione had dosed up on painkillers before setting off. She listened to Erik Satie in the car, and she insisted on cooking the Sunday meal when she arrived (even though her brothers were expecting to do that, and they'd brought all the ingredients). They ate at six o'clock, and it was when the men had finished washing and drying that Gregory demanded an evening stroll. No one liked to refuse him, even though none of their shoes were suitable for walking outdoors in the middle of winter.

The moon hung low on the horizon that night, and the bare trees beyond the hedgerows stood completely still. Halfway across the field, Gregory fell. His children were quietly horrified, but this tumble turned out to be no accident (or so he said): he'd decided, as he put it, 'to kiss the soil'.

He'd always been a bit of a hippy, and they were used to him doing quirky things and holding eccentric beliefs. They helped him uncomplainingly to his feet. I suppose they must have made quite a picture as they got him to the house. Red-haired Callum with his slight limp and gangly body; Ray, the photogenic one, with the large hands and confident step, and little Hermione with her too-long (in her own opinion) hair and her penchant for billowy dresses. Two clean-shaven men and a pony-tailed woman, forty-one, forty, and thirty-nine, respectively. Their father was suitably bent (since we're imagining a picture here), wrinkled and long-haired: he looked like Old Father Time, minus the beard.

Ten minutes later, when they were indoors, Gregory ushered them into his large kitchen, and told them to sit down at the old oak table.

It was then that they realised he had an announcement planned. They tried to prepare themselves for a bombshell, since that was the purpose of the old oak table. Previously, it had only been used for bad news: the bankruptcy when they'd been children; the sale of the art collection; their mother's cancer (terminal, as it transpired). They already wore sombre expressions. They supplemented them by folding their hands in their laps, avoiding each other's eyes, and trying, impossibly, to look through the polished wood surface at the carpet.

Meanwhile, still muddy from the field, Gregory took his accustomed place at the table's head. A sombre gloom reigned, hardly relieved by the diffuse table lamp in the corner. It felt like the prelude to some kind of gruesome confession.

"I won't beat about the bush," Gregory said. "You all probably remember years ago, when we went bankrupt. You were children at the time, but your mother and I never made any secret of what had happened. Nor about the fact that your uncle Nedrick, my older brother, bailed us out."

His three listeners nodded uncertainly, not sure whether, by doing so, they were committing themselves to something they'd later regret.

"In return for his help," he continued, "we agreed – that is, your mother and I agreed – to include him in the will. So, when I die, you'll each get a third of the house, which I expect you to sell… or not: it's up to you. But he inherits the surrounding land."

"I remember the whole thing well," Callum said gloomily. "Everything about that day is permanently etched on my memory."

"We thought it was much worse than it was," Ray added. "The word 'bankruptcy' having such nineteenth-century connotations: The Marshalsea Prison, the workhouse, that sort of thing. Right now, I don't think any of us actually *want* the field. We've all got good jobs, nice houses and loving families. We're in no danger of starving."

"Is Uncle Nedrick still alive?" Hermione said. "Last time we heard about him, he was in Australia, wasn't he? Given that he's three years older than you, he might no longer be with us. I'm not saying that would be a good thing, obviously. I don't think any of us really know him well enough to wish him either good *or* ill. And the field isn't a problem. Not for me, anyway."

Her brothers murmured their agreement.

Gregory smiled. "We probably wouldn't be having this conversation if I hadn't confirmed, very recently, that he's hale and hearty. Which is a scandalous irony, given all the illegal substances he's injected into his veins over the years. No, that's not the problem."

No one wanted to ask what 'the problem' was: it might look tactless, a kind of *for Heaven's sake, get on with it, Father*. They looked at the table again.

"The problem is," Gregory went on, "with me out of the way, he'll almost certainly sell the land, and with current government housing policy being what it is – *a zillion new houses by the middle of next year, don't care how and we don't care where* – the various developers will fall over themselves to get their grubby hands on it. Result: in eighteen months' time, it'll be covered in substandard executive houses with as much aesthetic value as a pile of cardboard boxes from a downmarket shoe shop."

"Are you suggesting changing your will?" Hermione asked.

"Would you blame me if I was? Put it like this: any cash he makes, he'll spend on navy rum and drugs. Knowing Nedrick – and that's another thing I confirmed, before you ask: that he hasn't changed - he'll be dead before they've laid the foundations for the first cardboard box. And don't imagine the money will come back to you. He's got about ten or twelve dependents from four broken marriages. They'll get the lot."

"If you change the will, they'll probably come after us," Callum said. "Nedrick will be expecting an inheritance. When he doesn't get it, he'll feel cheated - "

"Rightly," Ray said.

"And he'll probably pass his grievance on to the next generation," Hermione said. "People usually do. And if there's a lot of them, and they've - "

Gregory held his hands up. "Just a minute, everyone: I didn't say I *was* thinking of changing the will. I only asked whether you'd *blame* me in that case. Well, you've made your answer to that perfectly clear, thank you." He sighed. "The fact is, even if I wanted to, I couldn't. Nedrick was never the kind of person to overlook legal safeguards when he entered into an agreement. The things he put in place then also made it impossible for me ever to put a covenant on the land: *the inheritor must not allow building work to take place,* that sort of thing. You've got to understand, we went to Nedrick cap in hand. We could have lost everything. As it was, what should have been a serious car crash turned into several long miles of very bumpy road… at the end of which, we recovered."

"How did he ever get the money to bail us out?" Callum asked. "I thought he lived in a caravan."

Gregory chuckled. "He was an awful lot wealthier before he went to prison. He was King Croesus for a while. And yes, we knew that, at the time: we'd never have imposed on him, had we not known he had cash coming out of his eyeballs. We suspected – *knew,* actually, but we tried to pretend otherwise – that it was ill-gotten. And here we are, thirty years later. I suppose everyone gets what they deserve in the end, including me."

Hermione frowned. "Are you asking us to forgive you?" she said emotionally. "Is that what this is about? Because there's absolutely *nothing* to forgive!"

"I'll second that," Ray said.

"No, I've a different agenda," Gregory said. "Hear me out. When we first fell into dire straits, and it dawned inexorably on us that we'd have to appeal to Nedrick's generosity, such as it is, I came up with a plan. Part of it involved subtly guiding you three to turn you into what you now are. I wouldn't have done that had I thought I was *in any way* acting counter to your interests, by the way. I could have turned you into doctors, or architects, or lawyers. Instead, I turned you into three lovely historians with a penchant for archaeology."

"You never made any secret of what you were doing," Callum said amiably, "from what I remember."

"Archaeology was your big interest," Hermione said. "If you'd been a bad father, we might have taken other paths, but you weren't, and it always seemed sensible to develop the skills you'd nurtured in us. Thanks to you, we've had very successful careers."

Ray's eyes had been trying to stop his siblings going full steam ahead. He seemed to realise they'd failed, so he removed the light from them. He turned to his father. "What is this 'plan' you just mentioned?"

"I thought you'd never ask!" Gregory said jauntily. "Okay, there's no easy way to introduce it, because it's singular, and it involves risks, but I've spent a long time planning it – since you were children, in fact – and I'd like you to view it as the substance of my final wish. If you do this, I can die happy. But, of course, you're free agents, and if you say no, I'll respect that. As you said a moment ago, Ray, you've all got good jobs, nice houses, and loving families, you're in no danger of starving. I only want the best for the three of you. I always have."

"You're talking as if your death's imminent," Callum said. "You could have years left yet."

"Better safe than sorry," his father replied. "And I think we all know - "

"What exactly is your plan?" Ray persisted, trying to make it sound as if he was more interested than apprehensive.

Gregory sat up and folded his hands on the table. "Imagine if someone was to do an archaeological dig in those fields out there… and they were to unearth twenty prehistoric stones, in a wide circle. Imagine that. Those fields would then become a site of *national historical interest*. People would come from all over the world to see them. English Heritage would stake a claim to them, and it would probably end up buying them from Nedrick, who'd *have* to sell them, like it or not. There could be no possibility of building houses on them after that. Ever. And he'd get his money. Result: everyone's happy."

An astonished silence. The eyes of all three siblings started doing what Ray's had done a moment ago: trying to put the brakes on.

Ray let out an incredulous laugh. "You're asking us to *fake* a finding of twenty prehistoric stones in a wide circle? To *fabricate* the finding of a second Stonehenge?"

"It doesn't have to be *that* impressive," Gregory said. "More like the Rollright Stones in The Cotswolds, or Druid's Circle in Penmaenmawr."

Hermione coughed a laugh. "Oh, that's all right then. I was wondering where we were going to get thirty twenty-ton stones from, how we were going to bury them, then dig them all back up again. You know: *without anyone noticing*."

"Don't be silly, Hermione," Ray said. "There's a garden centre just round the corner."

Callum held his hands up. "Okay, okay, you two, you've had your fun." He turned to his father. "It's… an idea. And, er, it's pretty ambitious! Let's put all the logistical problems to one side for a moment. There's got to be a pretext for a dig. If the three of us start digging without any cause, and then we uncover the find of the century, won't people be suspicious?"

"I've thought of that," Gregory said. "I've got documents. There may actually *be* standing stones down there, for all we know."

"Down in the fields?" Ray said. "How did they get buried?"

"What sort of documents?" Hermione interjected.

"Not historical ones," Gregory said. "Visionary. I've met several visionaries over the years. They've *told* me there are standing stones down there. Stones that used to be standing," he added sheepishly. "In prehistory. They gave me signed affidavits to that effect. This was twenty or thirty years ago: like I said, I've been planning it for decades. They're all dead now – the visionaries, I mean - so they can't retract their claims."

"What do you mean by 'visionaries'?" Hermione asked, although, depressingly, she already knew.

"Spiritualists, some of them," Gregory replied: "remarkable people with a talent for finding hidden objects, often at a great distance. Men and women with paranormal powers." He paused, apparently to see what sort of an impression he'd produced. Registering that it wasn't a positive one, he sped up. "Now, I know what you're all going to say: *what sort of a pretext is that for a dig?* Universities are fortresses of unimaginative secularism, no *bona fide* member of the academy will ever accept 'visionaries' as a reason to do anything at all, you'll make yourselves laughing stocks."

"Something like that," Ray said, in as upbeat a manner as he could manage.

"Something *exactly* like that," Callum put in.

"Well, you don't have to suggest *you* believe it," Gregory said. "You tell them you have an eccentric old father, and thanks to said - admittedly also 'eccentric' – documents, you've decided to finally humour him. The end."

"Except that, if we're successful," Callum said, "which obviously we won't be, we'll be indirectly 'proving' the reliability of your 'visionaries'. Suddenly, we've opened a whole new can of worms. Because do you know how many backs that will put up? Dozens. And most of them won't even be in our faculty, or remotely related to it. They'll trip over themselves in an attempt to debunk us. And we'll be the casualties. Result: no more good jobs, and possibly – given that we've still got mortgages to pay off – no more nice houses, and perhaps even – given that professional and financial ruin tends to sabotage relationships – no more lovely families."

"The eventual sale of my house should go a long way towards paying off your mortgages," Gregory said, "but I take your point. However, there are ways round the problem. For example, you might 'discover' that the stones aren't actually ancient: at best they go back to the sixteenth century. Or the seventeenth, or eighteenth. And at that point, we've got something even better than we had when we started: an antique homage to prehistory."

"There would have to be a documentary counterpart to that," Hermione said. "The local historians would all be well aware of it, and they'd probably have found it a long time ago. A group of stones on its own, however unusual they might look, however curious their positioning, is never going to prove anything."

"It definitely wouldn't prove anything concerning *recent* history," Callum said, "although I don't think you can say the same for the history of pre-literate societies. A group of identically-sized large stones, equally spaced in an exact circle? That would strongly suggest *something* significant. However, I'm simply making a theoretical point. It's neither here nor there as regards the central issue. The point is, neither thing could be faked."

Gregory picked up a small cardboard box from beside his chair and set it on the table. "The documentary evidence is all in here," he said. "Or at least, copies. The originals are in a safety deposit box in the bank. I'd like you to look through them."

"I don't believe in that sort of thing," Ray said.

"Me neither," Callum put in.

Hermione shrugged her shoulders. "Come on, guys, let's keep an open mind, shall we? Or didn't you hear the words 'final wish'?"

Ray frowned. "I'd rather those words had been attached to some other aspiration."

"That's not how those words work," Hermione told him.

"All I'm asking is that you consider my proposal," Gregory said. "Like Herm just said: keep an open mind. And try to be accommodating. I know you'll find a way."

III.

You may be wondering how Hermione felt after all this talk about wills, final wishes and imminent death. The notebook is, as always, reticent about the matter of her own state of mind, but she does seem to have wept a little, although mainly over her father, not the difficult, possible impossible position in which she'd been placed. Perhaps she was beginning to merge their predicaments. She certainly sympathised with him in a way she didn't believe her brothers did. And she wanted to help him, even if that meant saving him from himself. As far as she could see, their best course of action might simply be to go through the motions of complying with his wishes. She was of one mind with her brothers in that respect, although probably more inclined than them to be indulgent.

They met the next day for dinner in Hermione's rustic kitchen in Hailsham. They agreed that they had to appear to be doing something. Ideally, though, in a way that was consistent with doing nothing.

For that to stand any chance of success, they had to know exactly what they were up against. They were researchers by nature, and they didn't usually act before gathering as much information as possible. The first thing – as obvious as it was unavoidable – was to look through the material their father had given them.

Hermione opened a bottle of red wine and took the box out from the cupboard above the sink. She'd already looked through it once, but she didn't consider it helpful to reveal that yet. She spread the contents on the table, and told her brothers to pick something and pass it on.

Half an hour later, they agreed: they'd learned as much as they were going to. It was exactly what they'd been told it was: a collection of written documents whose authors claimed paranormal knowledge of a wide circle of stones in the fields surrounding Beulah Cottage. All were signed, the names of the signatories printed beneath, and, in each case, they included a business address. Fertile material from which to launch an investigation? That was Callum's conclusion. "I think we should find these 'visionaries'," he said, "and possibly sue them. I know Dad said they're all dead, but I can't believe that. I'd imagine he paid them good money to make their pronouncements."

"I've spoken to him about that," Hermione put in. "He says he only paid them to find something of 'significant archaeological interest'. They all came up with the same thing. Independently."

Callum and Ray turned the same expression on her.

"Surely you don't believe that?" Ray said.

"It's also stated in writing in each document," she said. "And he's witnessed it. I doubt we have grounds for a prosecution. I wouldn't want to go down that route anyway. It's taking a sledgehammer to crack a nut."

"I've just read a book about spiritualism," Callum said. "*Servants of the Supernatural* wouldn't normally have been top of my reading list, but an aberrant father means needs must. Anyway, I can just about bring myself to concede that there may be one or two genuine 'spiritualists' out there. I mean, just for the sake of argument. But a whole regiment? Sorry, that beggars belief. The far better explanation is that Dad doesn't actually remember the facts. As he, himself, admits, he hired them a long time ago. In the intervening period, wishful thinking's stepped in, and possibly the beginning of Alzheimer's, and it's constructed an entirely more congenial – to him – narrative."

"And, Herm, he wanted to thwart Uncle Ned," Ray said. "Why *wouldn't* he have told them what to find? He's obsessed. I hate to say it, but it's a collection of fields. I don't understand why it holds such value for him."

"I got the impression he wasn't telling the whole truth about Uncle Nedrick," Hermione said. "I always thought they were on the best of terms, even nowadays. There's something he doesn't want us to know. Something important."

Ray scoffed. "He's old, and he's beginning to get mixed up, we all know that. You're right, though, just as a matter of interest: I've never got the feeling there was bad blood between them. Quite the opposite."

"What I find disgraceful," Callum said, "is the way each document warns against digging the stones up; the pathetically *transparent,* entirely *unoriginal,* utterly *puerile* way each author comes up with the same insurance policy. They were obviously afraid Dad might grab a spade. Well, how better to discourage him than with an implied 'curse'? Talk about desperate!"

Ray chuckled. "Mendacious psychics? Next, you'll be telling me the Pope's a Catholic!"

"It's not quite as straightforward as that," Hermione said. "I had a look through all these documents before I went to bed last night. Some of them specify exactly where the stones are. They don't just say, 'Somewhere within your seven acres; could be anywhere.' They actually say, 'X marks the spot.'"

Callum shrugged. "By the time the fifth or sixth psychic came along, that individual probably realised a simple, 'It's somewhere within your seven acres' just wouldn't do. Dad would have wanted far more than a repeat prescription: he'd have demanded greater and greater specificity as time went on. If the money was right, I'm sure said 'visionaries' were happy to oblige… but always with the 'Don't, for goodness sake, dig them up' caveat. Just to cover themselves."

"And they may well have colluded," Ray said. "All of them. Stone-finding-visionaries is probably a small, tight-knit community."

Hermione pulled a weary expression. "We've got to do something."

Ray leaned back in his chair. He took a pensive sip of his wine. "Let's not argue. We need to hire a private detective, guys. As you pointed out a moment ago, Callum, the signatories might not be deceased after all, and if whoever we hire can expose just one or two of them, that might re-set the discussion… such as it is."

Hermione and Callum agreed. They drank more wine and ate a jumbo bag of salt and vinegar crisps. They'd each contribute a third to the fee. As investigations went, it would probably be an easy one – the availability of the names and addresses of the people to be tracked down would ensure that - and so relatively inexpensive.

The next item on the agenda was how to appear to be doing something proactive in the meantime, something to please their dying father and produce the impression that they were three willing, cooperative, albeit slightly sceptical (they weren't prepared to relinquish that), children. Here, Hermione was the prime mover. She announced that she would assign a group of her undergraduate students to dig the fields. "This is how I'll sell it to them," she said: "my father, now old and frail, has a collection of fields which he has *allowed* us – not asked us: *allowed* us – to excavate. It's a one-off opportunity. I'm giving you free rein, ladies and gentlemen. Just see what you can come up with. Begin with metal detectors, maybe."

Callum gave a contemptuous smirk. *"Metal detectors?"*

"There might actually be one or two interesting things down there," she said. "We've got to give them *something* to play for, and maybe they'll come up with a few antique coins. They probably will. After that, I'll suggest places they might dig. I'll give them one of the 'X marks the spot' locations. From their point of view, it'll be an entirely random choice. I'll make sure Dad's in on the conspiracy."

Callum nodded sagely. "It's an excellent plan," he said. "The point is, you're right: we've got to go through the *motions* of doing something. Dad's getting more doddery every day, and maybe, once he realises it's a wild, wild goose chase, he'll re-focus, and decide to get some proper care. This way, we don't have to do anything ourselves, and, on the very slim chance that there really *is* something down there, we can take the credit."

IV.

We don't have to do anything ourselves. Afterwards, Hermione realised she'd been lumbered with the bulk of the work: Callum's and Ray's undergraduates weren't required to do anything at all. Which meant Callum and Ray weren't required to do anything either, not in that line.

She got verbal approval from the university authorities, and announced it in her weekly seminar the following day. All of her students were suitably excited, and began making plans there and then.

In the meantime, her father agreed to accommodate them all at Beulah Cottage for the duration of what was projected to be a two-week dig. The house had been virtually empty since his wife's death ten years ago, and it was easily big enough to lodge seven people who didn't object to sharing rooms, and who didn't necessarily mind sleeping on the floor.

The morning the dig was scheduled to begin, Hermione and her students arrived at Beulah Cottage in a minibus. She went for a walk alone in the fields while Gregory showed the others around. An early-morning mist lingered. It was damp underfoot and the sky was overcast, but not in a way that threatened rain. She expected to find the experience of being outdoors enjoyable, but she felt anxious.

Then it struck her: she was *supposed* to feel anxious. She was dying. Why did she keep forgetting? Well, not forgetting exactly, but as if it was all a dream. Unreal.

Maybe because keeping it unspoken *made* it unreal. Or gave it a smaller share in the real. Being alone meant you were in a community of one. Everyone in that community – one hundred percent of its population – knew your secret. 'Secret', in inverted commas, because right here, it wasn't one. Here, it was the commonest of common knowledge.

She turned around full circle. This whole bucolic expanse had been meant to stand in for a garden when they'd been children, but it had never lived up to its billing. It didn't have hillocks, or hidey-holes, or interesting trees, or anything really: you couldn't play in it in any creative way, it was too unrelentingly same-y.

Barren, almost, one might say. Perhaps the clay was responsible for that. The grass never really grew. Nothing much else did, except the occasional thistle, and even they weren't anything to write home about.

That anxiety again, redoubled.

No: it was more than the fact that she was dying. She wasn't afraid of death: it was just a good night's sleep. This was a distinct sense of the ominous, of something unpleasant; malevolent. She looked around herself for the feeling's cause: sometimes, seen out of the corner of the eye, the features of a landscape assumed distorted shapes that a person's unconscious thought it recognised, and it reacted to them affectively. Which was all psychologically normal.

But she could see nothing that might serve as the stimulus for such a process. And the feeling seemed to be intensifying.

She had to get back to the house.

Her phone rang. She took it from her bag – *Ray* – and picked up with considerable relief. Not exactly physical company, but the next best thing.

"We've had a bit of a breakthrough," he told her. "One of Dad's 'visionaries' is still alive and well - and living in a rest home in Crowborough, would you believe. Name of Martin Gersholm. Before I clear it with Callum, would you be happy to go and see him? I mean, alone? today?"

She expelled an indignant laugh. "Why me?"

"For a start, you're just round the corner. You are *at* Dad's, aren't you? But that's not the most important consideration. You're better at getting information out of people than Callum and I are. Partly because you're nice, and partly because you're an attractive woman. People warm to you."

She grimaced. She didn't like that sort of thing. "I don't recall you ever calling me 'attractive' before."

"Yes, well, maybe you are, maybe you aren't. I'm your brother so you can't expect an objective assessment, but you're a damn sight more - "

"Sexist."

"- Attractive than Callum or I am. And a smallish, attractive, pleasant woman walking into the room won't seem half as intimidating as a tallish, rather dubious-looking, pug-ugly man. Or two. Which would probably put anyone off."

"What's my mission objective? I thought we were going to threaten any living 'visionaries' with legal action."

"You, yourself, said that wouldn't be doable. No, you simply talk to him. Get him to admit that he was making it up. Maybe even offer him money."

"And then what? Drive him round here? Stand him there, in front of Dad, and get him to say, 'Sorry, Mr Portcher, I lied to you all those years ago.'"

"That would be the ideal, yes."

"But reality check: it's almost certainly not going to happen."

"We've already spent a lot of money finding these charlatans. You want to just write it off?"

She sighed. "I suppose what I'm saying is that we should have thought about this at the beginning. Seriously, what do we *want?* What am I going there to achieve? I mean, super specifically?"

"So you *will* go?"

"Er, what?"

"You just said you'd go. You implied it. Please. And the answer to your question is, just go for curiosity's sake. Maybe you're right: maybe we *should* have thought about this at the beginning. Obviously, yes, we should. But he might be ready to make a confession, and it's not an opportunity I think we should pass up. I'll tell you what: if you go and see him, and do your best to get him to 'fess up, I'll pay your share of the PI's bill."

She was almost back at the house now. What did it matter? She was on her way out of life, the universe and everything, anyway: she might as well make herself useful. "Okay, it's a deal."

"Good, because I've made an appointment for you. I'll text you the details in a minute or so."

He hung up.

V.

She arrived at The Marilyn Hills Care Home at 2pm, having briefed her students to simply explore the territory around Beulah Cottage for a few hours and report anything of interest after dinner. The nurse at reception took her name and led her upstairs and along a corridor to Martin Gersholm's room.

Hermione had tried to picture him on the way there, but she hadn't got beyond the stereotypical elderly man: thin, balding, slightly unsteady on his feet, rather slow, and dressed in nondescript clothes that, yes, were perfectly clean, but also subtly threadbare.

He surprised her by being only thin and balding. He stood up like a military man, and asked her courteously to sit down. The nurse brought them a pot of tea, which she poured according to their directions. He wore an olive suit and brogues and he looked disgruntled. The walls were covered in posters of astrological configurations, plus a large reproduction of the Rider-Waite-Smith Tarot deck. In some ways, it resembled a teenager's dorm room, except for the cross-stitched Bible quotation, in a wooden frame: *The wind bloweth where it listeth, and thou hearest the sound thereof, but canst not tell whence it cometh, and whither it goeth: so is everyone that is born of the Spirit. John 3.8*. Even so, it didn't look the kind of room an elderly, sartorial man might inhabit.

"I know why you're here," he told her, when the nurse had left. "It's an unusual name, Portcher. I assume you're Gregory's daughter."

She nodded. "You provided him with a signed statement to the effect that there are items of significant archaeological interest beneath his fields."

"And I stand by it. And I'd strongly advise most people against trying to recover those items. Not you, though. You're the daughter. 'Tiny Hermione' is how I remember you. You've grown since then. Not much, but enough."

She was surprised to find he knew her name. But of course, the nurse would have announced it. She didn't believe he remembered her.

In the meantime, she didn't want to alienate him. Which probably meant playing along with him - a bit. "I don't remember you at all. Please don't take that the wrong way. I don't remember anything at all about my father getting people in to assess subterranean matters."

He laughed. "Of course. Why would you? I don't think we were introduced at any point. I saw you from a distance. You were wearing a yellow jumpsuit – the colour of the sun: highly auspicious – and you had your hair in pigtails. I remember thinking, 'So that's her.'"

"Did my father point me out?"

"No, because he had no cause to. The reason I took such an interest in you, and why I found out your name, is because, as the daughter, you're predestined to dig those stones up. You're an archaeologist now, I presume, or something in that line?"

She frowned. She suddenly lost patience. "I suppose you think that, because you know what I do for a living, I'll also believe you have special powers of some sort?"

"Not at all. I wouldn't presume to underestimate you in that way."

"Well, I don't hold truck with anything of that nature. The supernatural, I mean."

"I knew your father very well. He and Nedrick both. They were both far, far wiser than me. You obviously believed I duped your father into believing there was something occult hidden beneath the fields he owns. You may even think I put the idea into his head. You're entirely wrong. He already knew. I simply confirmed it, and that wasn't even the reason he invited me round to your house. He invited me because we were friends. And the basis of that friendship was similar interests. He's just like me, only far more advanced." He grinned. "So please don't presume to tick me off, if that's what you're here for."

She had the impression he was trying to get inside her head. She shooed him out. "Tell me: what grounds do you have for thinking there's anything whatsoever under those fields?"

"None at all."

She hooted. "So you made it all up?"

"Sorry, I didn't quite finish my sentence. None at all ... *that you'd acknowledge or understand.* This entire conversation is already a waste of time, given your obvious prejudices. I suspected it would be."

"I take it you're not prepared to retract what you wrote?"

"Absolutely not. Why would I retract the truth?"

She finished her tea. "Well, thank you for agreeing to see me. I suppose that about wraps it up."

"Not so fast, young lady. You may not have anything more to say, but I do. Three things."

She'd been on the verge of leaving, but she turned to hear him out. She might as well. It'd be something to tell Callum and Ray later. Maybe.

"Firstly," he said, "in the same way that you're predestined to attempt to recover the stones, I'm predestined to help you."

She smiled bitterly. "Are you serious?"

"I'm in deadly earnest, as you'll shortly - "

"I don't need your help, thank you. I've got seven young, energetic undergraduates at my beck and call."

"Oh, they won't stay. Don't get me wrong, they'll want to. But one by one, they'll drop out. Not their fault. You and your family are immune to it, because you've lived there for so long. But it got your mother in the end, and now it's got you. It'll get them if they're stupid enough not to take the hint."

Her whole body had tensed. "Got me?"

He sipped his tea and looked at the floor.

Obviously, he knew. How - ? "What's 'it'?" she asked feebly.

"I don't know what 'it' is. Have you read *The Colour Out of Space?* HP Lovecraft? Well, 'it' is something of that nature, I'm guessing. Something unknown, and maybe unknowable."

She took a deep breath, put her fingertips on her forehead, rubbed, and returned to the real world. "Right. Okay. Leaving all that aside, you claim you're going to help me do the dig, even though you've just warned me not to let anyone do it."

"You're different. You *will* do it. And I'm only warning you because you're so young. I was young once. In those days, I wouldn't have helped you for the world. But I'm old now, and, as I say, I'm predestined, which – which I didn't discover until recently. So yes, I'll help you. Whether you like it or not. Whether *I* like it or not."

"I suppose I should be grateful," she said sarcastically. "What was the second thing you were going to tell me?"

"Find out about Cytherea Holmes. You've got an appointment with her, sometime in the near future."

"I've never heard of her."

"Very few people have, nowadays. And the third thing? Something to loosen that horrible pretend-scepticism of yours. Wait until there's a starry night. A cloudless sky and a new moon, ideally. Stand at the edge of your father's fields, and look directly upwards. After that, walk across them from north to south, then from east to west. Make sure you go all the way, and make sure you pass over the central point at least once. That's how I found the location of the stones. But you have to do it alone. It probably won't work if you're with your undergraduate flunkies."

She opened the door to let herself out. "And that's supposed to achieve… what?"

He looked blank. "Far be it from me to spoil the surprise."

VI.

Crowborough to Beulah Cottage was a half-hour drive. *Your appointment with Cytherea Holmes, Ma'am*. Mind games. He'd been trying to spook her. That was almost certainly how psychics tended to work, a kind of first- bamboozle-'em-then-sell-'em-your-snake-oil strategy.

When she pulled up in front of the house, the sun shone and a gentle breeze stroked the grass on the fields. Her father sat in a deckchair outside the big dining room window, wearing an overcoat. She couldn't tell whether or not he'd been waiting for her. Hopefully, nothing was wrong but, after her interview with Gersholm, she wouldn't have been surprised. She didn't believe in 'visionaries', but she did believe in coincidence, and more specifically, in this instance, in bad luck. He came over to meet her.

"Is anything wrong?" she asked him, as she got out of the car.

"Everything's going really well," he said. "We've actually found some Roman coins."

"Tunbridge Wells was garrisoned by the Romans. You know that. It shouldn't be too much of a surprise."

"It's a result, that's all. And it's better than nothing. Are you okay? You look a bit… shaken."

"Difficult morning. Don't ask. Where's the crew?"

"Still out in the fields. They seem genuinely enthusiastic."

"Good, although maybe they're just being polite. I'll go and find them."

"What would you like for dinner? We've got two vegans, so I thought, cauliflower stew?"

"You're not cooking dinner. Leave that to me. Tonight, we'll make a rota – me and the students, I mean – from which you're excluded. Although you are expected to eat with us. If you want to. You're welcome to. You don't have to. Someone different will shop and cook for us each day, until we've found these stones. Or not."

"I know you don't believe in them."

"Well, we've got 'maps' – I use the term advisedly – purporting to show their location. It should be an easy matter to determine which of the two of us is right."

"How are you going to introduce them to your students? The locations, I mean?"

"Very gradually. And subtly. So they don't suspect they've been produced by a 'visionary'. That's more than my reputation's worth."

"Yes, understood. And it sounds like a good idea."

"I'd better go and find them. They'll be wondering where I've gone."

She went inside and changed into her working clothes. Ten minutes later, she found her group sitting on the easternmost boundary. Four young men, three women. Two of the women ate sandwiches. One of the men vaped. They looked intense but reasonably content.

"How's it going?" she called when she was within hailing distance.

They turned to face her; perhaps they hadn't noticed her before. She noticed a change come over them, as if, yes, they were enjoying themselves, but they also had *news*, and they knew she wasn't going to like it.

"Liam feels ill," Kathy said.

She hadn't registered Liam till now, at least not in terms of him having a problem, but he raised his hand, and yes, he did look ill: he looked very ill indeed.

VII.

It took a week from arrival at Beulah Cottage to total evacuation. One by one, the students left the 'dig' (such as it was) and, because they were too poorly even to stay on campus, and it was suggested their complaint might be infectious, they went home. Their exact medical condition was never identified, but that may be because, to begin with, most illnesses don't admit of a totally unambiguous diagnosis, and no one ever asks the harder questions until matters take a turn for the deadly serious. For the moment, they were unwell, that was all. If they rested, they would probably recover. From the university's point of view, as it turned out, the most important (and useful) thing was the outbreak's common provenance. All the victims had succumbed at Beulah Cottage, under the sole jurisdiction of Dr Portcher, and Dr Portcher hadn't filled in the appropriate health and safety forms.

As for Hermione herself, only when the last student had gone home did an explanation for the outbreak occur to her, and it had to do with Martin Gersholm's experiment.

The night after she'd been to see him was, fortuitously, dark and starry. She donned a pair of wellingtons and a quilted jacket and crossed the fields in two directions. She was expecting nothing. Who was she humouring? Well, it couldn't be him, so it must be herself. At some level, he must have 'got into her head'. To her considerable surprise however, she'd only taken twelve steps when the stars entirely disappeared. They only reappeared when she reached the far boundary. For a second, she thought it must be clouds – such as were invisible from the ground. But clouds didn't work like that, surely?

Far from considering it evidence of anything supernatural, however, much less that it had anything to do with buried stones (how *could* it?), she took it to indicate that there was some kind of low-level atmospheric disturbance, perhaps originating underground. In fact, on balance, it made her less credulous of Gersholm and his fellow mystics: she could see how seeing all the stars go out might persuade such persons to conclude that their occult convictions were vindicated. She, on the other hand, was more level-headed.

She stayed on at Beulah Cottage after her students had gone home. She'd taken three weeks' research leave, and she might as well keep working. She saw no reason why she shouldn't do at least a bit of digging: she didn't think their illnesses were anything serious – food poisoning, maybe? - and she might not get another chance.

It took her seven days to realise that the mysterious phenomenon of the vanishing sky might be the very reason her students were becoming ill. If there was some underground contamination – my God, could it be *radioactivity* of some sort?

But how could something like that have got there?

Maybe Gersholm was right about something else: maybe she and her father had developed a kind of immunity, due to long-standing exposure.

But radioactivity wasn't the sort of thing you could develop an immunity to. So, no, it couldn't be that.

But there must be other candidates, things she wasn't familiar with: a gas, maybe; invisible in the daytime, but somehow light-shielding at night; an odourless gas. She didn't know much about earth science - just soil and its various cumbrances – so she was floundering about in the dark. She needed an expert's diagnosis.

Before that, she should really arrange another interview with Martin Gersholm, find out if he'd become ill during the time *he'd* been there (which couldn't have been *that* long a stay, surely?) He must have; lots of people must have. Otherwise, how could he know?

She called Marilyn Hills Care Home the next day. The receptionist put her on hold.

She hoped she hadn't alienated him on her first visit: she hadn't been rude, but she had been a little offhand. She should have known she might need to make a follow-up call, and been more diplomatic.

Mind you, he'd said he was predestined to help her. He could hardly do that if he wouldn't even speak to her.

"Hello?" A woman's voice. Not the receptionist.

"This is Hermione Portcher. I came to see Mr - "

"Yes, Dr Portcher, I know who you are. I'm Claire Pollson, the administrator here. We half-assumed Mr Gersholm might be with you. He left us just after your visit. He didn't provide a forwarding address, and he wouldn't say where he was going. No warning, he just packed his bags and left. We've been trying to contact you. I mean, we don't actually need to speak to him – he's fully paid up, and he's under no obligation to contact us, legal or otherwise -

but we're worried about him. He's been here a long time. Longer than I have."

"I - I'm sorry he's gone. He's definitely not with me. I hardly know him."

"Look, it's none of my business, and you don't have to answer if you don't want to, but could his decision have had anything to do with your visit? Please don't take that the wrong way."

"I don't know. I came to see him about a – a *psychic reading* he did for my father many years ago. I don't really believe in that sort of thing. I told him so, but I wasn't rude. I certainly didn't offend him. At least, I don't think so. I was hardly there for any length of time."

"If you do hear from him, could you please let us know? Just to set our minds at rest, that's all. We've tried the police: *uncharacteristic behaviour,* we told them. But you know how the police are. They're not remotely interested."

After she'd hung up, she remembered. *Cytherea Holmes*. Bloody hell, he actually *had* got inside her head. She Googled her, hoping she'd got the spelling right.

The only thing she could find was an essay in a collection called *Not So Disgusted, the Cool Side of Tunbridge Wells,* published by British Beatness Press – a vanity publisher, by the looks of it - in 1958, and apparently penned by an eccentric old woman called Ada Scott. It was available on EBay for £49.99 plus postage (*genuine 1950's beatnik fare! Very rare!*), but it was also available, on request, in the reference section of the library in Tunbridge Wells.

She couldn't be bothered with a wild goose chase at the moment. To heck with Cytherea Holmes. Instead, she called Callum.

Forget about Martin Gersholm, he said. Not her problem. "The obvious person to ask about the illnesses would be Dad. We've had visitors in the past, when we were kids. I can't remember whether they became ill or not, but I rather think they can't have. Dad would know. And why would he keep something like that quiet? Unless…"

"What?" she said.

"Oh, my God. The property value: *of course!* It'd drop through the floor, the field and everything! With something like that in the mix, it'd be worth peanuts! Look, Herm, you've got to forget it ever happened. *Got to*. Certainly don't raise it with Dad. He might be feeling guilty as it is, all those students dropping like flies. If you interrogate him, you might tip him over the edge, then he might shout it from the rooftops in an attempt to mollify his conscience. If that happens, where's our inheritance?"

"His death's a long way off, I hope. But it'd come out in any survey, surely?"

"We'll have to take our chances with that. When the day comes. Just because we might get killed later, doesn't mean we've got to commit suicide now. Just forget it."

"But that's immoral, isn't it?"

"It's not your call, Hermione. You've got me and my family to consider, and Ray and his family, and Uncle Nedrick and his entire bloody tribe. You're outvoted. Please, *please* don't say anything, Herm. For our sake."

"I'll only *ask* him."

"*No*. That's what I'm saying: *don't*. Don't do anything. Just get the hell out of Beulah Cottage and go home, and put the whole lurgy thing down to experience. If one day the chartered surveyors don't notice it, that's their fault. If they do… well, we'll cross that bridge when we have to. *If* we have to."

Later that day, Ray called. His line of argument was that their father *wanted* them to have an inheritance, he didn't *want* his good intentions for them sabotaging; they should indulge him, for kindness' sake. After he died – *when* he died, which might still be a long way off - they could all discuss it over a bottle or two of vintage wine, and she might come to a different conclusion, but, please, please, *please,* just hold your tongue for now.

She knew what he meant: hold your tongue *forever.*

That evening, she walked across the fields and noticed the stars disappear again. She was no longer doing Martin Gersholm's experiment, though. She was wrestling with her conscience.

She decided that she *would* broach the matter with her father. It was the right thing to do. She couldn't do it immediately, of course: she needed to look for an opening, raise the whole matter gently and tactfully.

Knowing that 'the right time' had a habit of never appearing unless it was given a little help, however, she gave herself a deadline. Within the next two days.

She laughed after she'd decided. Here she was 'looking for the right time'! When was she going to tell them *she* was dying? When was 'the right time' for that?

And then, she realised. Her brain flooded with endorphins. Her mouth dropped open, allowing air to flow over her tongue and her tonsils. She smiled beatifically.

It was never.

Because she wasn't going to die. She was never going to die. Despite everything the specialists said, and for all their morbid unanimity, she wasn't going to die. Never, never, *never*. Of *course* she didn't have to tell anyone!

Also: she didn't know how she knew that, except that probably, her brain was dying.

Let it!

The next day, she received a letter from the vice-chancellor's office. A student attached to her faculty had initiated legal proceedings against the university, and she'd been named as the principal party at fault. An urgent meeting of the board of trustees, convened to discuss the matter, had raised 'significant concerns' concerning her pastoral competence, and it had reluctantly decided to launch an internal inquiry. She was instructed to attend a disciplinary hearing, in two days' time, to decide her future.

VIII.

Of course, as I mentioned at the beginning of all this, the hearing was a foregone conclusion. A kind of show trial, really. I don't think the vice-chancellor was an especially vindictive man, but he'd been told to make budget cuts, and he wasn't the sort of person who liked a fight. Professional incompetence made it easy to get rid of someone; much more so than, say, if your area of expertise wasn't fashionable among would-be undergraduates, or if your research papers weren't appearing often enough in the relevant citation index.

The charge against her boiled down, slightly ludicrously, to the fact that she hadn't filled in the relevant risk assessment forms. In effect, that would make any insurance claims by students void. Her defence was that she had word-of-mouth approval from the relevant authorising office, and that she'd been eager to get on with the job.

In a way, she really was guilty, I suppose: those forms aren't there for nothing. But, in most circumstances, it's a slap on the wrist offence really, not a sackable one. I'm pretty sure they all knew that.

Anyway, I was given thirty pieces of silver. I called off the lawyers, Dr Portcher resigned, and we were all supposed to pretend the whole thing had never happened. From the trustees' point of view, we all lived happily ever after.

She tendered her resignation in the meeting itself. The board grudgingly accepted it. The vice-chancellor thanked her 'for not allowing the name of the university to be dragged through the mud' (a bit hyperbolic), and offered her a few words of encouragement: don't worry, you'll get another job, you've got a bank of solid research behind you, we will give you a reference if requested, never overlook the details again, tut tut, stay safe, etc.

As she left the main building, and got in her car to drive home for the last time, she burst into tears of anger and self-pity. She hit the steering wheel with her fists.

Her phone rang. *Ray*.

Bloody *hell!* She considered opening the window and throwing it across the car park.

Only that wouldn't work, because she had electric windows, and she hadn't even put the keys in the ignition yet.

"I'll call you back," she croaked.

"Don't hang up, Herm. I'm calling about Dad. Brace yourself. Are you sitting down? Yes? He collapsed about an hour ago. Luckily, not before he got to his phone. He's been taken to Pembury Hospital. It's *bad,* Hermione. I think this may be it, the final curtain. Callum and I are on our way over there. Drop whatever it is you're doing and come and join us as fast as you can." He sounded teary.

Suddenly, she didn't care about being 'let go' anymore.

IX.

She arrived at the hospital to find Callum and Ray waiting in the reception area, alongside twenty or so recent A&E arrivals in various states of misery and distress. The doctor took the three siblings into an office. Their father had suffered a massive stroke, he said, and was now in a coma from which he was not expected to recover. Sometime within the next few days, they would probably be given the option of switching off the life-support machine. They needed to prepare themselves for that.

When, three days later, the same doctor returned for a decision (clearly expecting their acquiescence, Hermione gauged). They told him they needed thirty minutes. They went into the car park.

"I'll kick the discussion off," Ray said grimly. "It's best for Dad. He's dying anyway."

"I hate to say it," Callum said, "but it's a no brainer."

Hermione filled her turn to speak with two seconds' silence. "I can't let that happen," she said at last. "Sorry, guys."

They turned to her as if she'd swept their feet from under them.

"Er… what?" Callum said.

She shrugged. "He's not suffering, so what's it matter if they keep him alive for another few weeks?"

Ray shook his head. "I really don't get what you're saying! What would that *achieve?* You heard the doctor's prognosis. He's not going to come round! And even if he does - "

"You may not remember," she said. "But we promised to investigate those stones under his fields. If he dies, the land goes straight to Uncle Nedrick. Result: we can never fulfil our promise."

Silence. Callum opened his eyes wide and shuddered like he'd ingested something bitter.

"*Was* it a promise?" Ray said. "Come on, Herm, are you *serious?* The stones *aren't there.* If you're going to prove something's not there, you've got to go over every inch of it. That's going to take a hell of a lot longer than 'a few weeks'."

"The locations are marked with crosses," she replied.

Callum frowned. "That's drivel, and you know it. Okay, what when you don't find them under those crosses? What if they're two or three feet to the left or right? As far as I'm aware, we're talking about 'treasure maps' drawn up by mercenary cranks. Even if they contain a germ of truth – just for the sake of argument, though I can't see how that's remotely possible, except by an almighty, seriously mindboggling, freakish coincidence - they're never going to be cartographically trustworthy. *How* reliable might they be? Eighty per cent? Hugely unlikely. Five, more like, and that's assuming my very generous hypothesis. So Ray's right: you'll have to dig every inch of it."

"I don't care," she said.

"Let's take a break," Ray announced. She saw him flick a 'come over here' look at her brother. They made a show of separating and considering for a few minutes, then they went behind a parked ambulance.

When they emerged, they advanced slowly on her, hands in pockets, looking at the ground.

"Look, Herm," Callum said. "I didn't know about you losing your job. Ray's just told me. I can see why you might want to do this particular dig. But we can help you in that regard. The great thing is, we're all in the same line of work. We've got contacts. And apparently you left 'for personal reasons', or something like that. You've got a great research record. We can get you another job, no problem."

Her mouth popped open. She turned to Ray. "How did you find out I'd lost my job? Who told you?"

"Come on," he said, "university archaeology's a small world. News travels. I can't - "

"So let me get this right," she said, "everyone knows I didn't leave for personal reasons – you said: 'or something like that' - is that correct?"

"I heard you were 'let go'," Ray said, "because one of your students – a complete wuss, by the sounds of him – became ill at Beulah Cottage, and decided litigation was too good an opportunity to pass up."

"We owe you," Callum said. "If it had been either of us, and our students, we could easily have gone the same way… as, er, you."

Her head was suddenly too high in the air for comfort. She sat on the pavement amongst the cigarette butts and put her hands over her face. So, all the things the vice-chancellor said about keeping her reputation intact: they'd been lies. And, of course, he'd put nothing in writing. Somehow, the truth had leaked out, and there wasn't a blind thing she could do about it.

Up till the hearing, she'd had a plan. She was dying, yes, but at least she could go out as a good archaeologist. Not great, just good. But her father would read the two or three obituaries in the specialist websites, and he'd feel proud. Which was as much as she'd ever wanted.

But now she had no job, no father, and suddenly, like a guillotine dropping, no prospect of being remembered. She was irretrievably beaten.

"We can help you get another job," Callum said again, though he sounded much less confident this time.

She wiped her eyes, got to her feet and tried to speak levelly. "Okay, if we're going to switch of Dad's life-support, we need to make a unanimous decision. That's what the doctor said, if you remember. Now, I'm not prepared to argue about it anymore. You haven't got my say-so, and that's the end of the matter. I'm going to dig those fields, and since I haven't actually got a job to go to, and no longer any prospect of getting one, I don't really care if it takes me the rest of my life. Dad will die naturally in the end. In the meantime, I'm going to do what I promised him I would. If you want to help me, you're welcome. But I don't expect you to. And yes, I know you'll be angry, but that's just too bad, I'm afraid. Now, I think the doctor needs to see all three of us together, since, as next of kin, we all have to sign the relevant forms. So, shall we go inside?"

"You're not thinking straight," Callum told her.

"What about the hospital bed Dad's taking up?" Ray asked. "Don't you think there might be other people whose need is greater? People who might actually *stand a chance of recovering?"*

She was already moving away. "Don't know. Don't care."

Ray and Callum fell into step behind her, and they all went inside.

She assumed the role of spokesperson. The doctor looked impassive. She could feel her brothers quietly seething on each side of her. When they all came out of the hospital, it was separately. The two men went to their cars without saying goodbye.

Tonight, they'd both phone each other and vent their fury. They'd progress from that to hatching childish plots designed to make her change her mind. They'd progress from that to the resolve to 'let her stew'. After about forty-five minutes, they'd hang up, and while they'd still be angry, there would be a vague sense of catharsis achieved through the exchange of vicious remarks; and also, perhaps, guilt: a faint sense that she was, after all, their little sister, and perhaps they'd gone too far. Then tomorrow would be a work day, and the daily grind would give the whole thing the perspective it deserved. They'd put it, and her, out of their thoughts. If, after that, they considered her at all, it would be as someone who was *stewing*.

She lived in Hailsham, but she wouldn't be going back there for a while. She drove to Beulah Cottage, parked her car outside the front door and walked into Tunbridge Wells. Two miles, which took much longer than she expected. She spent the afternoon drinking alone in The

Black Horse on Camden Road, her father's favourite pub. At five o'clock, when it was finally dark, she caught a bus back to Beulah Cottage: 'home', as she'd call it from now on. She'd begin digging tomorrow, assuming she didn't have too big a hangover.

The bus zoomed and halted, zoomed and halted. She sat behind two TWGGS girls, and a boy in a suit: Skinners, probably. Outside, the complete darkness framed houses with Christmas lights, and there were long processions of nothing.

Now that she wasn't fighting with them, she could see her brothers had a point. What did she have to go on? A collection of cranky 'maps' marked with X's, that's all. The likelihood of them signifying anything was – how had Callum put it? – that's right: he hadn't! *Infinitesimal*, that was the word. She laughed out loud.

Everyone on the bus turned to look at her, or that's what it felt like. *This time of the year, always some crazy drunk!*

The stop for Beulah Cottage was actually half a mile after the house. She'd never been on the bus before, so she didn't know about stops. She got off and tramped home along the main road, not really caring if she got run over (but please, God, let death come quickly), then along the everlasting front drive.

When she arrived at the house, she had the distinct impression she wasn't alone.

All afternoon, she'd been on the verge of some sort of religious epiphany. It had come from lots of different directions, and its content was always the same: *despite what you've always thought, there really is a God.*

There are no atheists in foxholes, so they said, and what was losing your job, and your father, and having your brothers set their stupid faces against you, and realising your life was literally at an end, and you were partner-less, and child-less, and destined to remain so, and you were just some other bus-people's crazy drunk, and the vice-chancellor had shown his, and academia's, complete contempt for you by lying to your face … well, what was all that if it wasn't a foxhole?

And it was Christmas, or nearly. Baby Jesus in the crib. The man who willed oneness with God, and before whom God Himself was forced to capitulate, and who re-wrote all prior history, and forced an everlasting route into Heaven for the entire human race by killing every vestige of his self, dying in the most humiliating, most painful, most protracted way possible?

She laughed again. Where on earth had *that* thought come from?

She wept. She staggered into the fields. Clouds covered the sky, so she couldn't see the stars disappear. She wished she'd bought a bottle of vodka in that convenience store on the way to the bus stop. One litre, that's all.

She walked ten or twelve metres, then did what she'd seen her father do, a few weeks' earlier, and partly for that reason: she threw herself to the ground and kissed the soil.

She sat up covered in mud. Then she knelt over and repeated the action.

To her surprise, her body seemed to fill with light and life. She suddenly had the sense that nothing bad could ever happen to her… or anyone. She looked up at the sky and saw the stars.

She realised what she had a week or so earlier: she wasn't going to die. She was never going to die. Never, never, *never*.

Wait a minute. The sky was cloudy, or had been a second ago.

So how could she see the stars?

Because they weren't stars. They were flecks of gold.

She guffawed. Golden *glitter? Nein, nein, mein Herr,* actual *gold!* Oh, how the mystery thickens!

She looked at the ground. It was flecked with tiny sparks.

Like she was on magic mushrooms or something (yet she'd never been *near* a magic mushroom – or anything!)

She looked at her hands. They were flecked with gold. Her whole body as well.

This wasn't an illusion. She wasn't dreaming. She wasn't drunk (well, yes, she *was,* but not completely!) Did this soil – did these fields – contain *gold?*

She wept again. She didn't want gold.

She did. Everyone did, dying or not. Gold was gold. It was beautiful.

She did, she didn't, she did. *It isn't gold – that can't be what you're seeing! That's not how gold works!*

This was presumably how the whole 'mental collapse' thing played out. Every psychologist in the world could probably recite its conventional stages by heart, and she was probably hosting them.

She felt nauseous. She wanted to vomit.

She was very drunk and made of gold.

No, she was dying, that was it: her brain was closing down. The alcohol had somehow fast-tracked her decline.

She could die out here if she wanted to. It was freezing. Her muscles would seize up and she'd get hypothermia, and she'd just sit there till her torso flopped over.

She didn't care, because she was ecstatic!

Then she remembered her brothers. They'd hurt her feelings today, but did she really want them to find her dead, in a muddy field? Okay, yes, they deserved to be taught a lesson, maybe, but not *that* sort of lesson. She still loved them.

And her 'vow'. She had to dig these fields.

She got up, trudged back to Beulah Cottage, went upstairs, undressed, showered, and got into the bed in the little room her father had always reserved for her.

She fell into a deep, delirious sleep, and was aware of not getting up for several days. Which might have been part of her dream, only there were a lot of dreams, and they were interspersed with snapshots of the bedroom in various conditions of light or dark. A man with a tender voice came in every so often, bearing a mugful of cold water. He got her to sit up and sip. Ray, or he seemed to be. He told her she was 'burning up'.

When she finally sloughed the confusion off, it was dark. She heard men's voices downstairs.

X.

She dressed in some old clothes and sneaked downstairs, hoping to reach the front door before they realised she was there. However, long before she reached the hallway, she recognised the voices.

Her brothers.

She went into the kitchen. They were sitting at the table eating bacon and eggs. They looked at her with astonishment. They put their cutlery down. Ray stood up and came over to support her.

"You're finally awake," he said. "Are you okay?"

Callum pulled out a chair for her. She told them she felt much, much better, thank you. She sat down. She asked what were they doing here.

"We had second thoughts," Ray said. "Just because we don't agree with you, doesn't mean we've got to stomp off in an almighty sulk. Callum and I both owe you, big time. We've already told you that. Your neck ended up on the chopping block. It could have been ours. And we've got a plan."

"We'll talk about that in a moment," Ray said. "Would you like something to eat?"

"I – I'll have an egg," she said. "Scrambled, on a piece of toast, please."

"Okay," Callum said.

No one moved. The two men moved in towards her with solicitous expressions. Obviously, they had something to tell her.

Their father had died. It had to be. She put her hand to her mouth. "Is Dad…"

"Still on a life support machine?" Callum said. "Yes. Just as we left him, a week ago. Nothing's changed in that regard."

"Herm, I want you to be completely honest with us here," Ray said. "I mean… can I ask… are you actually… *unwell?* I don't mean, lying-in-bed-shivering unwell, like you just were; I mean, you know… *might-never-get-better* unwell."

She took in a big dose of air. "I, er…"

"You've been talking in your sleep," Callum said.

"It might just have been a recurring nightmare," Ray added.

Silence.

She wiped her eyes, one at a time. "I've got a few months left to live. I don't want to go through the details. It's some sort of cancer… of which there are *a zillion* varieties, apparently. No, I won't have chemo, especially not now, but I wasn't ever going to, even before. I'm sorry I didn't tell you, truly, but I'm probably in denial, and I thought – irony of ironies – it might finish Dad off, and - and I'm sorry, all right? You probably had a right to know. I didn't want you to just find me just lying dead in a field, and I shouldn't have – maybe – I'm sure I *would* have told you later," she went on, "just closer to the – you know." She laughed. "Here I am, dying, and I can't actually *talk* about death! Talk about cultural mutism! *Closer to the day of my death*. Yay!" She took a deep breath, then exhaled. "There *is* an afterlife. Death's not the end. We will see each other again."

They pulled their chairs either side of her and hugged her from the left and the right.

She cried some more, then spluttered a chuckle. "Where's my scrambled egg?"

Her brothers rubbed away their tears and grinned. "Coming right up, Madam," Callum said.

"What's your plan?" she asked. "You said earlier you had a plan. What is it?"

As she expected, they looked keen to change the subject. She felt the same.

"Are you okay to go outside?" Callum said. "Of course you are: we won't start treating you like an invalid, unless you want us to."

Ray hooted. "*Invalid:* how politically incorrect is that?"

"You didn't hear it here first," Callum said, apparently chastened. "What I meant to say is, someone incapacitated, who feels in need of a helper. And no, Ray, I don't want to discuss that. One-nil to you, okay?"

"A typical university let's-come-to-blows-over-terminology show," Hermione said. "How entertaining."

"Come with me, Herm," Ray said. "Cal, switch the front light on, and remove the tarpaulin. I'll show her it from the bedroom. Save going outside. It's snowing again."

"Done," Callum said.

Ray took her hand, and they walked upstairs with her slightly in front, since the stairway wasn't broad enough for both of them. They went into the front bedroom. He drew the curtains, so she could look down on the driveway.

Just outside the front door, a pickup truck stood parked in the snow. Callum was down there. He uncovered the tarpaulin overlaying its rear to reveal ten huge granite stones, roughly hewn, each one slightly dissimilar to the others, but all in the approximate shape of baguettes.

"Your menhirs," he said. "Don't say anything – I know what you're going to tell me: that's cheating, and it's not what Dad wanted – but just hear me out. Okay, yes, we'll do a bit of digging. Me and Callum, not you. We'll have to, because we're going to pretend we dug these up.

We'll dig where the X's are. After all, we've got to dig somewhere, and that covers that particular base, if you see what I mean; kills two birds with one stone, so to speak. We 'dig up' those ten items down there, in the truck, then we position them as standing stones. We don't claim to have excavated anything prehistoric. We just set it all up: we're archaeologists, we're digging, we've found these mysterious-looking stones, they were all in a circle, we're setting them up with particular care and attention; we let people draw their own conclusions. Yes, it *could* be that we've chanced upon the find of the century, but it could *also* be that we're just doing it for fun, who knows?"

"I don't get it," she said. "I mean, I'm impressed. And grateful that you've gone to such lengths. It's an interesting plan. But what's the point? If there's nothing down there?" She suddenly realised the answer to her own question. She grinned. "Sorry, obviously a bit slow tonight!"

"Dad didn't want the field being sold to developers," Ray said. "This should put a stop to that. If, say, the locals get to like it."

She considered for a moment. "The locals? How on earth are we going to manage that?"

"Come on, Herm. Tunbridge Wells's own Neolithic stone circle? Or *perhaps* that's what it is, they can't rule it out? This is the town that, otherwise, only really goes back to 1606, with its not-so-fascinating origin-story of a nobleman whom nobody nowadays much remembers, finding a spring with an unusually high iron content? The tourist office will fall over itself to stop these fields being sold for houses, so long as there's the least bit of belief concerning the stones in anyone's mind. And who knows, we might be able to fake a *certain* degree of authenticity. I know we told Dad we couldn't, but that was a knee-jerk reaction, and it was meant to give him a reality check. But where there's a will, there's a way."

"What if someone sees through it? Won't you both lose your jobs?"

"Absolutely not. That's the beauty of it. If everything goes pear-shaped, we've filed a document in a security box in my bank, signed and dated, claiming it's a legitimate research-project, designed to investigate the extent to which it's possible to counterfeit something like this. And, of course, the whole thing's very postmodern. The Theorists – that's *Theory,* with a capital 'T' - will love us."

She smiled. "I think 'Theory', as it's called, went out of fashion in about 1993."

"Only because it won every battle it ever fought. It's invisible now mainly because it was so victorious then. I'm telling you, Herm, them Postmodernists, them Postmodernists is *gonna jus' lurve us!"*

"What about your wives? I mean, are Sally and Felicity on board with this? Do they even know about it?"

"Fully informed and one hundred percent supportive."

She nodded. Okay, yes, it could work. Who cared whether there was anything down there? There probably wasn't.

"Your scrambled egg's ready!" Callum called from downstairs.

"I love you both!" she replied.

XI.

Over the next week, she sensed they were having second thoughts. Each day, they went out into the fields, and when they came back, they were always taciturn and gloomy. Callum cooked, Ray washed up, and afterwards they watched one of their father's DVD's: *Dirty Harry, Saturday Night Fever* or *Chariots of Fire.* The only time they talked was when they thought she wasn't around, or listening, and then in low, complaining voices.

They were getting cold feet. Maybe the digging was hard, because the ground was frozen (but in fact, it wasn't); or maybe they missed their families (but they should have thought of that to begin with); or maybe they weren't essentially archaeologists, but archaeology lecturers (a subtle distinction, but common enough in reality). In any case, she'd have to confront them. They were here because they felt they 'owed' her. Their intentions had been noble, but they'd repaid their debt.

A week after Ray had taken her to the front window and shown her the fake standing stones (like Moses being shown the Promised Land, she reflected, and with much the same let-down at the end), she came downstairs to eat the leek and potato soup Callum had made, and found the two men exchanging grim remarks which dried up the moment she walked through the kitchen door. They turned to look at her, then looked at the table surface, as if that was the end of any meaningful discussion.

She sat down. Callum distributed the meals. They ate in silence.

"So what's the matter?" she said, when they'd finished.

They looked at each other, then at her, then at each other.

She smiled, she hoped warmly, forgivingly. "Look, it's obvious this isn't as good an idea as it must have seemed at the beginning. It's wintry out there, the ground's either a bog, or it's frozen, or too packed with clay, and you're missing your wives and your jobs. You've done your best, and I know you wanted to make this a success, and I'm touched, really, but you've got lives to lead and - "

Callum reached over and put his hand on hers. "It's not that, Herm."

The two men looked at each other again. *Shall I tell her, or will you?* Then at her.

"There *are* stones down there," Ray said. "They're exactly where Martin Gersholm said they'd be. And they're old. *Really* old. I mean, at least as old as Göbekli Tepe in Turkey, which is Neolithic. And they're… weird."

"'Weird' in what way?" Hermione asked.

"Come on, Ray," Callum said. "We've only uncovered three. Let's not get ahead of ourselves."

"Minerals," Ray went on, apparently ignoring him, "rather than rocks. I'm not a geologist, but we bought a book the other day. I mean, just for this. So far, we've got chrysoberyl, corundum, and something else which doesn't appear to even be *in* the book. I mean, how is that - "

"It's *got* to be fake," Callum said. *"Got to be*. It's too bloody crystal-y New-Agey. Someone's having a laugh, and at our expense. We've got to find Martin Gersholm. I'll bet my bottom dollar he knows *exactly* what's going on."

"And someone's watching us," Ray said. "All the time. We've both got this strong, crazy sense of being watched." He turned to face her. "Is it you?"

"It's not me," she said.

Callum scoffed. "Of course it's not. Some actual person couldn't produce that feeling - as you well know, Ray, since we've been over it several times. It can't be Hermione. Or anyone real. It's in our *minds,* that's all. Something strange is happening – by which, I simply mean that we're digging up strange things, and it's made us self-conscious. That always happens when you make a significant archaeological discovery, especially if you're in charge of the excavation. You always start thinking, 'What if someone got here before me?' or 'What if someone else steals the credit?' It's just everyday psychology, that's all; nothing with any foundation in the real world. No one's watching us."

Ray pursed his lips. He nodded and shrugged. "Agreed, I suppose."

"Can I have a look at what you've unearthed?" Hermione asked.

"Be our guest," Callum replied. "We knew you'd want to. They're still half-buried and they're going to take a lot of getting out of the ground. They're a lot bigger than the ones we brought over for the mock-up."

They put on their wellingtons and overcoats and trudged across the fields with torches. It snowed. There wasn't much to see in each case: just a wide hole about nine feet deep, with about five feet of excavated stone sticking up in the middle.

"It's early days," Callum said, "but they look like equidistant points on a circle. Which means there should be fourteen in all. And the minerals – well, they look like they've been chosen for hardness. I don't suppose you're familiar with the Mohs scale?"

"Enlighten me," Hermione replied.

"It's a measure of scratch resistance," he went on. "One to ten. Talc's one, diamond's ten. Diamond will scratch corundum, which is a nine, but not vice-versa, and so on." He gestured at the stone sticking up beneath them. "That's corundum. The other one we've been able to identify, chrysoberyl, that's eight and a half."

"These things were made to last," Ray said. "Whoever made them."

Hermione laughed. "They can't be *ancient,* Ray. Where would they have got the technology to fashion something like this, out of materials that are almost as hard as diamond?"

"My feeling exactly," Callum said. "They've got to be modern. They're someone's idea of a practical joke. The obvious prankster being Dad. He did say he 'manoeuvred' us all into becoming archaeologists."

"Just so he could play this *one* prank," Ray said sardonically. "We moved here when I was three and you were four. Do *you* remember a fleet of mechanical excavators, outside, burying fourteen megaliths? Because I don't. Quite apart from the probably bankrupting expense of producing something like this. Uncle Nedrick might have been 'King Croesus', as Dad put it, but *we* certainly weren't, even before the actual bankruptcy."

"Maybe this was what caused it," Callum said.

Ray turned on him. "Are you insane? Think about what you're saying, how plausible it sounds!"

"Very *im*plausible, you're right," Callum admitted, after a moment. "If there is a prankster, it can't be Dad. The obvious next choice is Martin Gersholm."

"Who isn't plausible either," Ray went on, "for the precise reason that *no one we could conceivably know* is." He turned to Hermione. "Yes, and that being established, the only other alternative is that they're ancient. Very ancient indeed. Listen, this is my reasoning: only in the twentieth century did humankind develop the technology required to craft fourteen objects like this, and bury them to a depth of several metres without anyone in the locality knowing about it – that is to say, quickly. But we've rejected that possibility. The contemporary world has the means, but no real motive and no opportunity. So where to next? Well, they didn't have the capability in any other historical time period that we know about. Ergo, they must have been put here during some *pre*-historic period, one that we know nothing whatsoever about. Or – get ready for HP Lovecraft, now – the stones landed here from outer space; just, coincidentally, in a circle. Which is, of course, stupid. Don't you see? Ockham's Razor rules out anything other than the prehistoric hypothesis."

They'd started walking back to the house. Hermione pulled her coat more tightly around her. "But if there was a prehistoric society with the technology to create these, they'd have done other things too, surely? Build skyscrapers and space rockets, for example."

"Maybe they did," Ray said. "As I've just said, we don't know anything about them."

"We'll get a much better picture when we've excavated the whole thing," Callum said. "Until then, we're just whistling in the wind."

"This is the find of the century!" Hermione said. "You *do* realise that, don't you? I assume you're going to notify The British Archaeological Association?"

Ray harrumphed. "You'd think so, wouldn't you?"

"Absolutely not," Callum said. "Not until we're sure it's not some sort of fraud. It could be the next Piltdown Man, for all we know, and I'd rather not go down in history as another Charles Dawson. Look, you've just heard Ray's argument, Herm. Here's mine, and it's based on two indisputable facts. One: if it really is prehistoric, no one in the modern world would be aware of it. However, we know that some people in the modern world *were and are* aware of it: namely, all those 'visionaries' who came to see Dad. Martin Gersholm for example. Two: as Ray's just so eloquently argued, only the modern world has the industrial means to pull something like this off. Now, put those two facts together and your only possible conclusion is that the whole thing must have been fabricated relatively recently. Unless you believe in the paranormal, of course. Which *you* may or may not, but I'm pretty sure The British Archaeological Association doesn't. They'll want to know how you knew, and when we tell them the truth – it was all down to a series of maps drawn up by the likes of Madame Sosostris, famous *clairvoyante* – we'll be laughed out of town. We agreed that much at the very start."

"That's what we were arguing about," Ray said, "when you came into the kitchen. What do you think?"

She laughed. "You want me to take sides?"

"We promise not to take it personally," Callum said.

They walked in silence. A few minutes ago, she'd been all for shouting the discovery from the rooftops. But Callum was right. Looked at objectively, it didn't add up.

"Definitely hold fire," she said at last. "The whole site's not going anywhere, and we need to look at it from the point of view of someone impartial. What might someone on the BAA board make of it? Well, from that person's perspective, it'll seem very suspicious that here we've got three archaeologists, one of whom has just effectively been fired, two of whom are her brothers, all of whom are now holed up together on a relatively impromptu dig, without helpers, and that their brilliant, mind-bending discovery just happens to be in the grounds of the very house in which they all grew up. The BAA will take all of that into account, and they'll run a mile. And that's before they've even noticed the supernatural elements. It won't even occur to them to give us the benefit of the doubt."

When they went indoors, ten minutes later, she ran up to her room in a state of high excitement. She switched off the lights and opened the curtains and, as her eyes gradually adjusted, she saw the fields lying in front of her. At some point, their parents had bought them. They'd bought exactly these fields within which the fourteen-stone circle lay.

How did they know?

They *must* have known! Who buys fields and just lets them lie fallow? Doesn't do *anything at all* with them?

It was a mystery she had to solve.

XII.

She had a strong feeling the solution lay somewhere within the house. Although she'd lived here as a child, she'd never really been allowed to explore all of it, and, at the time, that had never seemed a problem. Her parents' bedroom had been off limits, of course, but also the loft, and she had a strong sense that her answers lay somewhere up there, in one or the other… or both.

The bedroom yielded nothing, as she'd half-expected. The loft could only be reached by a stepladder, which had to be brought in from the garage, and its door, which lay flush with the landing ceiling, was lockable and always kept locked. When she'd been younger, she'd been told the loft was where the family kept their valuables; living out here, in the middle of nowhere, they were especially vulnerable to burglars (so the story went), and while the loft might *look* easy to get into, actually, it was more or less impregnable! Which she'd taken to mean: the key was well hidden and so was the stepladder.

The stepladder hung on three brackets in the garage. It took her an entire day to find the key. She looked in drawers, under beds, in cupboards, in ceramic pots and cardboard boxes, on tiered shelves, behind everything on the bookcase, in wardrobes, under cushions, deep behind the backs of sofas. Her brothers were outside in the fields all this time, otherwise they'd undoubtedly have stopped her with a maudlin, *You need to rest*.

She finally found what she was looking for in a blue glass jar with 'Misc. Stationery' written on, in black marker pen. She poured the paperclips and mini-bulldog clips onto the kitchen table and discovered, to her surprise, not a single key, but a key ring. Nevertheless, she knew immediately: this was it.

She took the stepladder from the garage, and the torch from the kitchen. She went upstairs to the loft hatch, and nervously climbed to the point where she could unlock it. To her surprise, it opened outwards, and she nearly lost her balance.

She realised she was looking at another door, this one slightly smaller. She unlocked it. It opened inwards, and she found herself staring into deep darkness. She switched on the torch, and swept the beam back and forwards. There was nothing to see, but then she could only be pointing it at a ceiling. What did she expect?

She hauled herself into the opening, wondering if the ceiling would bear her weight. Of course it would. She sat on the ledge, looking down at the ladder, and suddenly she felt dizzy and a little scared.

She should do a quick scout around and get out. Now she knew how to get inside, she could come back any time she liked.

To her relief, she found a light switch. Flicking it, she found herself confronted by a small, bare room with four wooden walls and a door at the far end. She retrieved the key ring and unlocked this second door. More darkness within, but she felt entitled to expect a light switch now, and, yes, there it was.

This second room was very different to the one she'd just left. It took her a moment to realise it was heptagonal in design: seven walls covered with geometrical figures and sentences in Latin. A round table stood in the middle, like an altar, with a brass plate on it. Against each wall stood a chest: presumably, the family 'valuables', although that no longer seemed remotely plausible. Both ceiling and floor were divided into seven triangles whose points met at the centre.

For a few moments, she was so astonished, she forgot entirely what she'd come up here to find.

That's right: evidence that her father had known what was under the fields outside.

Which seemed almost irrelevant now. What *was* this place? It looked like some kind of ritual enclosure!

Had her father been a freemason all this time?

She didn't think so. But what else - ?

Her brothers might be on their way back. She didn't know why, but she didn't want them to find her up here. It wasn't to do with them tut-tutting. No, they might think she'd known about it all along. Their first question would be, Why didn't you tell us? It might look as if she had a lot of explaining to do, which she didn't, not at all.

Seven large chests against seven long walls. She had to focus. Written material, that's what she was looking for. Anything relating to the house, or in her father's handwriting; either would be a good starting point.

She opened each chest in turn. Well, whatever else the contents might be, they weren't valuables, although they did look antique. Bells, lamps, candlesticks, urns, framed pictures, Orthodox Christian icons, and lots of old-looking books, nearly all in Latin or Greek.

Eventually, she found what she was looking for. A leather-bound volume, about the size and thickness of an average hardback, in English, and apparently in her father's hand. She stood up, closed the chest, and left both rooms, switching off the lights on her way out, and listening for any indication that her brothers were downstairs. She'd need a ready explanation. She couldn't think of one.

She descended the ladder, re-locked the door and the hatch, and quickly returned everything to where it had been an hour ago. Once the stepladder was back in the garage, she took the leather-bound book she'd just found to her favourite armchair in the living room. A thin covering of mist outside made the light dimmer than it should have been, and added a sense of something lurking just beyond the limits of visibility. The room's stillness augmented it.

All at once, she felt a twang of compunction. Her father had taken pains to hide this book. Should she really be reading it?

Well, it was too late to turn back now, and what could she possibly gain from leaving it unopened? A virtuous feeling, that's all, but not much of one. The truth was, her father probably wasn't coming back, and he'd left her with a host of questions to which she deserved answers. Far from prevaricating, she should be getting going. She drew her feet onto the chair, laid the book in her lap and began to read.

It was a journal, rather like her own notebook in some ways, but written over a longer period, and several decades ago. After an hour, she realised it fell into two parts. The first concerned her father's travels with his brother, Nedrick, in the 1960s, in search of 'esoteric knowledge' - presumably the hippie sort. They'd journeyed first to Jerusalem, then to a place called Damcar, in Yemen, then to

Alexandria in Egypt, then to Morocco, before they crossed into Spain, where the travelogue section ended.

The second part described their 'findings'. Some of it was in her father's hand, others in what was presumably Nedrick's. She anticipated a mixture of cod philosophy and psychedelic ramblings, and she wasn't entirely disappointed.

Their principal concern was the distinction between science and magic. Magic, they thought, differed from religion in being an alleged science: if x, then y, in a way that the connection between the two was objectively invariable, and independent of any subjective concern.

They then hypothesised that there might be a universe in which science and religion were reversed; in which what was science in this world was magic in that, and vice-versa. How could they find out? The vast size of space meant that interstellar travel was impossible by conventional means. Which must mean that there was some *un*conventional means by which it *was* possible.

She didn't follow the logic of this at all – it looked like the worst kind of wishful thinking - but it seemed connected to their conviction that there was a God, and that 'it' – God - had laid the entire universe at our disposal. Its characteristic mode of communicating with us was via riddles, none of which were insoluble. Most of the old riddles had been solved by the discovery and application of scientific method. The chief outstanding riddle – the riddle to which the twentieth and twenty-first centuries would be devoted - involved finding out how to travel inconceivably long distances in infinitesimally short intervals of time. Like every riddle, it was resolvable, but it would involve us radically revising our ideas about how knowledge was attained. Between empiricism and rationalism, then, there must be some third way. Or maybe it wasn't a midway point; maybe it was far above them.

All this ruminating about knowledge and how to obtain it gradually gave way, in the journal, to an increasing insistence that there really was somewhere, on the other side of the galaxy, where things were vastly better than they were here. The journal seemed to suggest that this was the brothers' main, if not exclusive, concern. It culminated with a confident assertion that they had found a way to open a channel between here and there.

… Which had something to do with Beulah Cottage, apparently. During the last half of their peregrinations, they'd spent a long time looking for something specific, the precise nature of which they considered too obvious, but also too incredible, to commit to writing. Whatever it was, they found it in a collection of adjacent fields, about a mile outside Tunbridge Wells, with a house attached, and they bought the entire estate at the asking price.

Where they obtained the money was a mystery: the journal was all but silent about that. Yet it did mention a 'business' they'd started… without supplying the smallest clue as to its identity.

Hermione immediately suspected it had something to do with drugs. Where did sudden wealth usually come from? Either outrageous good fortune or something nefarious. And Nedrick had gone to prison in Australia for drug-related offences. (Hadn't he? She was beginning to doubt everything now!) Drugs could explain why he'd emigrated, while his brother had stayed here: perhaps

Nedrick had found the sudden wealth harder to give up, or perhaps he'd been addicted to some substance, or perhaps his earnings were their insurance and only a radical separation could isolate it as such, or perhaps he and Gregory had argued… or maybe a combination of all of the above. In any case, her father's claim that Nedrick had come into possession of the field in exchange for a debt-rescue package looked significantly less credible now. Clearly, both brothers had a long-standing interest in everything here. They'd wandered round the Mediterranean for nearly ten years looking for it, so they'd have been loath to part with it on any basis whatsoever. That meant any 'loan' would have been a matter of existential necessity, not of fraternal generosity.

But she didn't even know whether there *had* ever been a loan. Maybe it was just some story her father had cooked up, because the truth was too conventionally wacky. She didn't know *what* the truth was anymore.

She did, however, know what she had to do next. That evening, she found out where Uncle Nedrick lived, and how to contact him. It wasn't difficult: her father hadn't bothered to hide the necessary papers. She sent him an email, with two photos of her bothers' excavations. She wanted to keep it cryptic, reel him in with a teaser or two, so it simply read, 'Come quickly!'

To her considerable surprise, he turned up at Beulah Cottage the following day. Even more astonishing, he'd brought along forty-five members of his family, four generations in all. They'd come to England the minute they heard about Gregory's stroke, so they'd been here some time. They didn't say *how* they'd heard: to her shame, she hadn't told them, and her brothers hadn't.

According to Nedrick, they'd intended to relocate here for years. They'd been waiting for 'this day'. They'd brought tents.

XIII.

This is where it all gets less clear; I mean, in terms of reporting the procession of events. The notebook gets increasingly sketchy, but what's obvious is that the next few months were revelatory. I will confine myself, to begin with, to the bare facts as she recorded them, plus what I've been able to deduce.

First of all, it appears her illness went into 'spontaneous remission' (read Dr Jeff Rediger of Harvard Medical School, if you don't believe me: the important point is - in case you doubt my reliability - it exists). In the normal course of events, she should have died, or at least gone into a morbid decline, but she didn't. Quite the reverse. Even stranger, *no one* got ill, which, given what had happened to the students, was the opposite of what might have been expected. Meanwhile, the stones – all fourteen of them - appeared at exactly the points they were supposed to. A perfect circle.

A change seems to have come over all three siblings. Yes, they were being watched, but the watcher was more than benign.

As for Ray and Callum, well, one might imagine that two men on an avowedly eccentric dig, one that shaded extemporaneously from days into weeks, and weeks into months, would try their spouses' patience; that there would be hard questions to be answered, accusations to be met, entreaties offered, ultimatums, tears, blistering rows, pot-shots at emotional blackmail, bouts of abject begging, etc. But the opposite seems to have been the case. The wives happily took their children out of school and moved lock stock and barrel *into tents* on the fields outside Beulah Cottage to be with their husbands.

I'll repeat that word. *Happily*. The two Portcher Mses were far more forgiving than their husbands' employers. Both men lost their jobs after hearings held *in absentia* (although let the records show they'd been invited to come along and defend themselves). By this time, their hair had grown long, and they had unkempt beards, and a strange way of not seeming to care very much at all about the future,

The fields owned by Gregory Portcher were effectively a large campsite now, but with permanent residents. Obviously, this raised concerns for the local council. And of course, the neighbours were less than enthusiastic. Especially when groups of itinerant musicians started arriving at the beginning of March. The whole thing started to look like a permanent Glastonbury Fayre, as anarchic as it was colourful. It also resembled an unexploded bomb.

Gregory passed away in hospital at the end of April. Technically, he died alone, since none of his family was physically present. Hermione's notebook records that, when she received the news, she cried for ten minutes. Then she laughed. By this time her hair had grown longer than her brothers'. It was streaked with grey and visibly matted.

By mid-May, all fourteen stones had been raised to ground level. There were about a hundred and fifty people living in the fields now, of whom the Portchers and their relatives constituted roughly fifty percent. The others were a ragtag assortment of New Agers previously connected to an end timer called Roddy Samhain, who had disappeared (for the second time) in 2022, and whose followers expected his imminent return in The Apocalypse (capital 'T', capital 'A'). There seems to have been no friction whatsoever between the two halves of the community, to the point where it seems somewhat artificial to even speak of it as two halves.

The next thing that happened was that Martin Gersholm apparently joined them. I say 'apparently'. Virtually nothing is said of him, other than that he appeared at the end of June, and was received with 'a meal of barley wine and good bread'. I suppose we could probably read that literally, although disappointingly, at this point, there is a lot in the notebooks that is either overtly symbolic or straightforwardly delusional. Descriptions of orchestras in the sky, for example, or manna on the morning grass, and one extended account of how someone brought Cytherea Holmes to the community, and how everyone went down on one knee, and how she was wearing a brown lamé dress and pointy mustard-coloured shoes, and how she was also Queen Elizabeth I, and so on and on, including how she actually ruled the community for a while, sitting on a throne made out of hazel leaves and gemstones. In the afternoons, apparently, everyone in the camp practised magic. One keeps expecting to read that Oberon and Titania appeared and danced a jig.

One thing is confirmed by the historical evidence: the fields, previously so bare and featureless, suddenly became fecund. Shrubs appeared everywhere, and seemed to grow unnaturally quickly. Well, it was summer, after all, and it may be that some things had been brought in, fully grown, from outside. But even so, this had always seemed like sterile land before. According to the notebooks, someone had finally asked The Fisher King the right question, only the Fisher King's kingdom didn't extend beyond this little parcel of fields.

What are we to make of all this? In my opinion, most of it is best understood as the too-vivid dream-life of a traumatised woman (rather than as - is also possible - evidence of incurable psychosis, or deep-rooted recreational drug use). Hermione Portcher had lost her job, then her father. Her sense of self (including her daughterhood) was heavily invested in her identity as an archaeologist. She had lost everything very suddenly.

The Cytherea Holmes dream, incidentally, is one of several extended fantasy-narratives. I will not bore the reader with the others. Suffice it to say, a diary of dreams, however curious, stops being useful as a historical record. With regret, at this point, I am afraid to say, we must put Hermione Portcher's notebooks permanently to one side.

Luckily, we have reliable documents concerning matters outside the community. We know for a fact that the council – motivated partly by the neighbours' complaints and the media's indignation - was concerned that the fields had become an illegal campsite and a permanent folk festival, auguring all the problems associated with shanty settlements, viz. petty crime, litter, anti-social behaviour, lack of sanitation, etc. In addition to which, there were the fourteen standing stones, for which planning permission had neither been sought nor granted. The tents needed to be cleared, the occupants relocated, and the 'stone circle' dismantled.

Not everyone in Tunbridge Wells was anti-, of course: one never finds complete unanimity in these sorts of cases. But most people probably were. Which is, of course, entirely understandable in my view.

A lot of preliminary legal work had to be done if the 'squatters' (an imprecise label, since they had the proprietor's blessing) were to be removed. Any eviction would have to be undertaken on the grounds of unauthorised use. An ongoing event of whatever kind plus a campsite, was legally required to comply with the Licencing Act of 2003. However, the Portchers had obtained neither a personal nor a premises licence, so, under any reasonable interpretation of what was going on there, they were in breach of civil law. And that was without taking into consideration the seven relevant bylaws that could be brought to bear against them. Bailiffs would therefore be required, and a court order, and the police would have to be present, in case the eviction became violent. Oh yes, and possibly an ambulance. All in all, it looked set to become an expensive operation.

The court order was served on May 21st. The next day, two representatives from the borough council's department for planning and building control – Steven Willesdown and Alison Grolle, both in their thirties, and dressed smart-casually - visited Beulah Cottage, hoping to thrash out a compromise. They spoke non-confrontationally to Ray, Callum and Nedrick about how the campsite was impacting the local community. They gave them forms to fill in, so that whatever it was they were trying to do might be re-arranged, someday not too far in the future maybe, on a secure legal basis - not to say a healthy commercial one!

The three interviewees made conciliatory noises, and for a few days, the council was optimistic about having resolved the crisis, but another week passed, and it was obvious their hopes had been misplaced. Willesdown and Grolle made a follow-up visit at the beginning of June. They were received every bit as amicably as the first time; but again, nothing altered.

Forced eviction now looked like the only alternative. June 21st was the preferred date: a month after the court order. It would be undertaken as a sudden incursion at 11pm, giving the authorities the element of surprise, and thus minimising the potential for violent resistance: it was, after all, customary for occupants to throw things, chain themselves together, kick, punch, shove, hurl excrement, let fly with makeshift projectiles and weaponry. A well-timed ambush could put paid to all that before it began.

The obvious problem with a night-time raid was the lack of visibility. Things tended to get confused in the dark; you didn't necessarily know who your enemies were. To solve it, the bailiffs would wear hi-vis jackets, and a long row of arc lights would be switched on the moment they breached the perimeter.

At 7pm, on the scheduled evening, six officials did a preliminary survey of the perimeter of the fields from the outside. They expected to encounter lookouts, but they completed their recce without meeting anyone, and they were all pretty certain they hadn't been clocked. It augured well.

They held a meeting in central Tunbridge Wells at 9pm. The chairman – an experienced bailiff: a fifty-year-old ex-squaddie with a Cornish accent - told them that the first objective was to surround the house and prevent it being used as a fallback by the occupants. This was the job of 'The Advance Team', a selection of fifteen of the most experienced personnel. The remaining bailiffs – 'Secondary Teams A, B and C' - would then enter the site from three different directions. The objective was to occupy the fields, remove the tents, and get as many people off the property as possible, all whilst avoiding violence. The police would be on hand as an extra level of protection, because everyone knew how emotional these things could become: there were always one or two desperadoes happy to end up in court charged with assault. The chair concluded by instructing his team to *talk* to the occupants if at all possible, to *try engaging them in reasoned dialogue*.

At 10.30, the police began discreetly closing off the roads surrounding the Portcher's property. The bailiffs silently got into position on the perimeter, carrying their hi-vis jackets in dark bags for the moment. At 10.55, they donned them, and waited for the signal to move in. Three decisive blows of an old-fashioned whistle.

They came at 11.01, just after the news that the house had been secured. As far as the leader of The Advance Team had been able to ascertain, there was no one inside Beulah Cottage at all. Secondary Teams A, B and C were clear to proceed.

They advanced in several ranks, and methodically crossed the perimeter. The technicians with the arc lights followed them.

And… no one knows what happened next. At first, the bailiffs thought they'd been outsmarted: they'd brought along a set of lights which they partly hoped (though this was never made explicit) would temporarily blind the occupants, giving them a few precious seconds' advantage.

In some sort of grotesque reversal of fortune, they were now looking into a blinding light. They couldn't remotely distinguish even the forms of the people they were supposed to evict. A potential disaster.

At the very least, a calamitous loss of the initiative. Which, depressingly, could only mean one thing: they were in for a hard battle.

They shielded their eyes, moved backwards in a self-possessed (but, one suspects, quietly livid) withdrawal, and shouted composed instructions to each other about regrouping, keeping calm, spreading out, etc.

Then they realised that, somehow, they were *outside* whatever it was. It wasn't *beams* of light they were up against, but something odder. More of a pavilion; something translucent, perhaps, and possibly inflatable, with an encompassing boundary.

Whatever it had been originally, however, it gradually transformed. Within half a minute, it resembled an upside-down tornado whose base encompassed the fields, and whose highest point ended – if it *did* end - somewhere out of view in the sky.

It lasted no more than twenty seconds. According to *The Courier*, people all over Tunbridge Wells saw it. From a distance, it looked like a luminescent vortex, or a grotesquely wide bolt of lightning, but directed from earth to the sky, rather than the other way around.

Then it disappeared.

A few seconds later, the bailiffs overcame both their disorientation, and their furious indignation, and re-entered the Portchers' fields in a concerted charge (with accompanying battle-cries), expecting a prolonged, excrement-throwing battle.

But their charge fizzled out in puzzlement, frustration, and every appearance of farce. There was no one here.

No tents, no occupants, nothing to indicate that the land had ever been a campsite, or anything resembling one.

And definitely no standing stones.

XIV.

According to Wikipedia, "St. Elmo's fire is a weather phenomenon in which luminous plasma is created by a corona discharge from a rod-like object such as a mast, spire, chimney, or animal horn in an atmospheric electric field."

So that was the explanation. Ninety-two people had disappeared from the face of the Earth in a phenomenon which, although rare, at least had the virtue of being something that secular-minded, intelligent, urbane people could get their heads around. *St. Elmo's fire*. And it was good for Tunbridge Wells, something the tourist office could capitalise on.

The 'disappearances' could be accounted for in the obvious manner: the occupants had left the site *en masse* when they'd realised the situation was hopeless. They'd gone their separate ways shortly afterwards, and, since all of them were the kind of people who regularly lived beneath the radar in any kind of civil society, they had effectively disappeared. 'Disappeared', that is to say, in virtual, not real, terms; in inverted commas. They were somewhere, obviously. Somewhere tragic, most likely: begging or staggering about like deranged persons, either mad, on drugs, or drunk. If you were to pass Hermione Portcher in the street, or Ray, or Callum, and even if you'd worked alongside them for twenty years, you probably wouldn't *see* them. In an all-too-commonplace way, they'd become unrecognisable. And let's not forget: theirs were the most well-known faces in that particular community. The others had all been *non-faces* from the outset.

Reading beneath the dream imagery and heavy symbolism in the final few pages of Hermione Portcher's notebook, it is clear that she thought she was in permanent, intimate contact with God, and that God was coming to take everyone in the community away sometime in the near future.

Talk about Waco!? Where she expected them all to go, she never says, even in her most cryptic ramblings. I know a few people, even today – less rational, more 'intuitive', more 'spiritual' people – who share her conviction. No St. Elmo's Fire for them.

But, with respect, I do think we should keep God out of it. The universe 'shrank' about five hundred years ago, when humanity realised the Earth wasn't at its centre. God suffered a corresponding demotion. However, now that we know the universe is virtually infinite, we haven't revised our theology at all. We still tend to think small. Consider, though: there could be *anything at all* out there; beings we cannot imagine, embodied in ways we cannot conceive, straddling entire star systems. And I think it highly likely that, from our feeble human point of view, they'd strongly resemble gods.

As for the *real* God, assuming such a being exists, and that we could encounter 'it', how would we even recognise it? More, given its utter transcendence, and the stupefying size of the universe, why should it bother with us? No, I doubt it was *God* Dr Portcher encountered, though I am willing to accept it may have been *something*.

You see, I keep coming back to that 'planet' she claimed to find talk of, in her father's journal. *Was* it a planet, in the sense in which the term is normally understood? I don't know. His journal was lost, along with virtually everything else in the 'fire'. Yes, there were elements of real fire. I haven't time or space, or the inclination, to go into that here. Have a look in the archives of the Tunbridge Wells library, if you're interested.

But that may be where they all are now; that 'planet'. And it may not be as congenial as they'd hoped.

But of course, I am speaking ironically. The truth is, Hermione Portcher was an unreliable narrator. To give but one example, that heptagonal chamber she claimed to discover in the loft at Beulah Cottage: it doesn't exist: I've been up there. It's lifted straight from the pages of *The Chymical Wedding of Christian Rosenkreutz*, if you must know, by Johann Valentin Andreae. Seventeenth century. The stones her brothers are supposed to have excavated: ditto in terms of their non-existence.

Or at least, that is what we've been led to believe. It fits with the least mind-bending story. Fourteen standing stones, each at least a ton in weight, don't just disappear, even in a spectacular conflagration.

The problem is, some people definitely did see them. Postmen, neighbours, council officials, ramblers; lots of people saw them.

There's another alternative. Maybe it was all a carefully staged piece of theatre. The notebook, a piece of fiction, intended as such from the outset, the stones made of *papier-mâché*. The occupants dispersed, laughing up their sleeves, somewhere like Islington or Camden.

Or perhaps *I'm* the unreliable narrator. That heptagonal chamber, maybe it really *did* exist! Perhaps I read the story of Cytherea Holmes in *Not So Disgusted, the Cool Side of Tunbridge Wells*. Maybe I thought, 'Everyone thought *her* story was fiction. I should publish this account in an obscure little anthology somewhere. Hopefully, it'll get lost, and it'll turn up in a few decades' time as a curiosity, and no one will even consider the possibility that it might all be true!'

Yes, maybe I know far more than I'm letting on. Maybe I even know where Hermione Portcher is!

Or maybe not. My God, how to steer a course between two radically unreliable poles? You must feel like you're in the depths of space, dear Reader, a billion light years from home! Is your head spinning yet?

A point of minor interest, and this *is* true. The two council employees, Steven Willesdown and Alison Grolle, were supposed make a third visit to the Portchers' before the bailiffs went in, but they refused. Challenged by their line-manager, they claimed to have 'seen something that shouldn't be there'. And they definitely didn't want to see that whatever-it-was again. They never elucidated. More: it later turned out that some of the bailiffs had undergone a similar experience.

What interests me about all this is that it exhibits *in extremis* what I suspect may be true of all stories whatsoever. What we have is a number of episodes, events and actions which we can put together in a dozen or so different ways, all broadly consistent with the facts as such, yet involving some minor inconsistency that we agree to overlook for the sake of constituting it as a story. Because we *want* a story.

The question is, why does something like this have to be a story? Why does anything? Why not just say: this was Hermione Portcher… about whom we know next to nothing?

The Mesmerist

I.

Helen Battersby Van Dijk looked through her front window onto Mount Sion road and stepped back to where she was less likely to be seen. She hoped she hadn't been too late. Sometimes when stalkers achieved eye contact, they saw it as auspicious, a foretaste of future triumphs.

"It's that man again," she said.

Tom sat examining his phone on the other side of the living room, his feet on the pouffe. He looked up. "The fifty-something guy with the sideburns? The one you claim is watching the house?"

"He *is*. He looked across at us *again* as he passed. I mean, as if he was sizing the place up. Like the other three times. He didn't look at any of the other houses in the street. Just this one. And this is the fourth time he's been past."

"In four days. Was he wearing a suit again?"

"The same one, by the looks of it. Why?"

"Just: maybe he's an estate agent."

"Why would an estate agent be looking solely at *our house?* We've only just moved in! He's – he's come back."

Tom got up as if it was his unpleasant duty. "Let me have a look. We should really get some net curtains. Next time we're in town, remind me to - "

"We should really get a dog."

Tom made a show of appraising the object of his wife's anxiety, then he met her eyes with a no-need-to-worry expression. "He's probably just a fan. And maybe he lives nearby. Come on, Helen. Like you say, we've only just moved in. We're not entitled to draw sweeping conclusions about individual passers-by. This could be his regular route into town, for all we know."

"A fan, you say. Possibly. But then, there are good fans, and there are stalking ones."

"Or maybe he's just a normal guy on his daily walk to somewhere completely innocuous. This isn't like you."

"It's not his *regularity* that's the problem, Tom. It's the way he looks at the house."

"A fan, then. He must be."

"You're not listening to me."

He sighed, flopped sideways onto the sofa, put his legs up on the arm, and went back to his phone. Helen sat on the antique chair and pulled her feet under her. She began to play with her brown hair, making little pigtails, then undoing them.

Maybe moving here had been a mistake; perhaps they shouldn't have left London. But then, her agent had said it wouldn't be a problem: *take your mind off the baby business, you could always adopt, meantime somewhere posh like Tunbridge Wells could be good for your career – makes it look like you've made it, or everyone thinks you have - and Davina McCall lives there, and there are some nice little bistros, and it's only an hour on the train*, etc. And the acting roles hadn't dried up, far from it. She was still only twenty-eight, and Tom seemed happy, despite the bad news, and even though he had a longer commute in the morning, and he was ten years older than her, almost middle-aged, so he should probably have been moaning by now, and –

There was a knock. Three decisive raps at the front door.

She half-sprang to the window, trying to gauge the optimum distance for seeing without being seen, but knowing in advance that there wasn't one; not with that sort of person. And it *was* – it was *him!*

No sooner had she advanced than she realised she'd miscalculated. She lurched back and reoccupied the chair.

Tom had already risen. "I take it that's your secret starer. If he asks if you're in, are you?"

"He knows I am, so yes, no point acting like a shrinking violet. Assuming I'm right, I mean, and… yes, I know I sound paranoid. Yes, I *do* sound paranoid, don't I?" She held up her hand. "Stop, Tom. I'll answer it. I'll take my own advice, and I'll get it over and done with into the bargain, have a showdown, if necessary. You stay here and discreetly take a few photos. If he's as dodgy as I think he is, we may need to go to the police."

"Good luck getting *them* interested. Tell him cold callers aren't allowed round here."

She strode into the hall and opened the door, every bit as decisively, she hoped, as the man outside had knocked. She donned her *warranted annoyance* persona.

The caller was thin, blond, with thick sideburns but no beard, and the sort of narrow eyes and thin lips that Helen, thanks to her cameo appearances in four soaps, had learned to associate with untrustworthy people.

"How can I help?" she said irritably.

"I'm sorry," he replied. A slight French accent, but it might have been put on. "I was just passing, and I, er – do you *live* here?"

She smiled thinly and began to close the door. "Sorry, I don't have time to chat. And cold callers aren't allowed in this area."

"No, please, *stop!*"

She did, but only because he'd justified her previously fake indignation. Now, she could shut him out with a clear conscience.

... If it came to that. He was still talking. "I actually – my great-great-great grandfather used to live in this very house, you know. Born in seventeen eighty-three, died – or rather killed - in Tunbridge Wells, in eighteen-ten, at the age of twenty-seven. A practitioner of animal magnetism. The Comte de Mauripois! An exile. A member of the nobility. If only he'd lived four more years, he'd have seen Louis the Eighteenth ascend the throne. Then all would have been well! He came to England in seventeen-ninety, and for a long time, they lived in - "

She didn't know what was coming, but it felt like the prelude to some momentous request. "I – I'm sorry, I've got to go," she said.

"I just wondered if I could have a look round your house someday. It doesn't have to be today, obviously. Just sometime."

"I don't even know your name."

"*Please* don't close the door!" He thrust his foot impetuously across the threshold. "My name's - "

Tom appeared from the living room. "What the *hell* do you think you're doing? Get your foot out of our house!"

"I own this house!" the man exclaimed, removing his foot and reddening at the same time. Suddenly, he looked on the verge of tears. "It was taken from my three times great grandfather illegally! It belongs to *me,* as his direct descendant! I'm just asking for a look around, that's - "

The door slammed him out. Tom and Helen looked solicitously at each other.

Tom strode into the living room. "He's walking away," he said, obviously trying to sound reassuring.

Helen joined him and looked through the window into the now empty road. "Did you get any photos?"

"Lots. We need to call the police. They almost certainly won't do anything, but if we don't call them, and then that – that *crackpot* comes back, we won't have a leg to stand on."

"Do you think he *will* come back?"

"I think… Yes."

"We should have got his name!"

Tom scoffed. "It wouldn't have been his *real* name, Helen. Next, you'll be telling me we should have invited him in, just to get it out of his system!"

"I wasn't going to say that. But yes, maybe."

"We need to hire a private detective, just in case. And get a house sitter, for when we're out. And possibly move, assuming he's the dogged type, which I agree, we've no reason – yet – to assume he is. But he probably is."

II.

For a couple of their age and social status, the Battersby Van Dijks had a typical diary of social engagements, and the following week found them at dinner with Ruth and Michael Strawson, in Culverden Down. The Strawsons were in their seventies, grey-haired and not very good at cooking, but Michael had been in charge of BBC Children's TV in the 1990s, and he and his wife took a close interest in Helen and Tom, one that was mostly neighbourly, nevertheless mingled, from time to time, with wistful aspirations to mentorship. They listened attentively to the story of the mysterious caller, hmm-ed over the bit about the Comte de Mauripois, nodded with concern at Helen's accounts of her nightmares, and re-hmm-ed as Tom described his overwhelmingly strong sense of being followed since the ominous visit. Finally, dispiritingly, Ruth recommended that the Battersby Van Dijks both see a therapist.

"As I understand it," Ruth said, "this man hasn't been back, and it's the worry that he might do you some harm that's provoking *your* nightmares, Helen, and *your* anxious feeling of being watched, Tom. You've just moved house; big upheaval. The buzzy, up-to-the-minute capital to sedate, sylvan Tunbridge Wells; big change. And then, of course, there was the fertility news. You're feeling fragile, and this – *whoever-he-was* just happened to tap into that. A therapist could help you rebuild your mental resilience. Of course, you may not believe in that sort of thing. 'Too American', some people say. Well, more fool them, that's my view."

"I wish whoever-he-was *would* come back," Helen said. "I ended up feeling rather sorry for him. I mean, about two hours after he'd gone."

"We can't just keep calling him 'whoever-he-was'," Michael said. "We need to give him a name."

"The problem with us seeing a therapist," Tom said, ignoring him, "is it sets our seal of approval on one particular interpretation of what's going on, namely that there's nothing behind it."

"Well, Helen's *dreams* can't be real," Ruth said. "Even if she's sleepwalking occasionally."

Tom was about to put a slice of potato in his mouth, but he put his fork down. "I know this is going to sound whacky, but Helen and I have talked about it, and we both think there's something more than mere psychology to this. We still haven't told you about the photos." He seemed to realise what he was saying. He shook his head self-depreciatingly. *"More than mere psychology*: of course, we *would* think that. If it went on long enough. Is a week 'long enough'? It'd be one of the symptoms."

"What photos?" Michael said.

"Tom took a few photos of Mr Grandson," Helen said. "While he was outside, and - "

Ruth hooted. "Really, that's what we're calling him?"

"Mr Whoever-he-was," Helen went on. "And not one of them was any use. The suit was good, and the shoes, and the surrounds; everything except the head. Which looked – and I'm not joking – like it belonged to a – a *slug*. I know that doesn't sound very charitable, but it's true. Show them, Tom."

But Tom was already jabbing his phone. He positioned it in between Ruth and Michael, and flicked slowly through the pictures.

"That *is* creepy," Michael said. "Point taken, Helen: you really weren't being flippant."

"How *could* they have come out like that?" Ruth asked. "I mean, I don't know much about photography, but that's not something I've ever seen before. If he was moving, his whole body would be blurred."

"You've shown these to the police?" Michael said.

"We stopped short of that," Helen replied. "We reported the incident, just for 'insurance' purposes: we didn't want them saying later, 'why didn't you tell us about the first time?' But showing them the pictures seemed pointless, and possibly even counter-productive. They might have laughed."

"And even worse," Tom said: "thought I wasn't very good at photography."

"It's not a joking matter," Helen told him.

"What about a private detective?" Michael asked.

"We considered it," Tom said. "Seriously… for about ten minutes. But there's virtually nothing to go on. And, now that I think about it, you're right. It's been over a week and we still haven't had a return visit. Though that doesn't alter the fact that I can't help thinking he's watching me, from somewhere, nearly all the time."

"Did you feel he was watching you… on the way over here?" Ruth asked.

"The whole journey," Tom said. "Helen felt it too. Which is mad, of course. He'd have to be in a car, and he'd have to have known what time we were going to set off, and he'd have to have a reason. I mean, if he wanted to break into the house, he'd watch for us going out, yes. But he wouldn't follow us over here."

"We've got a house-sitter tonight," Helen said. "Just so we know he can't break in."

"My God, you really *are* spooked!" Michael said. "I know it's not a long-term solution, but would you like to stay here tonight? You're welcome to the spare room, and you might get a bit of sleep. Ruth and I could go over to yours, settle up with the house sitter and look after the place till morning."

"Like Airbnb," Ruth said, "but without any of the exoticism or anticipation or excitement."

"That's very kind," Tom replied. "But we couldn't impose. Besides, I've got my work things over there, and I've got an early start in the morning." He looked at Helen. "Or that's the assumption I'm working on. *All things being well.*"

She smiled apologetically. "Tom means, assuming I haven't made my usual journey downstairs, into the non-existent cellar whose door is located beneath the carpet in the living room, and down four long flights of stairs to open the trapdoor at the bottom." She shuddered. "God, I can't make light of it. It's the same dream *every night,* and it's turning me into a nervous wreck!"

"We haven't even *got* a cellar," Tom said gloomily.

"Which is why I said, 'non-existent'," Helen told him tetchily.

"What's under the trapdoor?" Michael asked.

Helen shrugged. "That's when I always wake up."

"Enough," Ruth said. "When I said you should both see a therapist, I didn't mean just any old therapist. I had someone specific in mind."

III.

Lionel Rosembaum really wasn't just any old therapist. Sixty-two, portly, something of a dandy, with a chevron moustache and a shaven head, his grandfather, David, had been one of the leading lights of the British psychoanalytic movement in the 1920s and 30s. Lionel himself had trained as a psychologist. He had a consulting room on Upper Grosvenor Road, just before the junction at the town centre. He described himself for professional purposes as a therapist because he thought it sounded more congenial. He was known for solving difficult cases, but his reputation had soared after two local council workers called Steven Willesdown and Alison Grolle had been referred to him for post-traumatic stress. Both believed they had seen ghosts during a routine visit to what later became known as the 'St. Elmo's Fire house'. His clinical breakthrough came when he accepted their insistence that there were, after all, supernatural elements to the whole affair. If that effected a cure, he thought, what did it matter? In any case, it wasn't the *seeing* of the ghosts that mattered to them, it was the felt significance of their experience, the interpretation they'd put on it: namely, that the world was a much less knowable, far less hospitable place than they'd previously believed. Such a conviction wasn't conducive to mental ill health in itself. Lots of perfectly normal, well-balanced people held it. Luckily, being a Jungian, he'd always been determinedly agnostic about the whole business of ghosts.

Helen and Tom Battersby Van Dijk's experience and their subsequent upset looked to be a case cut from a similar cloth, and thus not as difficult to resolve as it might conceivably have seemed to most other mental health professionals. However, Lionel Rosembaum had a full complement of patients, so he had to decline. He listened patiently as Mrs Strawson tried to change his mind, all the time insisting that, much as he sympathised with the Battersby Van Dijks, it simply wasn't possible to add to his existing professional commitments.

Then she mentioned the one thing that could possibly have overturned his reluctance, and which completely blindsided him. The Comte de Mauripois.

In order to make sense of this *volte-face*, it is necessary to know that Lionel Rosembaum considered himself a master of the art of hypnotism. Over the years, his proficiency in that domain had provided a succession of keys to apparently intractable cases. As a thank you, and also because he thought he might one day make it his specialist subject on *Mastermind*, he did all he could to acquaint himself with the theory behind it, and its history.

As far as he knew, he was a world expert on The Comte de Mauripois. True, he had only read one book on him, but it just so happened that, in this case, and as far as he knew, that one book was 100% of all possible knowledge, and he owned the sole extant copy. As yet, The Comte didn't even have a Wikipedia page (though it was Lionel's ambition to one day write one).

The Interesting Life of Pierre Albert Bernard de Sale, Comte de Mauripois, Mesmerist and Tragic Exile, had been published privately in 1956, in a single edition print-run of one hundred copies, and its author – Dr BLN Pike - had apparently written nothing else and left no other mark on the world. As far as eBay, Bookfinder.com and everything else on the internet knew, the other ninety-nine copies of *The Interesting Life* no longer existed, which presumably meant they'd been binned, burned, pulped or dumped. In Lionel's view, that was not entirely surprising: not only was the book's subject matter poorly organised and badly communicated, not only did it end in 1800, ten years before the end of the subject's life, but *The Interesting Life*, etc. had to be one of the worst titles ever devised (it didn't even fit on the spine). Nonetheless, posterity's loss was his mild good fortune, and properly re-written, repackaged, and retitled, the Comte's life story – assuming its ending could ever be discovered - might perhaps make some future author a tidy sum of money.

Mrs Strawson was still singing the virtues of the Battersby Van Djiks, with the difference that she'd converted him now. He had to be careful not to appear to capitulate too quickly: Mrs Strawson might suspect something strange, and she was exactly the type not to rest content on an easy victory: she'd probably try for another at some point. So, over the next twenty minutes, he gradually allowed his reservations to fall away, each one accompanied by a wistful little sigh. Finally, he made his acquiescence sound as reluctant as possible: perhaps he *could* make space for them, after all, very well, all right, yes then, but just because it's *you*, Ruth, only because it's *you*.

IV.

When the Battersby Van Dijks turned up for their appointment, three days later, they struck him as typical young executive types, although he knew they weren't, not really. She was apparently an actress (so not an executive) and, although he worked in BBC programming, he looked at least ten years older than her (so not young). Still, between the two of them, it was half correct. Now, all that remained was to find out if they were neurotic, and if so, how acutely.

Which was a foregone conclusion, really. In his experience, the middle classes were all neurotic, nearly one hundred percent of the time, and he included himself in that assessment (how he constantly worried about his three suits smelling 'stale', the length of his fingernails, the shine of his shoes, etc.).

The Comte de Mauripois couldn't be overlooked, though, and he certainly couldn't be allowed to slip out of the equation. Best not be too hasty in providing a cure and sending them on their way.

Luckily, Mrs Battersby Van Dijk – Helen – was having bad dreams. Bad dreams cried out for hypnosis. Mr Battersby Van Dijk – Tom – thought he was being followed. Which didn't demand hypnosis, but didn't preclude it either. And hypnosis was his first and highest love. So: hypnosis it was.

First of all, Lionel got them to recline on his couch – he'd always believed patients felt reassured by the clichés, so the couch was a fixture – and got them to explain what had brought them to him. Then he put them into a trance and asked them in detail about the things they'd outlined in Stage 1, to see if any fresh detail came to light.

He quickly realised Helen was by far the most interesting of the two. Or rather: she was interesting, he wasn't. Tom's anxiety attacks (which is all they were, really) revealed themselves to be, at root, nothing more than psychologically displaced concerns for his wife. Noteworthy, of course, but hardly original. No, Helen was the genuine one; her issues were not so easily soluble. And perhaps not soluble at all.

Her conscious, on-the-couch relating of her dreams was unremarkable. Under hypnosis, however, whole new vistas came to light. She claimed to know much more than who the Comte de Mauripois was; she could relate entire episodes from his life. Four of the most unlikely were attested in *The Interesting Life of Pierre Albert Bernard de Sale, Comte de Mauripois, Mesmerist and Tragic Exile:* his being caught in a rainstorm in the channel in 1790 (mixed hailstones, rain and 'shards of what looked like charcoal'), his first impressions of Folkestone (he was 'intoxicated by the odour of herrings'), his broken index finger in 1794, his discovery of the 'questionable pleasures' of tea, and of a mysterious 'Mrs Fletcher', in Margate, in 1795.

After Freud and Jung, and the whole miserable paper mill of modern neuroscience, for any psychologist to find a case which, as a consequence of its otherwise irresolvable complexity, *had* to become personal, was – for all its career-destroying potential - to have hit upon the Holy Grail.

Praise be to Helen Battersby Van Dijk!

As regards her remarkable knowledge of the Comte, there was only one possibility really. There had to be another copy of *The Interesting Life* somewhere in Helen's past. Perhaps the library where she'd gone to university? Some libraries stocked every obscure tome under the sun. She was twenty-eight, and she'd left Essex seven years ago. Ample time for her to 'forget', and for her unconscious mind to have appropriated the whole thing, in order to fulfil its own recondite agenda.

Which might, in turn – just *might* - mean that she and Tom had – almost certainly without meaning to - fabricated their cold caller's claim that he was descended from the Comte. Tom would have got it from her.

… If there had ever really *been* a cold caller at all!

Lionel needed to keep all this to himself for the time being. Meanwhile, he could get in contact with the library at Essex University, and see if they had a copy of *The Interesting Life* on their shelves. If they had, then bingo.

But, for some reason, he didn't consider it very likely. Even though he'd already convinced himself it was the only plausible explanation.

Still, she must have come across it *somewhere.*

Hypnosis might reveal the answer.

Meanwhile, he should re-read *The Interesting Life*. On some level, it probably held the key – or at least, *one* key – to all this. He'd bring it into his office tomorrow, read it in between patients, and keep it in his desk drawer so the Battersby Van Dijks wouldn't see it. No point in spooking them even more drastically.

Not yet, anyway.

V.

A week later, Tom and Helen sat side by side on the couch in his Edwardian-feeling consulting room on Upper Grosvenor Road. Without looking at each other, they joined hands. Lionel sat at his desk, facing the window. He wrote for thirty seconds, then transferred himself to the brown leather armchair facing the couple, this being his usual signal that he was ready to share his conclusions. He crossed his legs and rested a notebook in his lap.

"I've believed since the beginning that there might be an imbalance in the amount of anxiety each of you feels," he began. "That is to say, without underestimating the seriousness of the problem, that one of you feels more apprehensive than the other. I can safely say we've now established that. My more interesting conclusion is that the uneasiness generated by the two of you together is circling and re-circling, using your emotional connection to create something resembling a feedback loop. The problem therefore escalates as time goes on."

"So, what are you suggesting?" Tom asked. "That we should separate for a while?"

Helen squeezed his hand. "Please, no."

"Which of us is the more anxious?" Tom said.

"It's me, isn't it?" Helen said.

"I'm not suggesting you should separate," Lionel replied. "I think, in this particular case, that might make matters worse." He smiled apologetically. "And yes, Helen, it is you."

"I knew it," she whispered.

"What you're saying in your conscious state," he told her, "doesn't match what you're saying under hypnosis. Obviously, that's not an accusation, not at all; it's a disinterested observation about what's entirely to be expected. It's the whole point about hypnosis. It sometimes brings things to the surface that our conscious minds don't want to acknowledge."

"What sort of things?" Helen said.

"What do you know about seven 'iron children'?" he asked her.

She turned an uncomprehending look on Tom, then back on Lionel. "I don't – I'm guessing it's something I said under hypnosis? But I – I've no recollection of saying anything – and certainly no memory of what I must have meant. What *are* the 'iron children'?"

"On your nightly walks downstairs to enter your non-existent cellar," Lionel said, "you frequently come across what seems to be an iron 'sculpture' – a piece of welding, really, so you say - depicting seven huddled, elated-looking children, all female, all more or less infants. According to your own description, it's about three feet tall and five feet wide. It appears to you at various locations in your house – on the landing, at the bottom of the stairs, in the living room. You never stop to examine it, perhaps because of your" – he read from his notebook – "'strong feeling that it has always been there, and always will be'."

"I still can't remember a thing," she said after a pause.

"Can I ask you both," he went on: "how certain are you that this cellar *you* keep visiting in your dreams, Helen, is actually non-existent?"

The couple exchanged bewildered expressions.

"The carpet was already there when we moved in," Helen said, as if the question had begun to make sense. "It was a new carpet. And fitted. And it's nice. It seemed ridiculous to replace it."

"There's no cellar in the property deeds," Tom said. "We've got plans of the house going back to the middle of the nineteenth century. But, well, we haven't actually looked. Why would we? We'd have to think Helen had some kind of psychic powers. We'd have to *care* about that. Whereas all we actually care about is stopping the nightmares and the anxiety attacks."

"All I'm thinking," Lionel went on, "is that the factual non-existence of the cellar might be a matter worth verifying first-hand. In some arcane manner that we can't replicate, Helen could have learned that there *might* be a cellar there. Overheard a neighbour, perhaps, or read something. Maybe you heard it as a rumour, Helen, mentioned idly by the previous owner, or maybe you heard that some houses on Mount Sion *do* have cellars, and your unconscious mind retained that, and worked on it. In any case, indisputable proof of the cellar's non-existence might help tackle your problem."

"It'd be a start," Helen said.

"We'll do it today," Tom said. "Soon as we get in. And, er, what if there *is* a cellar?"

Lionel smiled. "Then we're a little closer to being able to explain, and possibly therefore stop, the sleepwalking." He chuckled. "Beyond that, if it exists, it must have been closed up a long time. It's probably at least knee-deep in water."

Helen clicked her tongue. "Presumably, it'd need pumping out or something."

"Possibly," Lionel said airily. "Would you mind giving me a call when you've found out one way or the other? I don't suppose you'll have any luck, but, either way, it will have a bearing on how we proceed from here on."

"It'll probably take a few hours," Tom said. "But yes, no problem."

"What about the iron children?" Helen asked. "What do you think that part of my dream means?"

"I'm still considering that," Lionel said. "What I'd like you to do, Tom, is, the next time Helen sleepwalks, follow her with a notebook, and write down *exactly* what she does. I would ask you to take a video, but I doubt you'll be able to get very close, and it'll be dark. In any case, what *you* notice – how *you* read her behaviour – may be equally, if not more valuable than a bit of footage. We can go down the video route later, if necessary."

"Will do," Tom said.

They exchanged the usual slightly awkward farewells. Lionel followed them into the room next door, where his receptionist, Sandra, a middle-aged woman in a beige trouser-suit and her hair in a bun, booked them another appointment for five days' time. "But call me if there are any new developments," he told them, as they left. "Or if there's anything you think I should know. And don't forget to tell me what's under that carpet of yours."

They were his last patients of the day. When they'd gone, he went back into his office and removed *The Interesting Life* from his desk drawer. He wasn't very keen on it at the moment: it had let him down. Not only had Essex university library never heard of it, but they had no idea where to obtain a copy. And he'd paid forty pounds for the fancy 'international inter-library search' facility.

But to make matters even worse, Helen claimed never to have heard of it either, even under the deepest hypnosis.

He sat down in the armchair, and took the bookmark out from between pages 94 and 95. Nearly halfway through: it finished on page 204 with the author's remarks about

Napoleon crossing the Alps in 1800. Just before that, there was a little bit about the Comte's mesmerist career, but not much: disappointingly, the major biographical developments in that domain must have come later, between 1800 and the subject's untimely death in 1810.

So, not much to look forward to. *The Interesting Life* seemed a lot duller now than it had when he'd first read it, ten years ago. And it had been dull then. Still, it was research. It had to be done.

Three hours later, he'd reached page 167. Seventy-two pages: abysmal progress, on the face of it, but the author's bad writing wore him out. And perhaps he felt a little under the weather.

He looked at his watch. 7pm, time to go home. He could call in at *Subway* on his way. Bit of a detour, but it beat cooking.

His phone rang. *Tom Battersby Van Dijk*. He picked up. "Tom!"

"We've had all the downstairs carpets up," Tom said. "Or *I* have. No sign of a cellar door, or anything resembling one. Pretty much what I expected, really. I'm not sure how Helen's taking it. She's watching TV in the other room. She's not keen on upheaval."

"I think it was probably worth it."

"I've hired some men to re-fit everything tomorrow. The house should end up looking as good as new, assuming they're as reliable and competent as they say they are."

"Fingers crossed. And thank you for letting me know."

He was about to end the call, when Tom blurted out: "There's, er, one other thing I think I ought to tell you."

"Oh?"

Pause. When Tom started speaking, it was at speed, in a morose tone, as if he was excited, but about something ominous. "The house next door to ours, on the higher side: it's got a 'sold' sign outside. Which was news to us, because we didn't even know it'd been for sale. The houses up here are all detached, and so far, we've pretty much kept ourselves to ourselves. The neighbours didn't come round to say hi when we moved in, so we figured, fine, but why should *we* run after *them?* Anyway, it turns out it was unoccupied all this time. And on the market, apparently, with a prestigious estate agent in London. However, Helen thinks she's seen – we still don't know what to call him: *Mr Grandson*."

"Seen? In what way?"

"Seen him coming and going from that house. She's convinced he's the buyer."

"And… am I right in thinking that *you haven't* seen him?"

"I've been busy with the bloody carpets all afternoon. Meantime, she was upstairs, watching the street from the front window, as she seems to do a lot at the moment. Anyway, long story short: I went round there, knocked, no reply. Looked through the window; it's vacant, no doubt about that. No furniture or fittings whatsoever. Anyway, Helen says she saw him go inside quickly, then leave. I'll definitely try again later."

"And you've called the estate agent?"

"Yes, for all the good it did. Mind you, I knew in advance it was a long shot. Data protection; more than their reputation's worth. Anyway, the reason she's sitting down in the other room right now, watching TV, is because I made her. She's got a big glass of gin and tonic, plus four slices of ham and pineapple pizza in a box. Not the sort of thing we usually eat, by the way, but desperate times and that. Hopefully, she'll nod off soon. With any luck, she'll be inebriated enough to sleep through the night. Yes, that's what we've come to."

"Anything specific I can do to help? I'll be leaving the office to go home in a moment. If you need anything in the way of shopping, I could pick it up on the way, drop it off. Save you having to leave Helen."

"We're fine, but thank you for the offer."

"If you change your mind, give me a call. And keep me posted of any new developments, if possible. We may need to move your next appointment forward."

After he'd hung up, he transferred *The Interesting Life* to his briefcase and set off for home.

No, he wouldn't bother with *Subway*. Or get anything to eat at all. For some reason, he was feeling a little off-colour now.

VI.

When he got in, he undressed, went in the shower, donned his pyjamas, put his phone on his bedside table, got under the covers, and switched out the light. He wondered if he had Covid. Nothing he could do about it, if so. A good night's sleep should put him in a better position to judge whether he was actually ill at all; he might just be overtired. He looked at his bedside clock. 8pm. The earliest he'd turned in for quite some time.

… Which might be why he couldn't get to sleep. After an hour of turning onto one side, then the other, and trying his feet in different positions, he decided he needed help. *The Interesting Life* was just the thing: probably the most boring book in the world. If anything could send him to sleep, that could.

And a small glass of Jameson's.

Or a hot chocolate?

No, Jameson's was easier.

Five minutes later, he sat up in bed with two pillows behind him, sipping his Irish whiskey and reading. Only thirty-seven pages left.

It took him four pages before he'd finished his drink. Then the book slipped out of his hands, and he knew he'd done it. Sleep, here he came. He put *The Interesting Life* into his bedside drawer, switched off the light, and got down.

It took a few widely separated moments of fleeting wakefulness to reassure him that he really was asleep. He next picked up his bedside clock at 2am. He went straight back to sleep.

The next time he awoke, it was still dark. He lay on his side. He had a vague sense of being unable to move. Maybe sleep paralysis, as they called it. Not that it mattered: he wasn't intending to go anywhere.

It struck him that his bedside table looked strange. Illuminated somehow.

No, it wasn't the whole table. Just the drawer. The glow was coming from inside the drawer.

Then something very odd happened. He got up, opened the drawer, took out *The Interesting Life,* went to sit in the armchair on the other side of the room, and began to read.

Only, it wasn't him. He was still here in bed.

... So, yes, it must be a dream. Obviously.

But it was the oddest dream he'd ever had. He was in two places at the same time. Here he was, under the duvet – and there was another him – a *real* him – on the other side of the room, reading the biography of the Comte de Mauripois. He was simultaneously watching himself from the bed, aware of *being* in bed, and also on the other side of the room, sitting in the armchair, reading the book, whose contents were fully present to his eye. And yet this other him was wholly oblivious to the figure in the bed.

He tried to call out, but he couldn't.

On the other hand, he wasn't frightened. He was interested. He was a psychologist by profession, and this was the sort of thing he read about in academic journals. And Oliver Sacks, he'd made a career out of it. No matter that it was happening to him, and that it might be the precursor to madness. He could control that, surely?

Which was, he reflected gloomily, precisely what he *would* think.

His semi-anxiety didn't last very long, because he was entirely engrossed in the book. It was much fatter than the real version – some three or four hundred pages, by the feel of it – and the writing was much more lucid. Whereas the real book had come to a premature end in 1800, this one went right to the Comte's death, and beyond. Lionel was aware of knowing what it would say before he read it, but of having to read it anyway, and of reading at great speed, and with perfect retention.

The Comte de Mauripois came to Tunbridge Wells in 1800, specifically in his capacity as a practitioner of Mesmerism, a now long-discredited therapy 'discovered' by the German physician, Franz Anton Mesmer, in 1774. Mesmer held that the bodies of all humans (and all living things) possessed a vital substance which he called 'magnetic fluid', the distribution of which conditioned any given individual's health, or lack of it. By applying iron magnets to his patients' bodies, by sitting them, in groups, in 'baquets', tubs filled with water and fitted with iron rods, by making 'magnetic passes' over their bodies and thus 'mesmerising' them, he claimed to be able to cure or improve them. This latter technique is, of course, the ancestor of modern hypnotism. However, in the eighteenth century Mesmerism quickly took an esoteric turn….

…The Comte de Mauripois was attracted to Tunbridge Wells by its iron-rich springs. But he firmly believed that the local water contained more than mere iron, and that Franz Mesmer himself had analysed the composition of his 'magnetic fluid' with only partial accuracy…

… In 1783, Franz Anton Mesmer inaugurated The Society of Universal Harmony, designed to train future practitioners. The institution's first member, a Lyonnais by the name of Nicolas Bergasse, wrote a coded Mesmerist instruction book, whose contents could only be accessed using a cipher of cabbalistic signs. Pierre Albert Bernard de Sale, Comte de Mauripois was the Society's second

member. The Comte seems to have shared the most mystical beliefs of many of his fellow initiates. Several Mesmerist societies were linked to the Freemasons, and the sole surviving baquet in the 20th century is decorated with Masonic signs and symbols…

… The second stage in the history of Mesmerism, which led to its transformation into something more than a set of medical techniques, is connected to Amand-Marie-Jacques de Chastenet, Marquis de Puységur (1751-1825). Puységur focused on the 'sleeping trance' which had been just one item in Franz Anton's armoury. He quickly discovered that patients in a Mesmeric trance apparently 'knew' facts that should not have been available to them, and occasionally exhibited completely different personality traits. Eventually, some adherents came to believe that the mesmeric trance might open a door to the afterlife. In the second half of the nineteenth-century, Mesmerism evolved to become Spiritualism, although the process was underway well before the appearance of the infamous Fox sisters, in New York, in 1848. The Comte de Mauripois, as attentive readers will not be surprised to hear, was in the vanguard of that transformation …

… The Comte's first and only Mesmerist exhibition took place in the Bath House of The Pantiles on June 21st, 1804. The seven young ladies of prominent local families who sat, fully clothed, in his modified baquet reported feeling 'highly intoxicated' by the whole experience, and for several days they apparently retained such a feeling of euphoria that they wandered about (as several

particularly concerned fathers later attested) at home 'in a veritable trance'. It was to be several weeks before it became clear that something had gone critically wrong…

The book and the reader disappeared and Lionel found himself alone in bed and covered in sweat. His phone was ringing. *Tom Battersby Van Dijk*. He picked up.

"I – I – something awful has happened," Tom said. "I can't tell you over the phone. I need you here. Please, please could you come over? I'm going insane. I can't tell you over the phone," he repeated. "I need - "

"Give me twenty minutes," Lionel said. "I'm on my way."

VII.

Lionel arrived outside the Battersby Van Dijks' to find Tom standing in the street, dressed in his pyjamas and a pair of brown brogues, and looking deathly cold. He got out of his car.

Tom rushed to meet him. "Thank God you're here. Thank you. I – I know: I'm in my pyjamas!"

"Why are you outdoors?"

Tom laughed. "I've just realised, I haven't even got my dressing gown on!"

"You need to tell me what's - "

"Going on. Obviously, yes, of course. That's the *Mr Grandson* house," he said, pointing. "The one he bought, next to ours, obviously. The reason I'm outside is because I've been knocking on the door. Of his house." He swallowed. "I think Helen's – no, I *know* - Helen's in there. There was no answer, of course."

"She's in *there?* What makes you say that? I mean, did you *see* her go in?"

Tom seemed to diminish slightly, as if something intrinsic to him had just dropped away. "Not exactly, no. I'm sorry, I'm not making sense."

"We need to go indoors. You need to tell me what happened. You probably need to sit in front of a fire, or at least a working radiator."

Tom disconsolately led the way. Lionel had never been to the Battersby Van Dijks' before, but had it not been for the carpet and the underlay being half-folded over to reveal a significant expanse of floorboarding, it would have been roughly as he'd expected: TV, low coffee table with a selection of expensive magazines, velvet sofa, drinks cabinet, tastefully placed lamps, a few expensive-looking sculptural pieces, a Victorian fireplace with an overmantle mirror, and a bookcase with a selection of Jamie Olivers, a hardback copy of *Harry Potter and the Order of the Phoenix*, and a copy of *The Stage*. The sofa, the chair and the coffee table had all been shunted to one side to accommodate the doubling over of the carpet.

Tom gestured for Lionel to sit down, then he went to the drinks cabinet. He took out a big bottle of malt and two glasses, and threw his guest an interrogative glance.

"I'm driving, thank you," Lionel said. He sat down at the end of the sofa.

Tom poured himself four fingers of whisky, then came to sit at the other end. He held his glass up. "Sorry, but I need it. You might change your mind when you hear what

I've got to tell you. I mean, whether you believe what I'm about to impart or not. Definitely, if you do; probably, if you don't – because then you'll realise what a difficult case you've taken on. Cheers!" He took a big sip, gasped slightly, and sighed. "Helen's disappeared."

"Wait a minute. I thought you said she was next door. What do you mean, 'disappeared'?"

He laughed, manically. "We went to bed at the normal time. I had a notebook and a pen under my pillow, ready to describe any sleepwalking, just as you requested, but I didn't think there'd be any. Thanks to a seriously unsettling incident that occurred just after I called you, I was pretty shattered, so I wasn't even sure I'd notice if she went walkabout, but I was determined to do my best. Anyway, 3am, up she got. I must have been sleeping less heavily than I'd expected, because I was right behind her. Which is just as well, because she was off like a shot out of a gun. Nothing like her usual diffident sleep-self. She strode confidently across the landing, tramped down the stairs into the living room, stepped over the carpet - just there – and – and she pulled up - a trapdoor. That's right yes. She descended methodically out of view. I couldn't do anything, not in the time it took. I was stymied. And before I could even *begin* to pull myself together, she'd shut it behind her. And – and *now*, as you can see, there's nothing there: no door, no traces of a door, no possible way a door could ever have been there… and no Helen."

"Have you… I don't suppose you've called the police?"

"And told them what?"

"Yes, yes, good point."

They sat in silence for a moment. Lionel realised that he had to re-insert a dollop of sanity as soon as possible. Irrationality, if allowed time to take root, often became ineradicable. He didn't have time to consider his words, and time was of the essence, so he just said the first thing that came into his head. "Okay, you do realise that what you've just told me is literally impossible?"

Tom scowled. "I'm not an idiot, Dr Rosembaum, so yes. Thank you for that particular insight."

"Very well, here's my theory. You were unusually tired, due to this – we'll come to it in a moment, if you don't mind – 'unsettling incident' you mentioned. You *think* you got out of bed in pursuit of Helen, but you were dreaming. You dreamed you saw Helen do something impossible, and then you woke up. You didn't notice yourself pass from one cognitive state to the other, because the intensity of your emotions masked it. In the meantime, Helen had *already gone* sleepwalking somewhere. I mean, sometime before you awoke. It was your dim consciousness of that which provoked your fantasy that she was still present. Call it guilt, if you like. Have you checked the garden? All the rooms in the house? Outside in the street?"

"Yes, yes, yes, and yes. No sign."

"We should call the police. As your therapist – I'm a fully qualified psychologist, by the way – I can vouch for her mental condition. We simply tell them that she's out sleepwalking somewhere, and please could they keep a look out for her. That's all. Otherwise, she might get run over by a car."

"Good idea, except for the fact that I know where she is. She's next door."

Lionel nodded. "Okay, how do you think you know that?"

"I've been outside in the street. I heard her laughing. I heard where her laughter was coming from."

"Would you like *me* to verify that? Or are you so completely certain that you don't need a second opinion? Please tell me it's not the latter."

"It *is* the latter. But I'd also like a second opinion, if you don't mind. Mainly because I'd like to see the look on your face."

"I'm happy to oblige. But before I do, I'd be grateful if you could tell me something about the 'unsettling incident' you mentioned. The one you said made you go to bed feeling 'shattered'."

"Happy to oblige."

"Lionel smiled thinly. "Well, in that case, the floor's all yours."

"Nice of you to cede it. This evening, after I called you about taking up the carpet, I went to see if Helen needed anything. There she was, standing at the front window again, completely ignoring whatever was on the telly, which she hadn't turned off, or down. I think maybe she wanted me to think she was still watching it, because she jumped slightly when she realised I was behind her. She was frightened, I could see that. She told me she'd just seen Mr Grandson go into next door's again. And yes, she was certain it was him this time.

"I'm not sure what she expected me to do, but when I said I'd go round, she jumped at the idea: it would be a good move, providing I wasn't confrontational. And yes, I could see she was right. The boot was kind of on the other foot now. Whoever Mr Grandson was, or is, he's just turned into our next-door neighbour. No point antagonising him. Quite the opposite: it might be in our best interests to do a little grovelling. *I'm terribly sorry about when you knocked on our door, Helen and I were a bit out of sorts that day, I hope you can forgive us*, etcetera, etcetera. Anyway, I grabbed a very good bottle of wine from the kitchen cupboard - *Chateauneuf-du-Pape Cuvee Speciale*, forty quid a pop – to use as a 'welcome to the neighbourhood' gift. Surely, I thought, he's got to come around, see our side of things. And, thinking about it, there was no reason to believe he'd taken against us in the first place. Yes, I'd snapped at him, but he *had* put his foot into our hallway. We'd both behaved less than perfectly, so why wouldn't we both want to wipe the slate clean, make a fresh start? In a nutshell, I left the house feeling optimistic. I'd told Helen I'd call her, and get her to join me, once my charm offensive had worked. You might ask, 'Why didn't she just join you to begin with?' Well, the truth is, she's not very good at charming people. Don't get me wrong, I love my wife, but she can be a little… She's shy, sometimes, that's all, and it can come across as superciliousness. Not much of an asset for an actress, but she's genuinely talented, and that's what directors want. Sorry, I'm rambling.

"I knocked on next door's front door and waited. No answer. Tried again. Same. I went home, talked to Helen. She said she'd definitely seen him go into the house, and no, he definitely hadn't come out, so maybe he was in the garden? We decided to give it ten minutes. So, I went round again, knocked again. No answer. Tried a fourth time. Stood there like a complete muppet. At that point, I thought, 'why not go to the front window, have a look inside?'

Outlandish, I know, but by that time, I was beginning to think Helen must be mistaken. Maybe about the whole thing. Perhaps she was delusional. And, yes, I know how egregious an intrusion someone peeping through the front window might have seemed to anyone inside - how terrifying even - but I was desperate. As I'd got that bottle of wine out of the cupboard, I'd thought, 'maybe this is the answer, perhaps I can put the whole nightmare to bed now!'

"Anyway, that's what I did: looked through the front window into what must have been, or *was* technically, the living room. Which was completely unfurnished: clearly, no one was living there yet. And of course, there were no lights on. I was looking into a room rather like my own living room, but bare and gloomy.

"And then, I got the shock of my life. Mr Grandson just *appeared* from behind a wall. I don't mean supernaturally. No, there was a kind of semi-partition wall in the middle of the room, and he must have been standing behind it. He just stepped out, very decisively, as if he knew the effect it would have on me. Then he simply … *looked* at me. I collected myself with difficulty. I tried waving, tapping on the glass, smiling, holding up the wine. No response.

"And then – you think this story's been crazy so far, just wait till you hear this! - I got the impression that his face was… *dissolving,* becoming exactly like the face in the photo. Becoming something rather hideous. I say 'got the impression', but, believe me, it was no optical illusion. I suppose I *would* say that.

"Within a few seconds, I couldn't stay there any longer. As it was, I'd almost dropped the wine. I hurried home and locked myself in the bathroom for five minutes, so Helen wouldn't see how mortified I was. When I came out, she asked me how I'd fared and so on, and I said, 'sadly, he's still not answering the door', and we agreed that he must have gone into his back garden, then left the premises by his back gate. Or maybe he was asleep, or deaf, or just plain unsociable. In any case, we'd saved ourselves an excellent bottle of wine plus the inconvenience of having to give him the conventional neighbourly guided tour of our house – because that's what it'd have come to – and so we were the winners.

"But neither of us felt that way. *I* didn't, and I could tell Helen didn't, despite her wonderfully brave face. Somehow, we were doomed."

Silence.

"So should we call the police *now?"* Lionel asked. "I stand by my original theory, by the way."

"So how do explain the fact that I heard her laughing? That she's next door?"

"Tom, listen to - "

"You said you'd go and check. You said you'd humour me. 'Happy to oblige': those were your words, and on that basis, I told you what had brought me to this point. So, I've fulfilled my end of the bargain. Now it's your turn. And don't expect me to come with you. If I do, you'll probably claim I'm putting ideas into your head, and it's all your unconscious mind, blah, blah, blah, being influenced by yours truly. Not that you won't claim that anyway, probably."

"Tom, *you* called me round here. I'm not in the habit of coming out to my patients in the early hours of the morning. I'm here because I'm genuinely concerned."

Tom put his hands together in a prayerful attitude. "Of course, yes. Apologies. Genuine apologies." He wept. "Oh my God, I'm sorry, Dr Rosembaum. I'm just… Helen… I love her *so much*. If I've lost her, I don't know what I'm going to *do!*"

"Stay here. I'll be back in ten minutes." Lionel looked at his watch. 4.30am. He patted Tom on the shoulder in what he hoped was a reassuring, we're-still-friends manner, and walked out onto the street.

The house in which Helen was allegedly located looked like a face: wide, stupid eyes at the top, an open mouth, a bit like – and he knew it was hackneyed - *The Scream*. To dispel the illusion, he walked up to the front door. He was about to knock when he realised it was slightly ajar. For the first time that night, he felt unequivocally perturbed. He knocked anyway. He called, 'Hello, is anyone home?' then walked cautiously inside.

He was immediately aware of a presence. No one was at home – he felt that too, and equally unambiguously – but he definitely wasn't alone. The watcher, whoever or whatever it was, was robustly hostile, and possibly only one of a number.

The temptation to leave at speed was almost overwhelming, but he'd come here to do a job, and he was allowing his unconscious fears to take hold of him. He remembered Tom's words - *you'll probably claim it's all your unconscious mind, blah, blah, blah* – and tried to force a laugh.

He couldn't. Whatever was happening to him, it wasn't funny. His throat was dry.

He walked up the stairs, into all of the empty rooms in turn, and gradually – in some way he couldn't begin to account for - he came to realise that what Tom had said was true. Helen Battersby Van Dijk really was here.

There was no laughter, nothing audible or otherwise manifest to the five senses, but the conviction of her presence was irresistible - in a way it hadn't been even when she'd been physically in front of him, lying on his couch, or sitting next to her husband.

And somehow, it was horrible.

The house was uncomplicated. A ground floor and an upstairs: seven rooms in total, none furnished, all entirely empty. At his own estimate, it took him twenty minutes, including the exterior, to complete his survey. The garden felt like it was in another part of the world, or even on a different planet. Lurking shapes, dark tunnels, grotesque foliage. Throughout his exploration, he felt ridiculously self-conscious, ludicrously as if he was being scrutinised and found wanting.

When he finally closed the front door gently behind him, it was with considerable relief. Time to call the police. Tom would naturally wonder where he'd been, but he only needed tell the truth: he'd found the front door open, he'd had a good look around, he'd found nothing. He looked at his watch. 7am.

Which … hang on. *Seven o'clock in the morning?* He'd left Tom at 4.30! It had taken him twenty minutes at most to explore the house!

He suddenly noticed: it was light.

So, his watch wasn't wrong. It really *was* 7am!

How the …?

He walked back into the Battersby Van Dijks house. Disconcertingly, the door was ajar, but he realised that was how he'd left it. He was allowing himself to be spooked by association. But then, he *was* spooked.

Tom was asleep on the sofa. He jerked awake. "Where on earth have you been?" he asked.

It took Lionel a moment to respond. His reassuring lies dropped away like the petals of a dead flower. "I – I honestly don't know," he said.

VIII.

They told the police. Tom rang his BBC line manager. He explained that his wife had gone missing and that he needed at least a few days' leave to help coordinate a search. Lionel went home, bathed, changed into a new set of clothes and arrived at his office just after 9.30. He lumbered sleepily through a full roster of patients, returned home, and called Tom just after 6pm.

"I'm worried the police are going to start suspecting *me*," Tom said. "That's not my main worry, obviously. Helen's my main worry. I was just about to call you. There are two possibilities as far as I can see. Either Mr Grandson's abducted her – she mentioned he might be a stalker when he first came round here, and maybe that was a reliable intuition – or she's gone somewhere that's somehow 'important' to her; somewhere she might have mentioned under hypnosis? But then, I'm also aware," he went on, without allowing Lionel to respond, "that she must have woken up by now. Obviously she must. So where is she? Why hasn't she come home? Abduction's the only possibility."

"Have you mentioned all this to the police?"

"Absolutely. The problem's been convincing them that Mr Grandson even *exists,* let alone that he's behind her disappearance. He's not in that house. And the estate agent's not giving anything away; they say the police need a warrant. And I've no real reason to believe Mr Grandson had anything against us. *That non-existent person,* I hear the police thinking. And I realise I sound mad, even to myself."

"Could she be with a friend, or a relative?" It suddenly occurred to him that she might have decided to leave her husband, and this was her chosen means. Why hadn't he thought of that before?

Because nothing in her body language had suggested it, that's why. Not remotely.

But then, the mind didn't necessarily work that way. Unconscious desires were often at odds with everything a person thought they wanted.

"I've talked to her parents," Tom continued. "They were on holiday in Tuscany. They're on their way home. They'll investigate the relatives-possibility. As for friends, well, she doesn't have that many. Not close ones. I'm still ringing round, just on the off chance. No stone unturned. Meantime, I've got to stay here, in the house, in case she gets back. I've got the Strawsons here, being 'supportive'. The police want to speak to you too, obviously. They'll probably come round to your house at some point tonight. I take it you're at home?"

"I've just got in. It'll help that I can confirm she was as worried about this 'Mr Grandson' as you were."

"I should really be out there, on the streets, looking for her. But what good would that *do?* I wouldn't know where to *start!* Why has no one reported her? Woman in a lilac nightie, bare feet? If she was at large, someone would have noticed. She's been abducted. Pretty soon, I'll be the prime suspect, I know I will."

There was a knock at the front door. Lionel hung up.

Two policemen stood on the doorstep. Could they ask him a few questions in connection with a missing person?

He invited them in, sat them down, gave them tea. They wanted to know his connection to Helen, when he'd last seen her, how consistent he thought her sudden disappearance was with his diagnosis, whether he had any idea where she might be now, how long ago he'd been in touch with Tom. They knew nothing about his exploration of the vacant property next door to the Battersby Van Dijks'. He didn't volunteer anything. After half an hour, they ran out of questions, and wound up with a noncommittal, 'She'll probably turn up', a calm closing of the notebook, and a putting away of the pen. He promised to contact them if he got any more information. They all stood up. He saw them out.

Afterwards, he felt uneasy. He realised he'd been trying to string their visit out. Why? Whence the uneasiness?

He didn't know.

He'd been awake a lot of last night, maybe that was it. He was dead on his feet. Another early night seemed wise.

He hoped it wouldn't be as weird or as wearing as the last one.

It suddenly struck him that he felt exactly the same as he had last night, in the house next door to the Battersby Van Dijks. *There was someone else in here*. A mysterious sense of certainty, and it was getting stronger.

He did a complete sweep of the house.

He found nothing. But then, he hadn't expected a direct encounter. It wasn't that sort of intuition. It was the unnerving sense of someone both less *and* more than real. Less real like a ghost; more real like a… well, that was the sinister thing: like a *what?*

He changed into his pyjamas and got into bed. What alternative did he have? He left his bedside light on. Darkness wasn't an option.

He lay awake. Dawn came. The sun gradually illuminated the curtains and crept into the room. He switched his bedside light off. Outside, the noise of traffic increased. He stayed in bed, vainly hoping that sleep might finally overtake him, until his alarm went off. He got up at seven, breakfasted on toast and marmalade, drank two strong cups of coffee in a desperate effort to energise himself, and set off for work.

As he ascended the narrow staircase to his office, he suddenly felt ill again, just as he had after his last-session-of-the-day appointment with the Battersby Van Dijks.

Perhaps he'd overdosed on caffeine.

But no, that seemed too optimistic.

He stepped into Sandra's room and asked her to cancel his first two appointments. She shot him a quizzical look, but didn't ask why. He asked her not to disturb him.

He lumbered into his office. It seemed crazy to even consider it, but maybe he could get some sleep on the chaise longue.

But no, it *wasn't* crazy. This was his mental health! He'd gone through a lot in the past forty-eight hours, and there was no reason to think he'd find sleep any easier tonight; not if he still felt paranoid (and since he didn't know precisely what was causing it, why shouldn't he?) He'd burn out if he wasn't careful.

He laid his jacket gently on the armchair, removed his shoes, and went straight to the chaise longue. He wished he'd foregone that coffee now, but it couldn't be helped.

He took a long time getting to sleep, but when he finally succumbed, he knew he was dreaming and it felt as vivid as if he was awake. In this state, he put his jacket and shoes on, left the office at speed, and made for the town centre. He didn't know where he was going yet, but his 'body' seemed to have made up its mind.

He mounted the steps to the public library. Inside, it was much bigger, lighter and airier than he remembered. Futuristic, actually. Which was because he was dreaming, obviously, but the whole thing seemed so real, that he'd almost forgotten he wasn't really there.

A dark-haired man of about thirty, dressed in a tweed waistcoat, stood behind the loans and returns desk. He wore an accommodating expression. "How can I help you?" he asked.

"I'm looking for a specific book," Lionel told him. "I'm pretty certain you won't have a copy on your shelves, but there might be one in your reserve collection." He didn't know how he knew there was a reserve collection. But then this was *his* dream, so of course there was. "It's called, *The Interesting Life of Pierre Albert Bernard de Sale, Comte de Mauripois, Mesmerist and Tragic Exile.*"

The man's expression darkened. "We do have such a thing," he said.

"If it's not too much trouble, please could you fetch it for me?"

"We never let that particular book leave the basement. Not that we have many enquiries about it. Yours is the first."

The question, *If I'm the first, what made you decide not to let it out of the basement?* seemed pointless. Given that this was a dream, it could have no rational answer.

Nevertheless, he felt compelled to ask it. He followed the librarian through a glass door and down a metal staircase. "If I'm the first - "

"You *would* ask that," the librarian said contemptuously. "What annoys me about all this is that you still think you're *so* clever! 'Well,' you thought, 'the local library must have a copy' - as if the *rarity* of the book's the sole issue! Has it never occurred to you to wonder, not about the *book*, but about its *author?*"

"You mean - "

"'Dr BLN Pike'!"

"Why did you say it like that? I mean, as if in scare quotes?"

The librarian scoffed. His excitement decreased a notch. "Yes, you're right: almost as if there never *was* any 'Dr BLN Pike'; as if the name was entirely made up."

"I don't know - "

"Well, it was. Equally, there was no 'print-run of a hundred copies': that's also drivel." He stopped so abruptly that Lionel almost bumped into him.

The descent had become progressively darker: how much farther the stairs extended, Lionel couldn't see.

"Would you like me to tell you all about 'Dr BLN Pike'?" the librarian continued. "You know I'm going to anyway, because, from your perspective, this whole thing's a dream, and, well, you only have limited control over how it unfolds, haven't you? So be it, then, I'm happy to oblige. The thing about 'Dr BLN Pike' is, he thought he could emulate the great Pierre Albert Bernard de Sale, Comte de Mauripois. You know what happened to the Comte, don't you, Dr Rosembaum? No; you see, you don't even know *that!* Well, he launched himself, and those seven women he mesmerised, on the road to immortality. I don't know how he knew there was such a thing as 'the Big Bang', or that the universe had been, in its early stages, mainly ferrous – Physics didn't discover those things until at least a century and a half after his 'death' – those scare quotes again! – but somehow, he worked out that immortality could be achieved by physically reversing himself, with an exponentially multiplying velocity, through each of the universe's prior stages, and finally passing through the eye of the needle which is 'The Singularity': capital T, capital S. Somehow, the means to that regression was that *baquet* of his. Anyway, 'Dr BLN Pike' – real name, Roger Pearson, BSc. part-time civil servant, autodidact and amateur sword-swallower – somehow discovered all this – no one knows exactly how, but black magic's a plausible suggestion - and tried to repeat the feat. And failed. But not entirely. You see, he became immortal, but like poor old Tithonus in that hilarious Greek legend: stuck in the present, minus the consoling boon of eternal youth. In fact, Roger grew old exponentially, with the unpleasant result that, nowadays, he's not really recognisable as a human. Oh, *and* he's angry, incredibly angry. *And* insane, which may be for the best, since perhaps it helps him cope. Here we are."

They were in between two rows of bookshelves in an almost impenetrable, slate-grey gloom.

"Of course, what no one told Roger Pearson," the librarian continued, "is that there's only one way to follow the illustrious Comte – *truly follow* in his footsteps, I mean – and that's by descending *through* the cellar of whatever house he once lived in. I say 'through' not 'into' because, according to the story, that cellar's only the beginning of a long, long journey. Anyway, since no one can possibly locate the house anymore, let alone the cellar, it's academic. The worthy burghers of Tunbridge Wells – those who'd been affected, anyway - razed it to the ground with him inside it. Or that's the story; no one knows whether it's true or not: you'd have to know where he lived in order to ascertain that. It might simply be what they *wished* they'd done. The only *certain* thing is that the Comte vanished from the face of the Earth. But then, so did the girls. Girls, not women. They got younger and younger until, one day – poof! Maybe he went the same way. Of course, murder was a capital offence in those days, so there was probably very good reason to sweep every little fact of the matter under the carpet. In the locals' defence, most of them believed someone might try to replicate his - whatever-it-was – *experiment* on the Pantiles. And they were absolutely right, of course, but sadly, they were also a hundred years too soon to stop it. Poor Roger. He's down here, you know."

"What do you mean?"

"He lives down here. Or so I've been told. I've never seen him myself, but I have the information on very good authority. Of course, it's such a big place, that the chances of coming across him on a visit like this are infinitesimal. Anyway" – he plucked a volume from the shelf and handed it to Lionel – "there you are: *The Interesting Life*. I'm sure you won't mind making your own way back upstairs, will you?"

Lionel wanted to say, *Don't leave me*, but, as on the journey from his office, his actions were rigidly constrained. "Thank you for your help," he croaked.

He opened *The Interesting Life.* It was the expanded version – the same, he assumed, as the one he'd dream-read in his bedroom two nights ago – only this time, he was able to digest its contents at great speed. It finished with a description of the furore surrounding the seven women who had entered the Comte de Mauripois's *baquet* in 1804, how their families made vigorous attempts to find a cure, in tandem with desperate measures to conceal their plight, which, they felt, was worsening by the day. The girls themselves – to the extent that their reactions were recorded, and this was not an age in which young women's feelings on exigent practical matters were generally considered worth documenting - fluctuated between terrible anxiety and intense exultation.

The more he read, the more Lionel became aware of a menacing presence somewhere just nearby, the same one he'd intuited last night and the night before, but this time much closer, and far more focused. He flicked to the final few pages of the book. He read several ludicrous paragraphs about the prevalence of iron in the early universe. He tried to keep reading, but he realised the darkness was intensifying. And something was rearing up almost in front of him, with him in its sights. Yes, it was a *creature* of some sort – it was utterly *repulsive* - and it was going to – *ingest* him. *And he couldn't move!* My God, he had to wake up! *Wake up!*

"Wake up! Wake up, Dr Rosembaum!"

His eyes filled with tears of extreme trauma, as if his body thought filling them with water would somehow increase his ability to resist. He dropped the book ready to fend off the thing, but his arms wouldn't move. He screamed, but without sound.

He jerked awake to find himself lying on the chaise longue.

"Dr Rosembaum!" A feminine laugh. "I think you must have been dreaming!"

The real world sprang into view. It contained his office, and a woman's face – Sandra's? - and a smell like mingled soil and sweat. For a second, he was so relieved he almost wept with gratitude. Then he realised: that face: it wasn't Sandra's.

It belonged to Helen Battersby Van Dijk.

And he really was awake now. You might or might not know when you were dreaming, but you always knew when you were awake.

He was *awake!* Thank God!

He got to his feet. Meanwhile, Helen Battersby Van Dijk had retired to the armchair. She wore a lilac nightie –

presumably the one Tom had mentioned - and, as far as Lionel could tell, nothing else. Her hair was dishevelled. Her bare feet were muddy. There were thin scratches on her arms and her calves. She wore a wide grin.

Lionel found his throat and made it produce a sound. "How - ?"

"I don't really know," she said.

He suddenly had the odd feeling that maybe he'd misidentified her, despite all the compelling markers. Her face somehow didn't match Helen's.

Although, that might be the mysteries of makeup. Or lack of it.

But no, no, it wasn't.

"I went down into the cellar," she said, before he could conclude this line of thought. "Yes, there really is a cellar there. And - "

"Pardon me for interrupting. Does Tom know you're here? Do the police?"

She laughed. "What do the *police* want with me?"

"You disappeared. Tom called them. They're looking for you. And Tom's pretty frantic."

"I want to talk to you first."

He was a psychologist. He knew when to let a patient have her way. Tom and the police could wait.

"How did you get in here?" he asked. "I mean, did Sandra show you in?"

"Your receptionist? No, she was looking in a drawer. I just passed her office. I'd probably have said hello if she'd looked up, but she didn't. And your office wasn't locked. Apologies if I interrupted your sleep, but this is important."

"I'm very happy to see you. And frankly, it was more of a nightmare, so I'm more than glad to be back in the room."

"A nightmare about Roger Pearson, BSc. part-time civil servant, autodidact and amateur sword-swallower, if I'm not mistaken."

The room, apparently so solid since his awakening, suddenly did a full revolution. Maybe this *was* a dream, after all. If so, how the hell to snap out of it? "Er, how did you know that?"

"It's one of the many things I learned. Just listen. You don't have to say anything. There really is a cellar. And that man – Mr Grandson – who came to our house? He's the *actual Comte*. Yes, I know, it's amazing! He met me down there, in the cellar. And he's ever so nice. He's got all this mesmerist equipment, and, well, he wants me and Tom and Roger to join him. He really wants Roger: he didn't expect Roger to do what he did, and he feels bad about it, but he's open to me and Tom coming along, and, hey, why would *anyone* say no? Repeat: he wants us all to join him. He and his companions, the seven girls in the metal sculpture I told you about. They're not really children anymore. They were once, about five years ago, which is about a century and a half in their world. They went backwards in time, you see. They're all ages old now. Imagine that! Time, where they are, isn't like a straight line. Not exactly, anyway. It is, a *bit,* obviously, otherwise how could they still be going backwards? Strictly speaking, though, it doesn't exist. But then, it doesn't for any of us. Anyway, he wants me and Tom to join him, and bring Roger, and, er… That's it. Long story short, we won't be coming for any more appointments. I thought I'd better let you know."

"I see," Lionel said.

Silence.

"How did you get here?" Lionel asked. "I mean, you went down into some phantom 'cellar' – Tom says he saw you, by the way, if that's any consolation - "

"I don't need consoling. I'm ecstatic, or hadn't you noticed? Yes, Tom saw me. Of course he did, *because that's what happened*. But, please, excuse me for interrupting. Finish your sentence."

"How did you get here? You went underground, or that's what you think. Now you're back on the surface."

"I walked up a staircase and I found myself in Woodbury Park Cemetery. It's about five minutes from here, which I considered auspicious. And here I am."

Lionel realised there was no point gainsaying her. She clearly wasn't in her right mind. Yet she was capable of an accurate self-diagnosis, though not much of one: she really was ecstatic. In any case, it could be shock, or disorientation, or relief.

Or could she have taken some mind-altering drug?

No, she didn't seem the type.

Or she *hadn't*. People changed. She'd changed.

That unsettling feeling again: maybe he'd misidentified her. She both looked and didn't look like Helen Battersby Van Dijk.

"So, what are you going to do now?" he asked, partly by way of stilling his thoughts.

"In about five minutes, you're going to pick up your phone; you're going to call Tom, and Tom will come down here, and he'll say, 'Thank God you're safe', then – and it'll probably take him a few minutes, just as it's taken you – he'll look closely at me, and he'll say, 'Something about you is different.' And we'll laugh. And I'll say, 'Look at the crow's feet round my eyes. Or rather don't, because they've gone! And the lines around my mouth? Ditto.' And he'll say, 'You've – I don't know…' And I'll say, 'Become younger?' And he'll say, 'Yes, that's what it looks like, but…' And so on. There's nothing good about being younger, by the way. I used to think there was. By 'used to', I mean: yesterday and since being about twenty-five. But Tom will probably think it's good. Until he learns what I have. Then he'll realise it's not worth a fig."

"Okay, well, er, I suppose I'd better call him."

"There's one question you haven't asked. But I suppose that's probably because, unlike me, you're not thinking straight. Would you like me to tell you what it is?"

He spluttered a laugh, though he didn't feel like laughing. "Please."

"Okay, so there's a phantom trapdoor in the floor where Tom and I live. *Allegedly*. I can open it. Maybe Tom can follow me, if I hold his hand tightly enough. But what about Roger Pearson, BSc. part-time civil servant, autodidact and amateur sword-swallower? How's *he* going to join us? He is, after all, the main event, so to speak."

"I don't know the answer to that question."

"Everything's connected. You might recall that Roger entered you, just now, in that library. So, you've got Roger, and now that I'm sitting here with you, I've got Roger. In the name of research, I'm about to invite you to come and keep watch over me tomorrow night, on the shared assumption that I'll go 'sleepwalking' again, and you'll be able to provide a rational explanation for all the 'nonsense', as you see it, that I've been spouting since you found me sitting here, plus a scratch or two, M&S nightie a little the worse for wear, hair all over the joint, feet plastered with mud, but otherwise A-OK, right before your very eyes. As a devout rationalist, and a would-be scientist to boot, you'll have no alternative but to accept my invitation, hence you'll bring Roger Pearson, BSc. etc. to the party. Game, set and match. Which is the sort of thing it's conventional for a smart aleck to say in these sorts of circumstances, *n'est pas?*"

She not only didn't look like Helen Battersby Van Dijk. She wasn't even the same person. The former version had been shy, retiring and incorrigibly serious. This one –

"Time to ring Thomas now," she said.

IX.

He accepted her invitation to 'keep watch over her'. He arrived at the couple's house at 8pm. They offered him a drink. He accepted, and kept his hip-flask in reserve for the time being. When they went to bed at ten, he drained it. He already knew what was going to happen, and in the name of science, he wanted to tell himself he'd been drunk when it happened, so maybe... maybe it *hadn't* happened.

Yes, he was in danger of despising himself. Maybe he'd always know it *had* happened.

But how could he?

By 2am, he was sufficiently gone to be seeing double. He'd never been this drunk before, and, although he knew - obviously – that alcohol could do this to people, he'd always believed that perhaps he was different: perhaps it couldn't affect him to this degree. He stood on the landing. Suddenly, Helen Battersby Van Dijk appeared. She ran downstairs, clutching Tom's hand. A trapdoor materialised. A man appeared.

'A man': science be damned, name him, Lionel!

Roger Pearson, probably. BSc. part-time civil servant, autodidact and sword-swallower.

Helen pulled open the trapdoor. The three persons descended. The trapdoor closed. The trapdoor disappeared.

Lionel went to the drinks cabinet. He wanted to drink till he passed out, but, even in his present condition, he knew that wouldn't be sensible. He needed to leave while it was still dark. The Battersby Van Dijks had gone for good, and foul play might be suspected. And he might become the prime suspect.

He poured himself a large brandy, then wiped the whole house for fingerprints, laughing as he did so, because he knew nothing about 'wiping for fingerprints': it was something he'd picked up from American cop shows. Nowadays, they probably had more sophisticated ways of finding out who'd been there.

He poured himself another brandy before he left. He raised his glass. *To the US cops!*

He let himself out at 3am, closing the front door gently behind him.

He'd been drunk. It couldn't have been what it seemed. There had to be a rational explanation.

He looked at the sky. The universe lay spread out like a sparkly black sheet: stars, nebulae, constellations, galaxies, black holes, supernovae: astrology and astronomy side-by-side, as they always necessarily were.

My God, it was *beautiful!*

X.

Something loosened in Tunbridge Wells that night. Two months afterwards, a French historian from the University of Marseille – 'Professeure Mireille Daudigny' - discovered a memoir penned by The Comte de Mauripois in the archives of her university library. She then managed to uncover the story of his English adventures, including the seven women he'd supposedly magicked into thin air. After an initial double-take, Tunbridge Wells audaciously claimed him as their own, despite the fact that he was obviously a multiply debauched rake (*seven* young women, my goodness!)

The forgotten art of Mesmerism was revived on the Pantiles. After paying exorbitant fees for the privilege, tourists sat in *baquets* on the upper precinct, clutching iron rods and giggling nervously. Some even claimed to have supernatural experiences. But then, there were lots of pubs nearby, and anyone who'd just parted with a lot of money was naturally predisposed to wishful thinking. Thankfully, the local media outlets loved it. Tunbridge Wells is, to my knowledge, the only place in the whole world where Mesmerism, in its original incarnation, is still given a regular run-out. Probably because it chimes so well with all the 'Chalybeate' stuff. All in all, it's great fun.

Lionel Rosembaum died two months after the events recorded above. The illness he'd experienced on two occasions in this story turned out to be an aggressive form of cancer; nevertheless, his demise may have been aggravated by his 'misguided attempt' (as he put it) to cling to a rationalistic account of something that defied rational explanation, and his realisation that 'drunkenness' just wouldn't cut it. Against all the seeming odds, however, he died in a state of rapture.

A coda. For the benefit of those who believe in ghosts, his 'wraith' has apparently been spotted, by several reputable people, in the local cemetery on Benhall Mill Road, where he was buried; and always in company with two young men and a blonde-haired woman. I don't pretend to know how that is supposed to fit with the rest of this story, so please don't ask me. Anyway, it's a nice idea. Perhaps where he is now – if he's anywhere at all – nothing is absurd.

The Antique Jewellery Box

I.

Of all the cases I ever took on, I think Sophie Balaskas's was the most exciting - and spine-tingling! Oh, I don't believe in anything along the lines of the supernatural, not personally. But some people do, and since what people believe conditions what they see, hear, taste, smell, and think they've touched – it's a filter, in other words, through which they interpret the data – I believe that a good many honest people *think* they have firm *evidence* for the supernatural. As far as I'm concerned, what happened with Sophie Balaskas wasn't the stuff of ghosts, fairies, and demons, but, yes, it *was* strange. And it was what's sometimes called 'a roller-coaster'. I wouldn't have missed it for the world.

As you've probably guessed, I'm a private detective. As a species, we don't have much fun, as a rule; not at work: mostly, it's chasing documents, or spying on unfaithful partners, or finding out who's about to make a game-changing business deal behind someone else's back. I'm retired now. Male, white, sixty-four, slight paunch, grey hair – *grey* not *white!* - stumpy legs, bottle of scotch permanently to hand in my desk drawer (yes, I know, I'm a walking cliché!): Colin, that's me. How do you do, yes.

Anyway, you want to hear the story, I take it? The Sophie Balaskas story? That's good, because I'm going to tell you it anyway. Might as well. It makes me look interesting, and, as for you, what else are you going to do? It's snowing outside, and that wind's a nightmare: it's getting stronger by the minute. Look at the fir trees – *whoa!* look at them *go!* - Believe me, there'll be no skiing today, lady.

Okay, so, it all happened in Tunbridge Wells, a long way from here. I know what you're thinking: Tunbridge Wells, capital of stasis, the town where nothing ever happens and everyone's a Conservative. Well, actually, yes – and no. And it doesn't matter. Sophie lived there with her husband, Paul – well, she didn't live In Tunbridge Wells proper, she lived in *Southborough:* important distinction for some people, but to my mind Southborough's a part of Tunbridge Wells, like a suburb, but actually *attached* to the town, so that –

Yes, sorry, you're absolutely right: who cares? Anyway, Sophie and Paul, Sophie and Paul, Sophie and Paul. They were about forty-five. She had black hair. Quite tall. Olive complexion, I think her parents were Greek. He – Paul – was a bit of a health freak: liked to work out at the gym. Good haircut, slim; bit of an introvert, though. He had a harpsichord in the garage, and he wasn't a bad player, though he kept failing his Grade Three. Silver hair, stubbly beard, the sort of guy who wears sunglasses even when it's raining, which Sophie definitely wasn't. As far as I know, they were very happy together. They didn't have any children, which probably helped. They did have a myna bird called Spam, but it doesn't play any part in this story. You can forget about it if you like. I only mentioned it to indicate the sort of couple they were.

Anyway, one day Sophie walked into a niche little antique jewellery shop on the Pantiles and -

… The Pantiles. It's essentially a long pavement at the bottom of what's now the main part of Tunbridge Wells. With bespoke shops. The oldest part of the town. Anyway, she went into a shop there, and she came out with a jewellery box. About three centimetres by three by three, a perfect cube.

It was partly that which attracted her to it, so she said – her 'geometrical bent', if you can believe it; that, and the fact that it was covered with what looked like Egyptian hieroglyphics, but weren't. I mean, it looked like its creator had been *inspired* by Egyptian script to create something similar but obviously original, and, whoever that artist was, he or she had managed to paint the designs onto the box with astonishing skill. The finished product looked exquisite: her words, not mine. I'm not much of a connoisseur of jewellery boxes.

She paid the shopkeeper fifty pounds. He wrapped it in tissue paper, like they do in these places, and put it in an expensive bag with red string handles. On her way out, she bumped into a tall, thin man of about fifty. He wore a long grey overcoat and a collar and tie, plus he held a briefcase, so in that sense, he looked well-presented, but there was something about him, she said, that suggested the opposite. A certain something in his general demeanour, perhaps, and in the fact that, although his outfit was respectable, it was in poor condition, as if it had been through too many washes … or too few.

Anyway, that wasn't the only strange thing about him, not by a long chalk. Somehow, he seemed to know what Sophie was doing there. He knew she'd bought a specific jewellery box, and, not to put too fine a point on it, he wanted it.

I don't know how their exchange went, or precisely how fraught it was, but he offered her a hundred pounds, then two hundred, then – incredibly – a thousand.

Well, I ask you: what would you have done in her situation?

It's difficult to say, isn't it? Obviously, every new offer might simply confirm your suspicion that you've just made the purchase of the century. One hundred pounds: *gosh, it must be worth two!* Two hundred pounds: *wow, maybe it's worth four!* A thousand: *maybe it's worth ten!* And so on. You get the picture.

But then you get outside the shop. Mr Desperate-to-purchase with the briefcase has stomped off in an obvious huff, and you think to yourself: maybe it *is* only worth fifty, after all. Put it this way: the jeweller didn't look sorry to have sold it, and surely he'd know. Maybe it just had some sort of private, idiosyncratic value for Mr Desperate. In which case, you've just passed over the chance to make nine hundred and fifty pounds. How do you feel about *that,* Mug?

So, I can tell you how Sophie felt. It took all the pleasure out of her shopping expedition. She put the box in her bag, and when she got home, she gave it another appraisal. This time, she couldn't see what had attracted her to it in the first place. So not only had she failed to cash in on it, but she'd wasted fifty pounds. I dare say she felt angry with herself, and rather depressed. I'd have been inconsolable. Fifty pounds – sheesh; for *that*. But maybe she wasn't too put out. Some people have got money to burn.

She decided not to mention it to Paul – not because she was in the habit of keeping things from him: she wasn't – but because she simply wanted to put the whole dispiriting episode behind her. She put it in a drawer in the dressing table in the spare bedroom, where she hoped she wouldn't have to see it again for a long time. When one day, she finally re-encountered it, perhaps she'd feel sufficiently disinterested to put it on eBay. In which case, she might get some of her money back. If Mr Desperate saw it, she might get a lot, assuming anyone else cared to bid.

But they probably wouldn't.

II.

A few nights went by before she noticed there was a funny noise coming from somewhere within the house, and that it kept coming back. It sounded like gnawing, which is what she thought it was, to begin with. Rats.

Which was very disturbing, since… well, I don't have to explain why 'rats' is very disturbing, do I? The question was – and this was something she and Paul thought they'd have to ascertain before they called pest-control in – where *exactly* was it coming from?

They listened in vain at the skirting boards. They tried several nights in a row to follow the sound to its source, but it always stopped before they could pinpoint a precise location. It would begin in the early hours of the morning, when they were both asleep – a faint juddering at first, but gradually increasing in volume – and then die away to nothing when they tried to undertake a search.

By the end of the second week, it had become much louder, as if the rats no longer cared much about being discovered. Even so, it still tailed off before the crucial discovery could be made. By this time, Sophie and Paul were pretty much at their wits' end. I don't think it was the noise in itself; I think it was the thought that, the longer they left calling in some sort of exterminator, the more damage the rodents would likely have done. I don't really know why they didn't just ask the professionals to do the locating. Maybe they didn't like spending money – I mean, on that sort of thing; not on antique jewellery boxes of dubious aesthetic value, obviously.

In the end, it was Paul who made the breakthrough. He got up one night, and crept along the landing in his bare feet. He followed the noise into the spare bedroom.

A minute later, he called his wife.

She went to him. He was laughing: a good laugh: a laugh of relief. "Do you know anything about this?" he said.

The dressing table drawer hung open. Paul stood with the jewellery box on his flattened palm. It was vibrating.

"It's an antique," she told him. "I bought it in The Pantiles."

"And did you *know* it did this?"

"No, definitely not. Is that what the sound was?"

"I think so, yes. Hallelujah, if I'm right. I mean, not that being awoken at some Godforsaken hour every morning's a good thing, but at least we won't have to get someone in. Think of the money we've saved."

"*If* that's what's causing it."

He opened it and looked inside. "What's making it *do* that?"

"Maybe some sort of clockwork?"

"It would be visible. And you'd have to wind it up. And something would have to set it off. There's nowhere for a battery to go, and it can't be solar powered, not if it's been in the drawer all day; which I assume it has, since this isn't where you'd put your everyday stuff, is it?"

"I put it in there some time ago. I haven't had it out since."

He turned it over in his hands. "It's odd, isn't it? Quite interesting to look at. Anyway, mystery solved. No rats, no monumental expense. We can probably both get to sleep now, no matter how loud it becomes."

"I hope so."

So, back to bed. Over the next few nights, it continued to rattle, although Paul was right: without the implication of rats, it wasn't so bothersome.

Even so, they'd have to get rid of it. Given that it was definitely valuable, putting it in the bin wasn't an option.

III.

"I've got a friend of a friend coming to have a look at that jewellery box of yours," Paul announced, over dinner, a week later. "That is, assuming you still want to get shot of it, do you? How much should we ask?"

"Whoever it is can *have* it for all I care," Sophie said. "I'd just like to get a good night's sleep. Okay, I'm exaggerating: it's not that annoying. And it should be worth something."

"You paid fifty pounds for it."

"I'd take twenty-five. No, make that ten. Who's your buyer?"

"A 'Jeffrey Soames'. I don't know him personally. A friend of David's. David Lawson? In Accounts? You met him when we went to Il Vesuvio that time. Tall guy, jeans, Country and Western shirt - "

"The brogues with silver buckles man?"

"That's him. I got him interested just in time. He's leaving a week from now: some big firm in Leeds head-hunted him. All very underhand, and, of course, Management's furious. Anyway, Jeffrey Soames is a friend of his. A Physicist. I told him how freaked out we are by the fact that it keeps rattling, and that we're utterly at a loss to understand how it's doing it. I gave him – David, I mean - a demonstration at work, and he couldn't figure it out either. He took a quick video on his phone, showed it to his friends. Anyway, Soames apparently likes little puzzles, and he's been looking for the Holy Grail of a perpetual motion machine all his life – you know, like all Physicists do? – and David persuaded him to take a look at ours."

"Maybe that's really what it is. That man in the jeweller's seemed eager to get it off me."

"What man?"

She swallowed her pride. The reason she hadn't told him yet was because maybe it made her look stupid.

On the other hand, she hadn't taken advantage of 'an eccentric old man', as she now styled him; nor had she fallen for some kind of scam (which it *could* have been; had she accepted the thousand pounds, who knows? there might have been all manner of terms and conditions attached! and, in her eagerness to get her hands on the money and prove what a remarkably clever haggler she was, she might well have accepted them without due diligence. Next thing she knew: *bang,* there went her identity!)

This was roughly how she pitched it to her husband. She'd kept a clear head, and yes, she might not be nine hundred odd pounds better off, but nor was she worse off, and, on a level-headed interpretation, she might even have avoided a catastrophe for both of them. Everyone knew that Britain was now the scam-capital of the world.

"Well done, Soph," Paul said, reassuringly. "Better safe than sorry. I mean, let's face it, what's the likelihood that a secret agent in search of a perpetual motion machine would be hanging about on the Pantiles, at exactly the same moment you bought that jewellery box?"

"And that he wouldn't have known that that's what it was, until after I'd bought it?"

"Probably a crank. I mean, what sort of man wanders round with a thousand pounds in his pocket? No one. You had a lucky escape. Once these people realise you're interested, there's no getting away from them."

"Hear, hear."

So, all was apparently well that ended well. The odd thing is – as they later told me – neither of them quite thought this fully accounted for the facts. The man on the Pantiles remained enigmatic, despite their best efforts to consign him definitively to the category of cheats, fraudsters and round-the-clock mountebanks.

Jeffrey Soames knocked on their door two days later. A stout, bald man in a blazer and corduroy trousers, he had little tufts of grey hair growing from his nostrils and ears. He was a retired professor, he told them. They showed him the box, which remained annoying inanimate, and invited him to make an offer.

"You bought it for fifty pounds," he said, "and I understand you're eager to get rid of it. Would you accept fifty pounds? Once I've unlocked its secret – which shouldn't take me long, although, I admit, I haven't yet got a theory – it should double as a birthday present for my wife. Providing we can knock that infernal shaking on the head, I mean."

"Fifty pounds sounds more than generous," Sophie said.

He gave them five ten-pound notes, pocketed the box, shook both their hands, and bade them good night. They heard his car pull away outside.

And somehow, the conviction took hold of both of them – particularly of Sophie, but to some extent of Tom too – that they'd made a terrible mistake.

IV.

They were right about that, of course. You see, Sophie started, well, *seeing things*. There's no other way to put it, really… and I'm not insisting those things weren't there, but I'm not sure they *can* have been. That man she met, coming out of the jewellers – the one who offered her a cool K? – well, she kept spotting him out of the corner of her eye, and usually at the most unexpected moments. He'd be just in front of her in Sainsbury's and she'd register him as he disappeared into an aisle, and of course, when she went to look – no one; or she'd see him somewhere in town; again just before he slunk off behind a building, or into an alleyway.

Or in the countryside. Those were the worst ones, she said, especially at dusk… as you can probably imagine. And there's a lot of countryside in Tunbridge Wells – yes, actually *in* it. It's a peculiar town in that sense. Lots of expensive-looking old buildings, lots of trees, lots of slopes, and parts of it are quite downmarket, and then there's a completely modern bit: quite disorientating, or it can be. In sum, I'm sure the geography of the place didn't make things any easier for her.

It went from bad to worse, I'm afraid. It wasn't the *seeing* him that was the problem; it was the gradually increasing sense that their encounters were building to some unheard-of awfulness, something so far beyond her experience that she couldn't even begin to envisage it yet. This man felt like a representative of that. Whenever she caught a glimpse of his face, it looked - *eaten away*... yet as if that was completely normal where he came from. She began to expect it to happen to *her* at some point.

Mental health problems require mental health professionals, and she and Paul went to see a large number of those, all to no effect. Throughout her entire ordeal, Sophie insisted that the only way to begin to solve her problems was to treat them as if their cause was real; to take them seriously at face value. Most qualified practitioners considered that too much of a concession, which is why I think she ran through such a large number in such a short period.

Specifically, what she said she wanted was the box. She believed its return would precipitate her recovery, although she was never able to explain exactly how. It wasn't as if she'd found it comforting at any point during the period she'd owned it, or as if she'd had any attachment to it. Quite the opposite.

It was around about now that I entered the picture.

I'd never have been needed, had it not been for the fact that David Lawson – 'the brogues with silver buckles man'

– had moved jobs under something of a cloud. David Lawson was the Balaskas' only link to Jeffrey Soames. Finding him was thus a prerequisite for finding the hairy-nosed professor. Unfortunately, Paul didn't know him that well, and, for a variety of reasons, he wasn't able to find out where he'd gone. His colleagues behaved as if they were under an oath of secrecy. The firm that had employed him – Paul's firm - probably wouldn't have released any information about him anyway – data protection, and all that – but the fact that he'd left them in the lurch, giving so little notice before joining one of their biggest competitors, made them doubly loath to do so. They wanted to efface his memory, as firms often do in such circumstances. You can probably appreciate the difficulty of the problem.

Bringing me in was the last resort. Normally, when someone hires a private detective for the first time – especially if they'd never normally have considered such a thing in a million years – some day-old crisis has finally eliminated all vestiges of hesitation. In this case, Sophie had collapsed in Royal Victoria Place, just outside Fenwick's.

The Royal Victoria Place. It's like a big shopping mall, a kind of modern-day counterpart to the Pantiles, but at the opposite end of the town and – listen, it doesn't really matter, okay? It's not integral to the story.

Her collapse. No one knows what precipitated it, because, afterwards, she was unable, or maybe unwilling, to speak. She lay in bed at home, trembling and looking straight ahead all day. She stopped eating. The doctors didn't know what to do, not even the BUPA ones acquired at great expense.

Obviously, Paul thought he knew what had happened. He thought she'd seen the guy from the jeweller's, and the guy from the jeweller's had done something to put the fear of God into her.

When Paul came to see me in my office, a day later, he spent a long time explaining everything I've already told you, and of course I agreed to take the job. As I said earlier, it sounded like a barrel of monkeys. I didn't tell him that, obviously. I nodded solemnly, took a few notes, offered one or two vague reassurances, the sort of thing PD's are expected to do.

He asked me to do two things. Firstly, find the guy from the jeweller's.

Hmm, well, if he'd had nothing else to offer in terms of a goal, I'd have turned him down. I mean, the way he'd told the story, I wasn't convinced there was anyone to find. I don't think even *he* was a hundred percent sure.

Luckily, he'd foreseen my scepticism. So, the second part of my brief was to find Jeffrey Soames. He explained the difficulty, and, I must admit, I relaxed a bit. Challenging, but far from impossible.

We mulled over what we'd do when I found him. It wasn't even certain that Soames would still be in possession of the box, much less that he'd part with it, even for a significant sum of money. He might have solved its mystery and given it to his wife, he might have discovered something unexpected about it that made it worth its weight in gold, or he might have – well, why don't I let Paul Balaskas's fevered imagination take over here? Paul thought he might be a government agent, or a zombie, or a member of the Illuminati.

I don't know why he treated me to his theories: he should have realised they were a bit off-putting. No one wants to work with a crank. I tend to avoid crazies like the plague, but there are more of them in this business than you might think. Although, on second thoughts, perhaps it's not surprising: you're usually at the end of your tether when you hire a PD, so naturally you're going to be zany.

After he left, I got to thinking. The only way I was ever going to catch the guy from the jeweller's was if I accompanied Sophie everywhere she went. But it was too late for that, because she wasn't walking about anymore; not for the foreseeable, anyway.

Which meant I should concentrate on Jeffrey Soames.

As I'd anticipated, finding David Lawson was easy peasy. Simply a question of locating firms of a similar nature to the one he'd worked in alongside Paul, then narrowing my search to Leeds. Took me about fifteen minutes. Of course, I didn't tell Paul that. Not because I wanted any kind of extravagant praise, and definitely not because I wanted to string the job out, pump it for all the money it was worth. No, it was because, if he thought I'd gone to a lot of trouble, he'd be more willing to accompany me to Leeds. Think about it. He'd have to be the one to ask David Lawson where Soames was. Lawson would never give that sort of information to me, and gone were my days of putting thumbscrews on a mark, just to get him to sing.

I'm joking. I never used to do that, obviously.

The problem was that Paul wasn't keen on leaving Sophie alone, and, although she still wasn't talking, there were good reasons to think she didn't want to be left alone either. Thankfully, they had a wonderful neighbour called

Ms Something or Other, and she was able to come in for a small fee; I think she was more of a puppy-minder usually, but she was flexible. And, of course, they had the myna bird. Spam was always good company, especially with those pirate impressions. Anyway, he doesn't play any real part in this story, so just forget him. I've said that already, yes.

Bottom line, I managed to persuade Paul to come with me to Leeds, but it wasn't easy. We 'accidentally' bumped into Lawson in The Viaduct Showroom, a glam gay bar on Lower Briggate, and we bought him several martinis. He was scared at first. Why had Paul 'The Terminator' Balaskas come all this way, and what was he going to do to him?

Or that's how he acted. The alcohol pacified him, and once he found out we only wanted to know where Soames was, he relaxed completely. *Exhibited relief* might be a better description. So much so that he told us everything there was to know about Soames, including his date and place of birth, his two decades of charitable work for the RSPB, and most of the details of his colonoscopy six months ago.

Top fact: Soames lived in Tonbridge.

After grilling Lawson, Paul and I stayed overnight at a Leeds Travelodge – just to sleep off the alcohol – and in the morning, we drove back to Kent. I dropped Paul at home, then went to locate The Prof. I wasn't optimistic, and, as it turned out, things were far from drawing to a close.

V.

Soames's house was easy to find: a small detached bungalow just along from St. Stephen's Church. I wasn't too apprehensive about introducing myself: I'd recorded a video message from Paul on my phone, and I considered it ought to explain everything.

The problem was, he never seemed to be at home. Six times, I tried, over the course of three days. When he finally answered the door, he looked hostile.

Not unexpected. I just needed to show him I wasn't your ordinary cold caller. I won't dwell on the details of how I managed to do that, suffice it to say the video message played a large part.

However, he still didn't seem very pleased to see me.

Odd. Given that Paul – the MP4 version of Paul on my smartphone – had looked and sounded despairing, I'd expected Soames to be a bit more, like, *Oh dearie me, how can I conceivably help?* But he wasn't. He looked like he'd swallowed gripe water.

"What's Paul Balaskas's number?" he said.

"His phone number?" Stupid question, but I was taken aback.

He just glared at me. I realised my chances of getting an inch further depended on how fully I cooperated. And it had to be 100%. I didn't suppose Paul would mind. I unlocked my phone again and read out the number.

Soames instructed me to wait there, closed and locked the door on me, and left me standing on the step for five minutes. When he finally returned, he looked transformed. He wore an *Oh dearie me, how can I conceivably help?* expression.

"Come in," he said. "Can I get you a cup of tea?"

I politely declined. We went into his living room. A beige carpet, a brown leather suite, an oak sideboard, and a large framed portrait of Lady Gaga on the biggest wall. On the coffee table, in between the chairs, stood the contents of what looked like an average-sized drinks cabinet: an assortment of 70cl bottles of whisky, vodka, gin, rum, cola, and tequila, mostly half-empty.

"I've just been on the blower to Paul," he said. "If you're allowed to call it that anymore. Bloody cancel culture. Anyway, he says you're genuine. Sit down. Would you like a drink? I'm plastered, by the way. Pleased to meet you."

I politely declined the drink. "Did Paul tell you what I'm here about?"

"The jewellery box, yes?"

"He'd like to buy it back, if that's possible."

I explained what had happened to Sophie Balaskas, how she'd become more and more mentally unwell, until she'd finally suffered a nervous collapse, and how she'd previously insisted that getting the box back might aid her recovery.

"Do you know what Paul just told me?" he said, when I'd finished. "I mean just now, on the phone? No, of course you don't: you were outside, on the doorstep. He told me there were *people* watching his house."

"I'm not sure what to make of that," I replied. Paul hadn't said anything to me, but then, I hadn't spoken to him since we'd returned from Leeds.

"Well, there are people watching *this* house too, you may be interested to know."

"I see. And, er, you're suggesting that's something to do with the box?"

He laughed. "The thing is, I don't even think they *want* it. No, they want *me* to have it, so that when whatever's going to happen to it *does* happen, I'll be in the direct line of fire. Then, after assessing the damage, they can step in. Or not, depending on how bad it is."

"By 'they', you mean… who?"

"Government agents. MI5, probably."

"Okay, and does Paul Balaskas share your view?"

"Paul agrees with me. Mind you, they've probably got our phones tapped. So now they'll know we know." He passed his left hand roughly across his face. "I need to tell you what I found out about that box. You need to know. Or do you? Because, soon perhaps, if they think you know, they'll try to kill you. What am I saying? Of course they won't. No one would believe you. What would be the point of killing you? Or even me? Besides, they probably don't like having to do that sort of thing. They're spooks, yes, but most of them are university graduates with good degrees, they probably avoid murdering innocent people as much as they can. I really don't think it's at all necessary in our case, do you?"

"Perhaps when you tell me what this is all about, I'll be in a better position to judge."

"Yes, yes, good point, yes. Okay, here goes." He poured himself a large whisky. He drank it. "Here goes, yes. Firstly, there's nothing in that box that's making it rattle. Nothing I can discover, I mean. So, I made the mistake of taking it to an expert I know, someone in a higher education research unit, where I knew they'd have the equipment. Sharon Wilkes, in case you don't believe me: *Professor* Sharon Wilkes, of the University of Nottingham. I didn't think I had any alternative, and I was deeply curious. I wish to God I hadn't bothered. But I might as well tell you what she discovered. She was as disturbed as I was. She certainly didn't want to keep it, didn't want anything more to do with it. She says she didn't communicate her findings to anyone else, largely because that would have tied her inextricably to the object, and, as I've just said, she wanted to get away from it. But I'm pretty sure someone must have hacked her research, otherwise why are those people outside?"

I frowned. "Is that normal? For a scientist to find something 'inexplicable' and then try to wash her hands of it?"

"I take it that's a rhetorical question. No, of course it isn't 'normal'. Which indicates just how disturbing this particular discovery – or set of discoveries – is."

"I interrupted. Carry on."

"Schrödinger's Cat. You measure something, and, in the act of measuring it, you 'collapse' its duality, so that only one aspect appears. What if the whole of science is like that? So, the supernatural is well attested in everyday life, but whenever science is brought to bear, to investigate that life, its duality 'collapses' and only that part which is accessible to rational enquiry remains?"

I frowned. "I'm not sure what you're talking about. And *is* the supernatural 'well attested in everyday life'?"

"No one knows. It's an empirical question. Some pollster would have to investigate it."

I sighed. "I can't help feeling we're getting ever farther away from the point where you're going to tell me anything specific or useful."

"The first and most trivial thing she discovered is that it really *is* a perfect cube: down to the tiniest fraction of a nanometre. Disturbingly, everyone who sees it seems to recognise that fact intuitively. How? Unknown. The second thing is that the rattling's coming from … it's coming from somewhere *far away*. I mean, far away in the universe; *inconceivably* far away. Something's trying to get from there … to here."

"How can she possibly have discovered that?"

"I don't know, but she seemed absolutely certain. The intuition thing may be a clue. I mean, why tell me that people recognise 'intuitively' that it's a perfect cube? That bears no relation to physics, and it's of no interest to me, as a physicist. *Unless*… the intuitive knowledge she mentioned referred partly to *her own* non-verifiable comprehension? My hypothesis, then, is this: she intuitively *knew* where the rattling originated, she also knew she couldn't prove it, and thus she decided to, as you put it, 'wash her hands of it'."

"So it's just her bad feeling, then. A purely psychological explanation."

"Maybe. Or the intersection of the subjective and objective. Where *both* things are true – and neither. I'm saying, that's what she thought."

"Let's stick with the word 'psychological', shall we?"

"Okay." He poured himself another whisky. "You must have noticed something about this box: the way it seems to make everyone who comes into possession of it slightly deranged? First, there was Mrs Balaskas, then Paul: if I read our phone conversation correctly, he's not exactly the picture of mental health right now; then me, then Professor Wilkes."

"Possibly. What's your point?"

"You intend to buy it from me and give it to Paul. I'm advising you against that. I'm pretty sure it's not going to help his wife recover."

"You want to keep it here?"

He chuckled. "I want to put as much distance between myself and it as humanly possible. I don't particularly care what happens to it in the process, either. As you might expect, I've tried destroying it. It's totally invulnerable to hammers."

Before I could remark on this, we were interrupted by a high-pitched rattling. It lasted about thirty seconds, and grew progressively deeper in tone, before rising again. It faded away in the manner of something ascending to a pitch beyond human hearing.

Just before that, however, I got the peculiar sense that I fully understood what Professor Wilkes had meant. The rattling was obviously produced *by* the box, but somehow, something far greater lay behind it, and whatever it was felt both incredibly distant and horribly nearby, and not at all good-natured. Soames and I shuddered in unison.

"So what's your suggestion?" I asked.

"I get the impression you're pretty much a sceptic about all this. My suggestion is that you should tell Paul that I wouldn't give you the box, but that you're sure it wouldn't have helped anyway. I don't think he'll argue much. Then *you* keep it, see what happens. Maybe that'll give you a better idea of what you're up against."

"And of course, it'll get MI5 off your back."

"Yes, I suggested they were MI5 a moment ago, but that was when I thought I might as well pander to your scepticism."

"So who are they? I mean, who do you *think* they are?"

"I don't know. You're the private detective; find out."

"I'll take the box then, thank you. Could you write me some sort of introduction to Sharon Wilkes? I probably need to speak to her. I'll probably also try to talk to the jeweller on the Pantiles."

Soames went to the sideboard, opened the bottom drawer and came back with the jewellery box.

"No charge," he said. "In fact, *I* should be paying *you*." He watched me put it into my coat pocket with obvious relief. "Sharon won't talk to you. She's barely talking to me anymore. As for that jeweller, good luck, but I doubt you'll get anything out of him. There are a lot of missing pieces in this particular story. You'd be better off trying to find the man who offered Sophie a thousand pounds for it."

"Brilliant plan. Only, I'm not sure how."

He laughed sardonically. "Oh, now you've got the box in your pocket, I'm certain that won't be a problem."

VI.

It's totally invulnerable to hammers. Smashing it with a sledgehammer was the first thing I tried. And Soames was right. It wasn't just unbreakable; it was unscratchable. Which made it the scientific discovery of the century, surely? Why did someone like Professor Wilkes want to cut all ties to it? It might have made her name.

I took it back to Paul Balaskas and told him what Soames had advised me to do. Balaskas was paying my wages, after all; it'd have been morally remiss of me to keep him in the dark, and it would indicate that I was getting too personally involved.

Luckily, Balaskas saw the wisdom of Soames's suggestion, and, once he realised that it wasn't going to work a miracle cure so far as Sophie was concerned, he was perfectly happy for me to hang on to it. I think he foresaw himself going the same way as Sophie: the box was somehow beginning to haunt him.

Soames was right about the jeweller's: not only could I not find the particular vendor, but I couldn't even find the shop. There are several shops that might qualify as 'antique jewellers' on the Pantiles, and no one remembered selling it, or even stocking it. Strangely, none of them seemed particularly interested in buying it either, although I wouldn't actually have sold it: I was simply curious to ascertain how much they thought it was worth. Twenty pounds was the best offer. When I offered to take it outside and hit it with a hammer (on the grounds that any genuinely indestructible object has to be worth at least its own weight in gold, and possibly ten times that), they looked at me as if I was insane. *This is Tunbridge Wells. We don't* do *that sort of thing here!*

As for Professor Sharon Wilkes, Soames was right about her too. I'd like to use the old phrase, 'she wasn't returning my calls', but the truth is, it was a bit less and a bit more than that. She answered one call: she threatened to call the police if I kept pestering her.

Which was risible really. What she thought the police would do, I'm not sure. I wasn't scared of them – not in this particular scenario – but given her recalcitrance, persevering seemed a waste of my time and hers. I wrote her off as a possible source of help.

Of course, I started to see people. By that, I mean people who were apparently watching me from a distance with deep interest, and whose motives seemed discernibly malign, even from afar. Men and women, passing into, then swiftly out of, my sight-line, more often than not obliquely. They didn't look like MI5 agents: they were too clumsy for that. And why were there so many of them? One or two would have done. I had no idea what the man who offered Sophie a thousand pounds looked like - I'd asked her for a description, but she'd reported a curious blankness of memory – but I suspected he was amongst them.

The rattling continued, and intensified. It seemed to occur mainly at night, and for periods of between ten and thirty minutes. Being watched by phoney-MI5 bods was stressful enough, but this was of a different order. As I mentioned earlier, the rattling was only the surface aspect of it. What gave it its affective power was the overwhelming sense that there was something utterly unknown and unknowable behind it; something from a dimension where up was down, left was right, and light was an everlasting darkness; a place of gargantuan cites, where terrible things happened in complete silence, and where the silence was integral to the horror and …

Sorry. Got carried away. Often happens nowadays. Ignore me. Or rather don't, because you'll never hear the end of the story, will you?

I don't know whether you've ever come across a German theologian called Rudolf Otto? Wrote a slim volume on religious experience called *The Idea of the Holy?* I know what you're thinking: what's a private detective doing reading something like that? Bear with me. Otto claimed there were three marks of any deep religious experience. *Mysterium* – the sense of inscrutability; *fascinans* – the attractive power with which it seems to pull you in; *tremendum* – its terrifying, horrific face. This had all three in excess. The horror, definitely the mystery, but also the sombre fascination.

Like the Balaskases, like Soames and Sharon Wilkes, I began to lose my grip on reality. The jewellery box slowly became my whole universe. I don't know how, but it possessed a hypnotic grip; or to put it a better way, it reduced me to the sort of servitude usually associated with hallucinogenic drugs. All I seemed to do all day was wait for it to start rattling. I foresaw myself ending up like Sophie Balaskas, but I didn't care. By this time, I was drinking.

I lost contact with the Balaskases for a few weeks, then they stopped paying me. They didn't have to do that; they could have contacted me and, posed questions, talked things through, thanked me for what I'd done for them (which wasn't much, admittedly), requested an update on the jewellery box, asked solicitously if I thought I had anything further to offer, etcetera. It seemed inconsiderate to just cut me off, especially now they'd saddled me with the family curse, so to speak.

I felt aggrieved for a few days, obviously.

Until I learned that Sophie Balaskas had recently died, in terrible agitation, of unknown causes.

And that Paul Balaskas had followed in the same manner a few days later.

And that Jeffrey Soames was *also* pushing up the daisies: ditto as regards the agitation and causes.

How did I find all that out? Well, I happened to be sitting alone in my flat one night, drinking heavily and waiting for the beautiful rattle (yes, that's how it struck me now: I wasn't sure I could live without it, horrible – in another, parallel sense – though it was), when there was a knock at my door. I tossed back a double measure of brandy, and got up to answer it.

I found myself face to face with a middle-aged woman of roughly average height, with a blonde bob, a nose piercing, bulging eyes, and large ears sticking out from under her hair like china saucers. More noticeably, she was drenched, and covered in mud. She looked terrified.

"I'm Professor Sharon Wilkes," she said. "Do you still have that jewellery box?"

VII.

She didn't seem particularly surprised to have to step over six or seven empty bottles to get to the sofa. She sat down, then stood up again. She pulled another empty bottle from the upholstery behind her, and resumed her position.

"I don't suppose you're going to ask me what I'm here for," she said. "I imagine it's pretty obvious, isn't it?"

"Not really," I said. "You can't want the jewellery box, since you told Soames you didn't. You can't want to talk to me, since you could do that on the phone. So the ball's in your court, as they say… in tennis."

"How long have you been sitting here, drinking?"

"About a week. On the plus side, I've lost a lot of weight. I haven't really been eating, you see."

She nodded. "Ah."

"Why are you covered in mud?"

She either didn't hear me, or didn't want to reply. The rattling began. As usual, it lasted about thirty seconds, growing increasingly deeper in tone, before rising again and fading away. I watched Wilkes's expression fill with a kind of tortured rapture, and realised why she was here. She felt the same way I did about it.

"You do know about Jeffrey, don't you?" she asked quietly.

"What about Jeffrey?"

"That he's dead? And that the Balaskases are dead?"

I must have looked even more taken aback than I had a minute ago, when she'd materialised at the front door. I definitely didn't speak. She supplied the details, which all seemed to boil down to the same two things: terrible agitation and unknown causes.

"It's too much of a coincidence not to be that box," she concluded. "Which means we're going the same way. You and I."

I realised I'd known for some time that I was on a downward spiral, and that, uninterrupted, it could only have one conclusion. And that I had no intention of interrupting it.

Obviously, I didn't want to die.

Or did I? On some level, I must have done, otherwise why was I poisoning myself?

But I didn't want to go out in terrible agitation. No one does.

"What do you actually know about that box?" I asked, putting on my private detective's hat for what might well be the last time. "What did you find out?"

"Oh, a whole host of things," she said. "You see, I made the terrible mistake of looking inside it. While it was rattling. I opened it, and peered in."

It struck me strange that I'd never done that. For reasons unknown it had never occurred to me.

It seemed courageous.

"And what did you see?" I asked.

"Something's trying to get from there to here. By 'there', I mean somewhere in a different galaxy. I mean, it's in *our* universe," she added hurriedly, as if that made it better, "but another galaxy. Somewhere unimaginably far away, where nothing even remotely resembles here, including the laws of physics. If it gets through, that'll be the end. Or maybe the beginning, I don't know. It could be horrendous, or it could be wonderful, I honestly don't know. All I know is, I looked in, and what I saw was so far beyond my capacity to comprehend it that it - it shattered my mind. Just as that rattling shattered my mind, though not as suddenly and dramatically. Just as it's shattered yours, and the Balaskases' and Jeffrey's."

"Yes, I see. Well, thank you for letting me know. Would you like a drink, by the way? It doesn't have to be alcohol. I've got tea and coffee, and orange juice. By 'orange juice', I mean, squash. I haven't got any fresh orange juice."

"We're going to *die!* Don't you care?"

"The box is indestructible, so I don't see what we can do. What you can't change, you've got to accept: that's my credo. Keep calm and drink tea. Apologies. I'm still drunk. Do you have a plan?"

"I'll have a mugful of tap water, please. And yes, yes, I do. Why do you think I'm covered in mud?"

"I don't know," I replied. "I asked, but you didn't say anything."

She shrugged. I went into the kitchen and brought her back a cup of water.

"Do you know anything about the guys who I keep seeing out of the corner of my eye?" I asked. "Jeffrey thought they were MI5. Or he pretended to for a while – for about three minutes – for what he claimed was my benefit. But I'm inclined to agree with his final assessment: they're not secret agents of any normal description."

"You mean, any normal *human* description."

I hmm-ed. "I *didn't* actually mean that, but I won't quibble. So, getting back to the point, who - or what - are they? Do you know?"

"I don't know where they come from, or what precisely motivates them; I don't know whether they're good or evil. I do know they're not from this world. And that they don't want the thing coming through any more than you or I do."

"You've just answered your own question. If you're correct, then they're on our side. Ergo, they're good."

She laughed. "*Are* they?"

"What do you mean?"

"What if it's *the thing that's trying to get through that's good?* What if it's actually *God?"*

"God?"

"God with a capital 'G'! God has lost His way, he's been trapped on the other side of the universe for thousands of years, and he's trying to get back! And that little box, it's like a - a miniature *Ark of the Covenant* or something!"

She didn't sound remotely like a physicist anymore. To tell the truth, she didn't even sound sane.

I decided to let it pass. No point in antagonising her. Besides, she'd mentioned having a plan, so perhaps we could ditch the speculative stuff and switch to discussing practicalities.

"So what do you want to do about it?" I asked.

"What *we've* got to do is bury it at least ten feet beneath the Earth," she replied. "You're right, it can't be destroyed, but sufficiently far underground, it should become ineffective as a portal. I'm a physicist. Trust me."

I laughed, mainly at the 'physicist' bit. "I haven't got a better plan. I take it, from the state of your clothes, shoes, hair, hands, and face that you've actually begun digging the required hole?"

"And I had help."

"So, all I've got to do is give you the box?"

"Good try. No, I don't want to be on my own with it. And what if it starts rattling while I'm driving?"

"Ten feet down. How far have you dug then?"

"More than ten feet. Like I say, I had help. All you've got to do is put the box in your pocket, get in my car, sit there until I tell you we've arrived, then follow me, drop the box in the hole, and help me and the others cover it with soil."

"What 'others'?"

"The people you keep seeing out of the corner of your eye. I use the word 'people' advisedly: as I said earlier, I don't know who or what they are, or anything about them. All I can tell you is that, once I've done my bit, and you've done yours, they'll stop hounding us, and they'll go back to wherever it is they came from, and everyone will live happily ever after. It'll be as if none of this ever happened."

"Except for the fact that the Balaskases are dead and so is Jeffrey Soames. But we can't help that, I suppose."

"Sadly, no. Keep calm and have a cup of tea."

I shrugged. "Let's go, then."

VIII.

The hole she'd dug was at High Rocks, just over two miles from Tunbridge Wells: a stone age settlement turned picturesque nature reserve, punctuated by huge rocky outcrops. To my way of thinking, it was a risky place to dig a ten-foot hole, mainly because it was a site of special geological interest, and so probably well monitored, but maybe she'd factored that in; maybe she considered it so well looked-after, and host to so many tourists, that the chances of anyone ever unearthing what she intended to bury there were negligible.

Her car was an expensive-looking SUV, and, since it rained all the way, she had the windscreen wipers on full. The road was deserted, dark – there were no lampposts, and very few houses - and winding. The box began to rattle in my pocket as we set off, and quickly reached a pitch reminiscent of something in distress. It continued for the entire journey. After about a mile, I couldn't help feeling sorry for it.

I couldn't help thinking about Spam, the Balaskases' myna bird. I wondered what had happened to him, now that they were both dead. I hoped he hadn't been put down.

I was drunk as a skunk. Somehow, the myna bird and the jewellery box had come together in one big inner sob about how horrible life is to things that have no way of defending themselves.

Yes, I know I told you Spam didn't play any part in this story, but I was lying, okay? Unreliable, as the professional literary critics would call me. Or perhaps I didn't intend to tell you this bit, because, frankly, it's rather embarrassing.

I tried to rationalise my inebriated sentimentalism. Apart from anything else, what kind of reaction to something new and exciting is burying it? Sharon Wilkes and I ought to be ashamed of ourselves! What sort of a bloody *scientist* was she? Yes, I know I've asked that question already, but this time I'd like it minuted, Mme Secretary.

I can tell what you're thinking right now. Something along the lines of: that jewellery box sounds new and exciting in the same sense that Russian roulette does.

Yet I don't know: perhaps her, 'What if it's actually *God?'* had got to me. In part, paradoxically, because it was such a weird expostulation, but also because of the *mysterium, tremendum fascinans* I mentioned earlier. What else can do that to you? I mean, apart from God … or, at the very least, *a* god?

I expect you can tell what's coming, so I won't dwell too much on it. We reached our destination just after 2am. Sharon Wilkes ordered me out of the car. We walked through the woods in a howling thunderstorm for what felt like an age, always ascending. She seemed to know her way, although everything looked the same to me, which is to say, an amorphous jumble of dark blue columns and jet black in-between-bits, except during the occasional moment when it was all illuminated by sheet lightning. At one point we squeezed through what looked like a freshly cut hole in a wire-mesh fence.

The box hadn't stopped rattling since we'd left my flat, and, to my mind, it had become more and more pitiable.

Slogging through the woods, I reached a decision. I couldn't allow her to bury it. Neither science nor charity could possibly condone such a thing.

I thought it best to leave the necessary remonstrations until we both came to a halt. That way, we could talk face to face, and give each other our undivided attention. I was optimistic about winning her over. After all, she was obviously an intelligent woman, and I had a number of good arguments up my sleeve. She'd just allowed herself to fall into a rut of looking at the whole matter from the wrong perspective. If she buried it, she'd come to regret it, just as I would.

We eventually emerged into a clearing, and the ground levelled off. We'd reached the summit. I could see specks of light in the distance. We were both soaked through.

I turned to face her. "Where's the hole?"

"Not far from here. I need you to show me the box; just to double check you've still got it."

I laughed. "Isn't the rattling evidence enough?"

"I said, I need to *see* it!"

I removed it from my pocket. It vibrated energetically, and it was glowing slightly. To me, it looked beautiful, although that word doesn't remotely do it justice. I summoned all my courage and determination: time to begin my case for the defence. "Listen," I said, "I'm really not sure whether we should - "

Something emerged from the trees and gave me a colossal shove. I seemed to sail through the air and fall down the hill we'd just climbed. When I landed on my side, I was in considerable pain.

The truth, which was rather different, hit me in successive waves of horror. Perhaps it was too horrible for me to grasp in one go.

I was in a room. With no ceiling. Or no, it wasn't a room, it was a chamber of some sort.

No, no, no, wrong again. I was in a hole.

Oh my God, this was *the* hole. The *ten-foot hole!*

They were going to bury me alive.

As if to confirm that I'd finally got the right answer, soil began to pour down on me.

The silhouette of Sharon's head appeared. "I'm *so sorry* about this!" she yelled. To give her credit, she genuinely did sound upset: I think she was actually crying. "But what's inside that box is so terrible, nothing about it can be allowed to get away, and that means no one with a story to tell! They're going to kill *me too* afterwards! I'm going to submit willingly! We didn't think *you* would! I'm so, *so sorry!* Here!" She tossed something down. I was almost up to my knees in loose earth now, but I picked it up. A sheath knife. "It's just been sharpened!" she told me. "Cut your wrists! It's far better than being suffocated by soil! I also bought you this!" She dropped something else in. I picked it up. My eyes adjusted. A one-litre bottle of Glenfiddich. "It's a single malt!" she shouted. *"It's from the 1937 Rare Collection!* I'm really, really *sorry!"* Her head disappeared.

If all this sounds hilarious in the re-telling, well, strangely, it even seemed a tiny bit funny at the time. I'd just been pushed into a hole, I was being buried alive, I suppose I'd run out of shock. Droll with a dash of dread.

Meanwhile, the box was screaming. I picked it up. I opened it. I looked inside.

What I saw was a whirling mass of dislocated shapes, vortices, colours populated with what looked like tunnels.

Which not only doesn't begin to capture it; it's almost certainly an unavoidable falsification. Because the bewildered shock of falling into that hole was as nothing compared with the total incredulity that seized me now. I knew that what I was looking at belonged to a completely different order of things, that it wasn't remotely what it looked like, that my brain had constructed something trivially unknowable to stand in for the total opaqueness of what I'd ridiculously tried to make it process.

I'd only *felt sorry* for the thing in the box so far, but actually, pity isn't so far removed from love (I often wonder whether that's why we love animals), and that's what I now experienced. I'd ceased to notice that I was up to my waist in soil, that I was choking on what felt like airborne mud, that my eyes hurt, my throat was constricted, I could barely see. I put my fingers into the box and emerged with a little creature, shaped like an 'X', furry and obviously alive. It scuttled onto the back of my hand, then... seemed to disappear into it; into my hand, I mean. Into me.

I suddenly knew what I had to do, although, looking back, I'm not sure how and why it worked. My idea – if you can call it mine; similarly, if you can call it an idea (it would probably have struck me as unworkable in any other circumstances) – was to wait till I was covered with soil, then somehow *swim up* (yes, that's actually how I phrased it to myself) keeping my head just a few inches below the interface between the soil and the air. Unbeknown to my executors, as they filled in the hole, they'd actually be providing me with the means to climb out; which I would, obviously, once they'd gone.

How would I know they'd gone? No idea. I simply *knew I would*, just as I knew an awful lot of things, now, that I'd never known before.

Crazy though it all sounds, it worked. That's how I escaped, yes. Without that little creature, I'd have been a goner.

Mind you, I won't say there hasn't been a price to pay.

IX.

I still don't know what the creature is, incidentally, or why it's come here. I do know that the world changed significantly for me after it entered me. In a nutshell, it became much darker. Not night, exactly; subtler than that. Oh, I can still see perfectly well to read, and watch TV, and cross a busy main road, but it's as if the sun's permanently behind a high mountain.

In addition, I've got the constant sense that the reality in which we all live is but a small part of what's actually there; that there are profound levels of gloom, just a millimetre beyond our field of vision. Lifeless hills, deserted mega-cities, frozen stars. I do glimpse them occasionally, but never for more than a second.

What else? Oh, yes: I can actually gaze directly at the sun now. It looks black.

Anyway, on a more mundane level, after escaping from that ten-foot hole, I walked home, showered, went to bed, and then tried to carry on as if nothing had happened. I gave up drinking. I gave up working: nowadays, money just seems to mysteriously appear whenever I need or want it. Any amount. In a very real sense, I gave up living.

Two days later, the news was full of Sharon Wilkes. Her corpse, I mean, which had been found in the woods in Rusthall. The police said she'd been the victim of a 'ritualistic killing', but what they meant by that still isn't clear. They didn't release any details, and no one ever found the killer or killers.

I expect to live for a long time, by the way. A very long time. Again, don't ask me how I know; I just do. It's not a happy expectation.

It's far more than I can say for the people around me, however. Like the Ancient Mariner, I'm compelled to keep telling my story. The difference between me and him is that everyone who hears *my* tale seems fated to die soon afterwards. You will too, I'm sorry to say.

But then, that might not be a bad thing. The more time goes on, the more I'm inclined to think Sharon Wilkes was correct: it was a mistake to let the whatever-it-is thing enter our world. If I'm right – and I nearly always am, nowadays – it was an error of galactic proportions.

But I'm not infallible. I still don't know what it is. I don't even know if it's good or evil. It could be good. The God of the Old Testament does a lot of killing, doesn't he, and he's supposed to be good. Evil's usually easy enough to identify, but as for good? Good's often dressed in someone else's clothes.

In any case, what's done is done. As for what happens from here on, we'll just have to wait and see.

I say, 'we'. Luckily, you'll be long gone by then.

Books by James Ward

General Fiction

The House of Charles Swinter
The Weird Problem of Good
The Bright Fish
*Hannah and Soraya's Fully Magic Generation-Y *Snowflake* Road Trip across America*

The Original Tales of MI7

Our Woman in Jamaica
The Kramski Case
The Girl from Kandahar
The Vengeance of San Gennaro

The John Mordred Tales of MI7 books

The Eastern Ukraine Question
The Social Magus
Encounter with ISIS
World War O
The New Europeans
Libya Story
Little War in London
The Square Mile Murder
The Ultimate Londoner
Death in a Half Foreign Country
The BBC Hunters
The Seductive Scent of Empire
Humankind 2.0
Ruby Parker's Last Orders

Poetry

The Latest Noel
Metals of the Future

Short Stories

An Evening at the Beach
Wadhurst Ghost Stories
Tunbridge Wells Ghost Stories

Philosophy

21st Century Philosophy
A New Theory of Justice and Other Essays

www.ingramcontent.com/pod-product-compliance
Ingram Content Group UK Ltd.
Pitfield, Milton Keynes, MK11 3LW, UK
UKHW041953190726
13854UKWH00005B/1939

9 781913 851590